Disney

SET IN STONE

A TWISTED TALE NOVEL

CW00829193

MARI MANCUSI

AUTUMN
PUBLISHING

Published in 2023
First published in the UK by Autumn Publishing
An imprint of Igloo Books Ltd
Cottage Farm, NN6 0BJ, UK
Owned by Bonnier Books
Sveavägen 56, Stockholm, Sweden
www.igloobooks.com

© 2023 Disney Enterprises, Inc. All rights reserved.

All rights reserved. No part of this publication may be reproduced or transmitted in any form or by any means, electronic, or mechanical, including photocopying, recording, or by any information storage and retrieval system, without permission in writing from the publisher.

0323 001
2 4 6 8 10 9 7 5 3 1
ISBN 978-1-80368-543-4

Cover illustrated by Giuseppe Di Maio

Printed and manufactured in the EU

Disney

SET IN STONE

A TWISTED TALE NOVEL

To all my once and future readers
– you make this all worthwhile.

– M.M.

PROLOGUE

Bermuda – Present Day

"Higgidis... piggidis! Alakazoom! No, that's not right. That's not right at all!"

The waiter frowned as he approached the elderly man with the long white beard who had been collapsed on a deckchair in front of the resort's main pool for the past four hours, mumbling to himself. He was dressed like an overenthusiastic tourist, wearing a baseball cap, loud striped shirt and yellow shorts with little palm trees printed down the sides. On his feet were red Converse trainers, and a pair of yellow sunglasses obscured his eyes.

Ugh. Why do they always end up in my section? the waiter wondered before clearing his throat.

"Um, sir?" he tried. "Are you… all right?"

The man jerked at the sound of the voice, his baseball cap flying from his head and landing in the pool. He stared up at the waiter, pulling his sunglasses down his hooked nose, revealing a pair of piercing blue eyes that seemed far too sharp for an old man's face.

"Am I all right?" he repeated, as if astounded by the question. "Did you just ask me if I'm all right?"

"Um, yes?" The waiter took a small step backwards as the man struggled to get out of his chair, somehow managing to get his foot stuck in the straps in the process. When he tried to yank his foot free, the chair flew backwards, bonking him on the nose. The waiter flinched as the man let out a stream of nonsense words that seemed to be meant as curses – though none the waiter had ever heard before. *Oh, dear.* Maybe he should have left the gentleman well enough alone. Still, he was almost off his shift, and he needed to cash everyone out before he left.

"Can I… get you something?" he ventured. "The bill, perhaps?"

"Bill? Please! I don't need a bill! I need a time machine. I don't suppose you have one of those on the menu, do you, my boy?" The man ripped off his sunglasses and stared at the waiter, almost accusingly.

The waiter sighed, reaching for his mobile phone. It appeared he was going to need some backup on this one. "I'm so sorry, sir," he said as he frantically texted hotel security. "But I'm afraid we're fresh out of time machines here at the Bermuda Dunes Hotel." Was this man even a guest at the resort? Or had he wandered in from somewhere off the beach?

The man groaned loudly and stroked his rather impressive white beard. The waiter found himself wondering just how many years it would take to grow a beard of that magnitude. "I'm sorry," the man said. "It's just… I'm a bit out of sorts today, you understand. After all, time travel does quite a number on one's noggin, especially if you do it twenty-three times in a row."

"Of course it does," the waiter agreed politely. *The guests are never wrong.* "I'm, uh, always saying that to my wife."

The man nodded as if this made perfect sense. "It wasn't intentional, of course. All I wanted to do was spend a few days in 1960s Bermuda – get a little warmed up after spending all those weeks in a cold leaky tower." He peered at the waiter. "I mean, is that so wrong?"

The waiter agreed this sounded more than reasonable.

"But after a short R and R, I was ready to go home – back to medieval England. Which should have been a mere hop in the park for an accomplished wizard like myself. But instead, after casting my spell, I found myself still here in Bermuda – this time in the year 2634." He glanced around the resort. "A terrible decade, by the way. I don't recommend it at all."

He reached into a small suitcase by his feet, pulling out a tall pointed blue hat. It reminded the waiter of the sorcerer cap a character had worn in an old cartoon, and he wondered, for a second, if the man was going to claim it came from the future.

Instead, he planted it on his head. "So I tried again. And again. At this point I've bounced around half of human history. But I can't seem to leave this blasted island." He shook his head, nearly losing his cap in the process. "I just don't know what's wrong with me."

To be fair, the waiter had been wondering the same thing since he'd started the conversation. He tried to surreptitiously glance behind himself. What was taking security so long?

The man rose from his chair, shaking crisp crumbs from his beard. "You know what? I'll bet it's *her* doing." He nodded his head vigorously, as if agreeing with himself. "She's still mad that I won that duel fair and square – even though she completely cheated! Purple dragon." He rolled his eyes. "Of all the ridiculous…"

The waiter bit his lower lip. "You know, sometimes if you spend too long in the sun—"

"And now I'm stuck here and she's back there, and who knows what she'll try to pull in my absence? What if she goes after the boy again? He'll be completely helpless on his own!" His face crumpled. "We got in a fight, you see. Right before I left. I got mad and just abandoned him all by himself. Well, with Archimedes, I suppose. He's a very intelligent owl. But still..." He sighed. "Oh, Wart. I never meant to let you down."

He looked so despondent the waiter almost felt bad. "Look, I'm sure whoever this Wart is, he'll forgive you," he assured the man, patting him on the shoulder comfortingly. "In the meantime, maybe you should go take a little nap? I'm sure you'll feel much better if you just get out of the sun for a few hours and—"

The man looked up. "Nap?" he sputtered, shaking his fists as his long white beard swung from side to side. "Haven't you listened to anything I've been saying? I can't take a blasted nap! I need to get back to England pronto!"

"Now, now, sir, take it easy."

The waiter whirled around to see that two burly security guards dressed in matching khaki pants and dark glasses had stepped up behind him. He dropped his shoulders in relief. Backup. Finally.

"Let's get you back to your room," said the first one, taking a cautious step towards the man.

"You're going to feel much better soon," assured the second, going around to his other side.

"I'll take care of your tab," the waiter added, starting to feel a little bad for the old geezer. After all, he was probably someone's grandfather. Maybe this Wart person's, even? "Uh, what did you say your name was again?"

"My name?" the man huffed, suddenly dodging the security guards with a move that seemed far too nimble for an old guy. "My name is Merlin, of course. I'm the world's most powerful wizard." He stared up at the sky, moaning mournfully. "And if I don't get back to Camelot soon, the world as we know it will surely be doomed!"

CHAPTER ONE
ARTHUR

Over one thousand years earlier, in medieval England…

"Oh, Archimedes, surely I'm doomed!"

The young boy, Wart, recently crowned King Arthur, paced the cavernous throne room of Camelot Castle, shoving the altogether too-heavy velvet and metal crown out of his eyes for what felt like the thousandth time that day. He glanced over at the small brown owl, who perched on the armrest of his new throne.

"What am I to do?" Arthur asked mournfully. "I can't be king. I'm fourteen years old! Just a boy!"

"A boy who somehow managed to pull the legendary

sword from the stone," Archimedes, Merlin's highly educated owl, hooted back in reminder. "Which evidently makes you the rightful ruler of all England."

Arthur gave him a beseeching look, and the owl ruffled his feathers. "Sorry, I don't make the rules."

Arthur groaned, dropping down onto the throne. Which, by the way, had turned out to be the most uncomfortable chair he'd ever sat on in his entire life. Evidently kings didn't believe in cushions.

"I still don't understand how it happened," he mused, his mind going back to the day a week before when the so-called miracle had taken place. He'd been so excited to stand in as a real squire for the day after Kay's other squire, Hobbs, had mysteriously come down with the mumps. It was a great honour, after all, for a lowborn orphan like himself to serve a true knight of the realm – even if, in this case, the knight in question was his oafish foster brother, Kay. Arthur had been sure it would be the best day of his life.

Instead, it had turned out to be the worst.

The jousting tournament had been held to determine who would become England's next king, with the winner taking the throne. England had been too long without a king after Uther Pendragon had died with no heir, and it had thrown the kingdom into a dark age full of war and famine. They badly needed someone to don the crown and start making some rules around the place. And Sir Ector, Arthur's foster father, had decided his son Kay would be perfect for the job.

So when Arthur accidentally forgot Kay's sword back at the inn, he'd been forced to find another at the last moment – lest Kay be disqualified. And it was Archimedes who had first spotted the lone sword in the nearby churchyard, stuck in an anvil on top of a stone. How was Arthur supposed to know this was *the* sword in the stone – the one that would truly determine who would be king? It looked like any other sword.

Until he pulled it out of the anvil…

Not long after that, people were bowing to him. Knights and lords and ladies who had never given him the time of day, now calling him sire and Your Majesty and king. Claiming it was a miracle, ordained by Heaven itself. That Arthur was now the land's chosen monarch.

That Arthur, single-handedly, would somehow save them all.

"Why me?" he asked, staring up at the high ceiling of the throne room, which was decorated in rich tapestries of royal blues and purples and greens. "I'm no one. I wash dishes for a living. I shouldn't be king."

"Don't think I don't agree with you," Archimedes assured

him with a dismissive snort. "I told Merlin from the start he was wasting his time with you. But he saw something in you." The owl spun his head. "Maybe this was it."

"I wish he had warned me," Arthur grumped, thinking back to his kind but somewhat bumbling tutor. The wizard Merlin had seen fit to take Arthur under his wing the year before after Arthur had accidentally crashed through his roof, searching for Kay's lost arrow. At the time, Arthur had just been grateful for the attention, even if Merlin's unique brand of tutelage did frequently get him into a bit of trouble. After all, who wouldn't enjoy lessons that entailed becoming a fish or a squirrel or even a bird?

But those transformations hadn't exactly prepared him for being a king.

"If only Merlin would come back," he moaned. "He'd know what to do."

Archimedes flew from the throne up to a wooden beam near the ceiling. "Believe me, I want Merlin back as much as you do," he agreed. "I never realised how fond I was of the old fool until he bopped himself off to Bermuda."

"Blow me to Bermuda," Arthur sadly echoed Merlin's last words. "I know he was angry with me, but I never thought he'd stay away for good." He slumped his shoulders. "I should have turned down the squire job like he wanted

me to. I could have stayed behind at Ector's castle and continued my lessons with him. Then I wouldn't be in such a mess."

If only there were a way to reach him. To apologise. Merlin had been right about everything all along. But Arthur hadn't listened...

"Well, there's no use crying over wandering wizards," Archimedes chirped. "The point is, he's gone. You're king. And there's nothing you can do about it. So I suggest you stop moping about and start doing your duty." He flew across the throne room to the double doors at the end. "There are at least two dozen people outside, waiting to talk to you. You can't keep them out forever."

Arthur nodded miserably. He knew the owl was right. "Very well," he said. "Let them in." He tried to straighten his crown, which was far too big for his head, and sat up taller in his throne. Archimedes waited for him to be settled, then yanked the front doors open with his talons.

Suddenly the vast empty chamber exploded in sound and colour as the people of England poured inside to meet their new king. Arthur tried not to squirm as they dropped to their knees before him and practically kissed the ground at his feet. How embarrassing.

"All rise," he called out, trying to make his voice sound authoritative – like a king's. Instead, it sounded as squeaky as a mouse's. "Make an orderly line. I'm ready to hear your grievances."

Arthur had never known any actual kings prior to becoming one himself, mind you. But he had always just assumed being king meant being able to do whatever you wanted – whenever you wanted to do it. Unfortunately, the opposite was true according to Sir Pellinore, who had instated himself as head knight and official advisor once Arthur took the throne. A king had to attend to his subjects constantly, listening to their problems and trying to help solve them. Even if their problems were difficult.

Or just plain ridiculous.

Speaking of, an apple-cheeked woman with pale skin and freckles, dressed in a dusty white apron and powder-blue dress, pushed her way through the crowd, cradling a small brown chicken in her arms.

"Your Majesty," she said, bowing so low to Arthur that she almost dropped her chicken in the process. "I am in desperate need of your help."

Arthur nodded, beckoning for her to stand upright again. He wondered, not for the first time, if it was within his powers to outlaw bowing entirely – at least to a king. He'd have to ask Sir Pellinore later. "What seems to be the trouble?" he asked.

The woman thrust the bird forwards. "I am Mistress Mabel. And this is my chicken. I call her Helen of Troy. She's a remarkable bird. Always has an egg for me, every morning, rain or shine."

"That's… great." Arthur waited for the complaint.

"Well, this morning, I went out to her henhouse, and there was no egg! And no Helen of Troy, either! I searched the yard thoroughly, concerned that a fox might have come in and stolen her away in the night."

"But… you found her," Arthur suggested gently, gesturing to the chicken, which was clearly no longer lost nor eaten by a fox. "She's all right." He wondered if it'd be unkingly to ask her to get to the point.

"I found her… in my neighbour's chicken coop!" Mistress Mabel sputtered, her red cheeks ripe with indignation.

Before Arthur could speak, another woman shoved her way through the crowd. She grabbed the chicken from Mabel and yanked it in her own direction. Helen of Troy squawked in dismay, and a spray of feathers burst into the air, causing several people – including Arthur – to sneeze.

"Bless you," Archimedes whispered. "And good luck with this one."

Arthur sighed and turned back to the new woman in front of him. "I'm sorry. You are…?"

"I'm Ayn, the rightful owner of this here chicken," the new woman declared.

"I see." Oh, dear. Arthur's eyes strayed to the long line of people behind the two women, who were starting to look impatient.

Mistress Ayn puffed out her chest. "You see, sire, I woke up this morning, ready to get started preparing our family's daily meal. We were all well looking forward to a nice supper of roasted bird this eve." She licked her lips. Helen of Troy squirmed in her arms, looking a tad alarmed.

"So I go out to the chicken coop. And what do I find there but this *thief*!" She gestured angrily to Mistress Mabel at her left. "She was trying to steal my chicken! Steal food out of my poor, sweet kids' very mouths!"

"Helen of Troy is mine!" Mistress Mabel protested. "I hatched her from an egg!"

"A disgusting lie. I picked her up at the market on Monday," countered Mistress Ayn, crossing her arms over her chest. "And you can't prove that I didn't."

The two women turned to look at Arthur expectantly. Meanwhile, the chicken had managed to wriggle its way out of Ayn's hands and drop to the floor, which it pecked at. Arthur raked a hand through his hair, feeling nervous. He knew they wanted him to rule on whom the chicken truly belonged to. But how could he tell for sure? They both seemed utterly convinced the bird was theirs.

If only Merlin were there. He'd know what to do.

Arthur turned to Archimedes – who was the next best thing. "What should I do?" he whispered.

The owl ruffled his feathers. "I'm sure I don't know. Though chicken for dinner does sound quite lovely." He eyed the bird hungrily. "Maybe we should just take it for ourselves and settle it that way."

"But that wouldn't be fair," Arthur protested.

"You want fair? Then just have them split it in two," Archimedes replied. "One half for each of them. That would be *fair*, right?" He huffed. "And then we can move on from all this nonsense and get to the important matters of the day."

Arthur frowned. The owl wasn't wrong. But still... Something about it didn't sit right with him. His eyes travelled to the two women. Mistress Ayn was glaring at Mistress Mabel with a smug look on her face. Mistress Mabel looked close to tears.

And suddenly he had an idea.

"Very well," he declared grandly, addressing the women and the court. "Since I suppose we can't know for sure who the bird belongs to, how about this? What if we cut the chicken in half and you can each have half of it? That ought to solve your problem, right?"

He watched the two women's faces, holding his breath.

Ayn spoke first. "Half," she muttered. "Well, I suppose it's better than nothing. Though with my big family…" She trailed off, turning to Mistress Mabel, who, Arthur realised, had burst into tears. Arthur watched as she dropped to her knees in front of him, her hands clasped in prayer.

"Please, kind sir," she begged. "Your Grace. Your Majesty. Do not split Helen of Troy in two! If she must have her, then she must have her. But make her promise not to eat her and to let her lay her daily eggs. They're good eggs – the best in the village." She turned to Ayn, her face pleading. "You'd do so much better to keep her alive than eat her, I promise you!"

It was all Arthur needed to hear. He clapped his hands.

"I have made my decision," he declared. "The chicken – Helen of Troy – shall be returned to this woman here." He smiled down at Mabel, who was still on her knees before him. "For if she cares so much for the fate of a chicken that she's willing to give it away rather than have it be cut in two, clearly she is the rightful owner."

Mabel let out a cry of joy. She dived for the chicken. Helen of Troy leapt into her lap, and she hugged the creature tightly against her chest, tears streaming down her rosy cheeks. The crowd behind her broke into cheers.

Mistress Ayn grunted and stormed out of the great hall, slamming the door behind her.

"Oh, thank you, kind sir," Mabel cried, still weeping. "Finally, we have a true king. One who is so just and good and kind and fair." She rose to her feet, still cuddling Helen of Troy. "I will bring you eggs every day from now on! To thank you for your kindness." She bowed again, then turned and headed through the hall to the door, all the while being congratulated by the others waiting their turns.

"That was very good, boy," Archimedes hooted. "Using wisdom to gain knowledge. Merlin would be so proud."

Arthur beamed, all of a sudden feeling quite proud of himself. His first act as king, and it was a success. Perhaps this wouldn't be as hard as he'd thought.

"Your Majesty, if you're done courting chickens, we must speak of graver matters."

Or… maybe not.

Arthur looked up to see that Sir Pellinore had stepped up to the throne. The tall, thin balding knight looked quite distraught – with an expression under his thick grey moustache that sent a chill down Arthur's spine.

"What is it?" Arthur asked worriedly, not entirely sure he wanted to know.

Sir Pellinore gave him a solemn look. "We have word that a new threat is coming to London Town, Your Majesty.

An army of Saxon invaders is rumoured to be landing on our eastern shores. They have supposedly heard of your new… position… and likely seek to learn for themselves what mettle you are made of." He met Arthur's eyes with his own steely grey ones. "What should we do to answer their call?"

Arthur sank back into his seat, all his earlier bravado fleeing. While the fate of chickens was something he felt somewhat confident handling, the fate of the kingdom was something else entirely. Especially when it came to matters of war. What if he made the wrong decision? People could die. England could be overrun by invaders. Soon there might not even be an England for him to be king of.

He glanced over at Archimedes, but the owl had retreated up into the rafters. Coward!

"Um…" he stammered, turning back to Pellinore. "What do *you* think we should do?" Sir Pellinore was, after all, an actual knight. And much more versed in these types of matters.

But the elderly knight shook his head. "What I think doesn't matter in this case," he told Arthur. "You, my boy, are our king. You are the one the heavens chose. You are the one who must decide our fate."

Arthur bit back a groan. He'd had a feeling Pellinore was going to say something like that. He rubbed his hand on his chin, as if deep in thought. But in truth, his mind was basically blank. He squirmed on his throne, once again wishing he had a cushion. But all the cushions in the world couldn't get him out of this one.

What would Merlin do? he asked himself again. But this time he had no answer. Merlin had tried to give him a top-notch education, but none of his teachings had to do with battles or invaders. War wasn't the wizard's thing.

"Well, Your Majesty?"

Arthur could feel the entire court locking their eyes onto him, holding their breaths, waiting for his reply. Whatever came out of his mouth next had the potential to change the course of history. He did not want to say the wrong thing. He swallowed hard and opened his mouth…

"I think we should… I think we should…"

His voice trailed off as he realised everything had gone strangely quiet. The hum of voices in the hall had completely ceased. And when his eyes scanned the room, he realised everyone was standing very still. Not still because they were paying close attention, mind you. But as if they had been actually frozen in place. Even Archimedes was hanging above him – suspended in midair.

Then, suddenly, a new voice rose up beside Arthur. Thin and reedy and high pitched.

"Now, now, don't tell me our illustrious new king is *chicken*…"

CHAPTER TWO
ARTHUR

Arthur whirled around, shocked to find a hunched old woman standing next to him, seeming to have come out of nowhere. She wore long purple robes and the same style of pointed hat that Merlin favoured, though hers was a dark shade of violet. She leant heavily on a wooden cane topped with an elaborate carving of a dragon's head. As Arthur gaped at her, she grinned toothily back at him as if he were a long-lost friend, and even though he was pretty positive he'd never seen her before in his life, he felt a weird shimmer of familiarity wash over him as he gazed upon her face.

"Um, who are you?" he asked, warily looking around the room. "And why is everyone but us frozen?"

The woman laughed. It sounded like the tinkling of

tiny bells. "That was my doing, m'lord," she informed him, bobbing her head respectfully in his direction. "I wanted to speak with you privately, and they were all being so very loud." She paused, staring at him with strangely vivid purple eyes. "You don't mind, do you?"

"Um…" Arthur honestly wasn't sure if he should mind or not. On one hand, it wasn't right to freeze people against their wills simply to have a quieter conversation. On the other, it did give him some extra time to make a decision on the whole Saxon invader thing, which, he supposed, wasn't unwelcome. "Who are you again?" he asked.

"My name is Morgan," the woman informed him. "The marvellous Morgan le Fay. I am a wizard of some high regard. Surely you have heard of me?" She looked a little hurt to think that maybe he hadn't.

Arthur felt his cheeks heat to a blush. "I'm sorry," he said. "I'm sure you're quite well known. It's just… I don't get out much, you see. In fact, before last month, I'd never gone beyond the Forest Sauvage and my foster father's place. And now that I'm king, I'm not allowed to leave this castle."

"Poor lad." The woman – Morgan – put a hand on his arm and patted him comfortingly. Arthur couldn't help noticing that even her fingernails were painted purple. "And now you're king of all England. I imagine that kind of quick change of fortune is bound to make one's head spin."

"You have no idea," Arthur said with a sigh, looking out over his frozen court.

"Oh, but I do! In fact, it's why I'm here, my boy!"

"It is?" Arthur turned back to the woman, his eyes widening. Suddenly he put two and two together. "Wait... did Merlin send you? Is he all right? Why isn't he here? Is he still angry at me about the whole squire thing? Because I really feel bad about all that! I didn't mean to drive him away!"

Morgan laughed, holding up a hand to stop the barrage of questions. "Oh, my dear boy. You know Merlin! He's so flighty. So unpredictable. He wanted to be here, of course. But he had a little holiday planned. And you know how *those* can be. Don't cancel in time? You don't get your deposit back. And no one wants that!" She gave Arthur a knowing look.

Arthur swallowed hard, his mind whirling. He knew she was speaking English, but he wasn't quite sure he understood half the things she'd just said. But then again, that was how Merlin always talked, too. Maybe it was a wizard thing...

"Anyhoo, while dear old Merlin is enjoying a little R and R in the far-off future, I'm here at his behest to take over your education. And it seems, my dear little sparrow,

I've arrived just in the nick of time." She glanced out over the frozen court. "Now tell Auntie Morgan. What exactly seems to be the trouble?"

Arthur sank back down onto his throne, slumping his shoulders in relief. Finally, someone grown-up – and human (he stole a glance up at Archimedes) – who was willing to listen.

"I want to be a good king," he told Morgan. "I don't want to let anyone down. But I know nothing of battles and wars and invasions." He sighed. "It seems the Saxons – whoever they are – will be landing on our shores shortly. And it sounds as if they'll be up to no good when they get here. But I don't know what I should do about it."

"Oh! That's simple!" Morgan exclaimed without a pause. "You blow them out of the water."

Arthur looked at her, surprised. "What?" This was not quite what he'd been expecting her to say.

"Come on! Isn't it obvious? We have to show these silly boys they can't just roll up to England's shores without RSVPing first! It's simply not done! And quite rude, to boot."

"RSV-what?"

Morgan waved him off. "Look, it's all very simple. You round up an army of your very best knights. And you send them down to the shores to defend your land. Show them exactly what happens when they try to rise up under our rule!"

"*Our* rule?" Arthur scrunched up his face.

Morgan giggled. "Did I say *our*? I meant *your*, of course. For *you* are the king of England now! All because you pulled that sword from that stone." She motioned to the sword at Arthur's belt. "A marvellous miracle, don't you think?"

"I— I suppose..." Arthur stammered, starting to feel a little uncomfortable.

"Oh! He's modest, too! How adorable." Morgan pinched his cheeks, just a tad too hard. Then she clapped her hands. "Look, all you need to do is show them who's boss. And then they won't have a leg to stand on. Literally – if you cut off their legs." She giggled. "Just kidding," she added quickly, in a way that made Arthur wonder if she had been.

"Look, I don't want to hurt anyone," he told Morgan. "I just want them to go home."

"Oh, they will. A few amputated limbs and everyone will take off running." She laughed. This time it sounded a bit more like a cackle. "Well, not *running*, exactly." She slapped her hand on her knee. "Kidding! Kidding! Sorry! Sometimes I just can't help myself!"

"Right..." Arthur pressed his lips together, glancing up at Archimedes again, wishing the owl would unfreeze and help him. Maybe he could tell Arthur who this woman really was – and if she truly was a friend of his teacher's. She claimed Merlin had sent her. But she certainly had a very different way of looking at the world than his old tutor.

His mind flashed back to the day Merlin had turned him into a fish. They'd been swimming along in the castle moat quite happily when a huge pike with nasty sharp teeth had started chasing them. Merlin had refused to help, telling Arthur he needed to figure it out on his own. In fact, he still remembered the wizard's words. Something about the strong wanting to conquer you, but that you could defeat them using intellect.

Intellect – not violence. Because according to Merlin, *brains* were just as powerful as brawn.

What if he could trick the Saxons? Or better yet, try to befriend them? Maybe they could avoid violence. Maybe it could even work out in everyone's favour – having a new friend was never a bad thing…

He realised Morgan was still waiting for an answer. Sitting up straighter in his throne, he cleared his throat. He had to be careful. After all, friend of Merlin's or no, she was clearly a powerful wizard. He didn't want to make her angry by dismissing her outright. She might even refuse to unfreeze his court. And then where would he be?

"Look," he said, "it's not that I don't appreciate your

advice. I really do. But in this case, I think I am going to try something else first. Something more... peaceful." He shrugged sheepishly. "I'm pretty sure it's what Merlin would have wanted."

Morgan's smile slipped from her face. For a moment, she looked angry. But then, just as quickly as her smile had faded, it returned. "Of course, of course!" she agreed, patting him a little too hard on the shoulder. "You do you! You're the king, after all! You pulled the sword from the stone – all by yourself! So why would you want to listen to a silly old wizard who went so far out of her way to come and help you with your troubles? Much better to imagine what Merlin would do. The cowardly kook who abandoned you to this fate. Did he even say goodbye when he left?"

Arthur cringed. "Well, not exactly—"

"Of course he didn't. That silly boy!" Morgan snorted. "Anyway, I must be going now! So much time, so little to do!" she jabbered. "Or is it the opposite?" She tapped her finger to her chin. "In any case, have fun running the kingdom all by yourself! Hope you don't get invaded and suffer a fate worse than death!" She lifted her hand to a wave. "Toodles!"

And with that, she poofed into a cloud of smoke. When it cleared, she had disappeared completely. As if she'd never been there at all.

A moment later the court erupted into sound again, everyone talking and moving as if they had no idea they'd ever been frozen at all. Perhaps they didn't. Arthur felt a shimmer of unease as he looked to the spot where Morgan had stood a moment before, now completely empty. He wondered if he'd made the right decision.

Archimedes dropped down from his perch and peered at Arthur quizzically.

"Are you all right?" he asked. "You look like you've seen a ghost."

"I'll tell you later," Arthur said, waving him off. He turned back to Sir Pellinore, who was now once again expectantly waiting for his answer.

"Sire?" the knight queried. "What do you want us to do?"

Arthur drew in a breath. "I think we should invite the Saxons here," he blurted out before he could lose his nerve.

Pellinore looked shocked. "Excuse me?"

"We will invite them to the castle. And when they come, we will throw a great feast in their honour."

"You want to invite our enemies to a feast?" The old knight looked as if he was about to fall over.

"Yes," Arthur declared, feeling more and more confident about his plan as he thought about it. It was exactly the kind of thing Merlin would have approved of. "We will invite them here and speak with them as equals. See what they want. Who knows – maybe we can work out a peace treaty that will benefit us both. We may be different, but we're all human beings, after all. There's no reason we can't all get along."

For a moment Pellinore said nothing. Then he slowly nodded his head. "Very well, Your Majesty," he said. "You are the king. It's your call." But he didn't sound too confident about the whole thing. Perhaps he would have preferred Morgan's idea of destroying them all. Arthur sighed, looking out onto the court for support. Surely *someone* thought this was a good idea, besides him? But all he saw were worried, distrustful faces. No one seemed to approve of his plan.

Merlin would have approved, Arthur thought, forcing himself to remain strong. *And he's the smartest person I know.*

CHAPTER THREE
MADAM MIM

Merlin is such a meddling muck!

The Marvellous Madam Mim cursed under her breath as she poofed herself back to her little cottage in the woods, so furious at what had just transpired at the castle that her skin had broken out into pink polka dots all over again – an irritating lingering side effect of that horrific disease she'd suffered at the hands of that wily waste of a wizard. She glanced in the mirror, scowled, then snapped a finger. The elegant elder 'Morgan le Fay' vanished into thin air and Mim returned to her normal purple-haired self.

She stormed over to the fireplace, poking angrily at the ashes. Then she waved her finger, and a small purple flame sputtered to life in the hearth. Huffing, she plopped down on a nearby chair in front of her table of cards. But she was in no mood for games.

"This was not how it was supposed to go," she muttered to herself. "Not how it was supposed to go at all. Here I go to all the effort of faking a miracle, and where does it get me? A young sparrow with delusions of grandeur and no respect for his elders."

Mim spat on the floor. "Bleh!" This was clearly all Merlin's fault. As usual.

Perhaps she should have never meddled in the situation to begin with. But when she'd heard the announcement that they were going to have a tournament to decide on a king at last, she'd panicked. All these years she'd been working to ensure England stayed stuck in a dark age of chaos and confusion – a state Mim delighted in; it was just so much fun! And now they were going to allow some random knight in shining armour to rise up and start making rules again? What if this man united England? What if he brought peace and lawfulness to the land?

Why, that would be no fun at all!

And so she'd determined to take matters into her own hands. She had sneaked out late at night and used her magic to relocate the real sword in the stone to some kind of fancy theme park far in the future of a land yet to be called Florida. In its place, she'd fashioned a replacement.

A design of her own, which allowed the sword to be lifted from the stone by a person of her choosing.

And she'd chosen the least likely candidate of all.

"The looks on their faces!" she cackled in remembrance. "When they realised this scrawny little sparrow who couldn't even fit into his clothes was to be their king!" She thought back to all the fools bowing low before the boy and how she'd laughed and laughed from the sidelines. "How could they really believe he was the one?"

It was all just perfectly hilarious.

And if that wasn't victory enough, she'd gone one step further, getting rid of the only person who might have discovered her ruse. The meddlesome Merlin, who'd completely, unfairly cheated during their wizards' duel. She'd been on her way to demand a rematch when she'd overheard his owl say he'd gone to somewhere in the future called Bermuda. It took a bit of fancy spell casting – including the regretful sacrifice of her favourite warty toad, Martha – but she'd managed to track him down and scramble up his spell book while he was asleep in a lounge chair on the beach, making it impossible for him to magically find his way back home. Which meant he wouldn't be around to mess up her messing things up.

Yes, everything had been so perfectly un-perfect.

Until she'd spotted the owl in court today. *Merlin's* owl.

And he'd been talking to the boy.

She grunted in annoyance, remembering the moment she'd realised what she'd accidentally done. That of all the boys in all the world, she'd somehow managed to place Merlin's own protégé on the throne. It was an honest mistake; she'd never seen Arthur with Merlin before. At least not in his boy state – he'd been a bird when he'd come down her chimney and started the whole duel thing. How was she to know that this very same boy would turn up halfway across England in London on the day of the tournament, looking for a sword?

Mim liked bad luck. But only when it happened to other people.

At first, she didn't think it would be a huge problem. In fact, maybe it could even work out in her favour. What better way to get back at Merlin than to take over the 'education' of his favourite pupil? With Merlin gone, Arthur would be lost, confused, scared. She could slip right in and pretend to be his friend, offering up some oh-so-wise advice that surely he would follow, relieved to have a grown-up calling the shots.

She imagined with delight Merlin's horror when he finally realised what she had done. Taking his very own student – the one he had risked his life in their duel to protect – and moulding him into her own stooge, a fellow lover of the gruesome and grim! It would have been the best revenge she could have hoped for.

Unfortunately, it had not gone so well.

She scowled into the mirror, thinking back to the scene. Why, the boy had not listened to her oh-so-wise advice at all! Instead, the little boy king had some wonky idea of trying for a peaceful solution instead. Which was ridiculous, to say the least! After all, what young lad in medieval England wanted peace? There was no glory in that! No adventure! No dragons, even.

Merlin had clearly poisoned his young brain.

She sighed, brushing away the pile of cards. She needed a new plan. It was too late to put someone else on the throne – it would cause far too many questions. And she was still convinced Arthur could be turned to her side; he just needed something more convincing. Or maybe some*one*. Someone he could grow to trust. Someone Mim could use to feed him her fun ideas and make him act on them – ensuring more and more chaos the longer his rule. An advisor, maybe? Was there a knight she could corrupt? Maybe a servant?

A friend?

"Mother? I'm home!"

Mim's head shot up as her ward, Guinevere, stepped into the cottage, her arms laden with supplies she'd acquired at the market in town. Guinevere always insisted on buying groceries the old-fashioned way, no matter how many times Mim reminded her she could just conjure them up with magic – no muss, no fuss. (And no price tag, either! Let's just say being a wizard was marvellous, but didn't always pay the bills.)

Mim had been fostering Guinevere for the last thirteen years, after 'borrowing' her from her cradle in her parents' home back in the Summer Country. Mim had always thought it would be fun to have a child to teach magic to, and had somehow not managed, thus far, to produce any on her own. And so when she had discovered, in an ancient tome, that Guinevere's family lines ran deep and were rumoured to flow with fairy blood – the kind of blood that could help make one into a powerful wizard – Mim took matters into her own hands, not wanting such potential power to end up totally wasted on a royal lady in court who would never have a chance to properly use it.

Guinevere, of course, didn't know any of these pesky little details of her unconventional 'adoption' – a story Mim found far too boring for her liking. Instead, she'd told the young girl she'd rescued her from the evil wizard Merlin, who had killed her parents and tried to steal her away, which proved a much better bedtime story. Guin was *so* lucky that Mim had come by when she had and risked her own life to save the baby from the hands of that tyrant. And Guin should be eternally grateful her 'mother' had agreed to take her in afterwards, when she had nowhere else to go. After all, babies were stinky. And those midnight feedings? A major sacrifice for the sake of a helpless creature who couldn't even keep up with an intelligent conversation.

But it would all be worth it, Mim had told herself back then, once Guinevere started mastering her magic. And she would become a worthy heir to take Mim's place someday as the most powerful wizard in the land.

There was only one problem with it all. Guinevere hated magic.

Perhaps it was Mim's fault, she thought in hindsight. Perhaps the Merlin story had been a bit too dramatic to tell an impressionable four-year-old just before bed. But there was nothing she could do to take it back now. And as much as Mim tried to show Guin all the fun things that magic could do – fireworks! shapeshifting! rainbow-coloured ponies! – Guin remained thoroughly unconvinced. Hence the groceries. And the washing. And the mending. All things that could have been easily accomplished by a touch of magic, instead done painstakingly by her daughter's hands. While all of Guin's potential power remained untapped. Untouched.

Mim shook her head. Such a waste…

Guinevere set her packages on the floor near the door, then danced across the cottage to give her mother a warm hug. Mim indulged her for a moment – hugs made her itchy – then shrugged her off.

"What's wrong, Mother?" Guin asked, frowning as she studied Mim's face with her big brown eyes. The girl had the most amazing lashes, Mim thought grumpily. So thick and curly. And she didn't even need magic to grow them. "You look upset."

"Oh, I'm just fine, my dear," she assured her, patting her on the arm. "Did you get any slugs at the market today? I've been practically dying for slug soup for dinner."

"I'm sorry," Guinevere apologised as she walked over to her bags and grabbed one, bringing it over to the table. "I looked and looked. No one seems to sell slugs in London." She shrugged. "They did have some lovely apples, though." She reached into the bag and pulled out a shiny red apple, giving Mim a hopeful look.

Mim did not like apples. Especially ripe ones without any worms. They made her toot like a trumpet and tasted nothing like a good old slimy slug. But she only smiled and petted Guinevere's hand. The poor girl did try so hard to please her mother. Even if she did have lousy taste in food.

Guinevere began putting away the groceries, dancing a little as she went. As much as Guin didn't like magic, she *loved* to dance. Which had always given them something to bond over. Mim would sing and Guin would dance. And for a brief moment, it would feel as if it was just the two of them – together against the hard, cruel world – and Mim would realise just how lucky she was to have a daughter of her very own.

"It was wild in town today," Guinevere said as she placed some potatoes in the bin where they could sit until they properly rotted. "With the new king holding court and all. People were here from all over the kingdom to meet him."

Mim frowned, unhappy to be reminded of that ridiculous Arthur and his ridiculous court again. She still couldn't believe he'd basically thrown her out of the throne room, all because of some teensy-weensy suggestion that he start a war. Thank goodness everyone had been frozen at the time and therefore hadn't witnessed her humiliation.

Guinevere, oblivious, danced back over to the table. "It *was* pretty exciting, though," she added, her eyes sparkling a little as she grabbed a cabbage. "You should have been there. It was as if there was this energy crackling in the air. Everyone's waited so long for a new king. And to finally have one at long last! Why, they say he'll bring peace to the realm! Maybe even unite all of England!"

Mim swallowed back the urge to vomit. Seriously, this Arthur was nothing if not nauseating.

"Please don't talk to me about that usurper," she protested grumpily. "He shouldn't even be king, you know."

Guinevere stopped short. She turned to Mim, her large brown eyes widening in surprise. "What are you saying, Mother?" she asked. "Why shouldn't he be king? He pulled the sword from the stone, didn't he?"

He certainly had, Mim thought huffingly. Thanks to her. She really had to do something about this. She couldn't just sit back and let Merlin win after all.

Suddenly an idea began to niggle at the back of her brain. She looked up at Guinevere.

"Yes," she said. "He *did* pull the sword from the stone. But he wasn't meant to. It was all a trick. Concocted by that evil wizard Merlin to get his little puppet on the throne – so he could have all the power for himself and destroy England!"

Guinevere dropped her cabbage. It fell to the floor of the cottage with a loud thump. This was not surprising. She always got upset when Mim said the *M* word. She turned slowly to her mother, her face white with fear. "Are you serious?" she asked. "Merlin? He's behind the miracle?"

Mim smiled to herself. Now that was more like it.

"None other," she declared, liking this story more and

more as she made it up out of thin air. "And now Arthur is on the throne. Who knows what damage he'll do to our country?" She sighed loudly. "I worry for the realm, I really do."

"Oh, but this is terrible!" Guinevere murmured, pacing the cottage, rubbing her hands together in worry. "I had no idea. Everyone seems to love the new king so much!"

"A trick. A trap. Evil sorcery of the worst kind."

"So what do we do?" Guinevere asked. She dropped to her knees before Mim, clasping her hands over Mim's own. "You can't let Merlin get away with this! Tell me you have a plan."

Mim stroked her hairy chin, her fabulously big brain now whirring with excitement as a plan did begin to form. "I do," she confessed. "However, I don't think I can pull it off myself. I tried to go to court today, but he rejected my oh-so-generous offer of help. I think he might have been suspicious of my intentions. Which were entirely good, of course!" she added, lest Guin have any doubt. She dropped her eyes to meet her daughter's. "But perhaps if someone *else* were to go to court in my place. Someone more his own age…"

"Do you mean me?" Guinevere's voice echoed her surprise. Which, Mim supposed, wasn't unwarranted. Back in the Forest Sauvage, she hadn't exactly let the girl wander too far from their cottage in the woods for most of her life. For her own good, of course. And just in case someone recognised her and had the bad sense to call the authorities. Mim wasn't about to lose her useful protégé over something as ridiculous as having her real parents wanting her back.

But they were far from the forest now. And while Guin had grown to look irritatingly like her birth mother, no one here would recognise her. Mim would have to take a chance.

"Yes." Mim straightened, her plan solidifying in her mind. Arthur wouldn't suspect a thing from a sweet young girl like Guin. And Guin would do whatever her mother asked of her without question. "You will go to court and apply to be a dishwasher or dog walker or privy emptier or whatever random job they might have open at the castle for young ladies like yourself. This way you can be my eyes and ears on the ground."

Guinevere looked unsure. "Would I have to use magic?" she asked.

"No, no, of course not," Mim assured her, resisting the urge to lecture the girl about the benefits of having powers – she didn't need to start a fight. "You just have to be yourself. Befriend Arthur – make him trust you. Get him to tell you his evil plans, then report them all back to me. Perhaps you'll even discover a weakness. Something we can use to take him down."

"And put the rightful ruler on the throne instead!" Guinevere concluded, looking satisfied at the idea now that she knew it didn't involve magic. She rose to her feet, planting her hands on her hips. "I love it. It's perfect. And I know I can do it. He won't stand a chance against me." She smiled smugly. She might not be magical, but Mim had always admired her confidence.

"That's my girl!" Mim cried, feeling suddenly so much better about everything. She leapt up from her chair, grabbing a harp and strumming the chords. Guinevere clapped her hands, delighted, then broke out into a playful dance as Mim began to sing.

The evil Merlin thinks he's won.
But the game, my dear, is not half done.
For his lackey king is far too dim...
To stand a chance against the mighty,
magnificent, marvellous—

"Guinevere!" Guin broke in, finishing the song with a dramatic flourish.

Mim frowned. "That doesn't exactly rhyme," she muttered a little sulkily at having her song interrupted. But Guin wasn't listening. She was standing in the centre of the cottage, her eyes shining.

"Just leave it to me, Mother," she declared. "I swear I won't let you down. I will do whatever it takes to put this usurper back in his rightful place."

Mim couldn't help a small smile at the earnest look on her daughter's face. Yes. This was going to be great. Arthur would trust her confident daughter, giving Mim the perfect in. And Merlin – he would be so upset when he found out she'd stolen his pet and made him her own! She walked over to Guin, taking her hands and squeezing them tight.

"This will be just *marvellous*, my dear. Wait and see."

CHAPTER FOUR
GUINEVERE

After she received her assignment, Guinevere had hoped her mother would send her to Camelot Castle immediately so she could begin her quest to help unseat Merlin's pawn. Instead, Mim had told her it was best to wait until morning to start her journey, stating that it would be dangerous for a young girl to travel through the woods on her own in the dark where wolves and other nasty forest creatures might be lurking. Guin wouldn't exactly be able to save the world, she reminded her, if she became a wolf's midnight snack.

Of course, Mim could zap her there immediately using magic, but Guinevere chose to decline that option, saying she should probably cook dinner first anyway.

So Guin began to prepare their nightly meal, deciding on a hearty stew using the vegetables she'd found in the market. (She was still secretly grateful she hadn't found any slugs. Nothing against her mother, of course, but they were just so slimy!) She planned to make an extra-large portion of stew so Mim could eat it while she was away. After all, she had no idea how long she'd be at the castle. And she didn't need her mother resorting to magic again while she was gone just to feed herself.

After slicing and dicing the vegetables, Guin realised she didn't have enough water for her stew. And so she set out with two large buckets to the well just outside of town. It was about an eight-furlong walk, but Guinevere didn't mind the trek so much. It was pleasant, after all, to feel the warm sun on her skin and fresh air on her face.

It reminded her of the Forest Sauvage, where she and Mim had lived up until recently. Mim had decided one day (seemingly on a whim) to use her magic to poof their entire cottage furlongs away from its old spot and plop it down on an entirely new plot of land just outside of London – with them still inside of it. Mim insisted it was more convenient that way – rather than packing everything up and moving to a new place by horse and wagon. And Guinevere *was* happy to be able to keep her old room in the new spot. Though she admittedly would have preferred a less jarring way to go about it.

Magic. It was always so troublesome.

Speaking of magic, she still couldn't believe what that dastardly Merlin had managed to get away with. Or maybe she could – after all, it was just like the evil wizard to meddle in affairs that were simply none of his business. He'd killed her parents, for one thing. And he'd tried to kill her, too. Why, he'd quite recently barged into her mother's cottage with his bewitched owl for no reason at all, while Mim was minding her own business playing a game of cards. He'd challenged her to a duel, forcing her mother to use her magic, then cheated by giving her a near-fatal disease. It had taken weeks for Guin to nurse her poor mother back to health.

The man had to be stopped. And if Guinevere could help in any way? Why, she was more than happy to do so. She'd been longing for revenge as long as she could remember. And finally she would get her chance.

She wondered what Arthur would be like. Mim hadn't allowed her to attend his coronation, so she'd never caught sight of his face. She could imagine it, though – probably rough and scarred from the many battles he'd fought. And his shoulders would be very broad. He'd be tall, too. Guinevere was pretty sure all kings were tall. And likely barrel-chested – maybe with a cleft in his chin. She pictured him draped in heavy ermine robes and decked out in stolen jewels as he sat languidly on the throne, working to destroy a kingdom that he should never have been allowed to rule to begin with.

But that wasn't going to happen. Not on her watch.

When she arrived at the well, she realised there was someone already there: a boy, around her own age, with a mop of sandy-coloured hair on top of his head. From his simple undyed cotton tunic, woven belt and plain shoes, she assumed he was one of the nearby villagers, come to gather water at the well.

Except he didn't have a bucket. And he was peering down into the water with a strange longing on his face.

She waited for a moment, hoping he'd just leave on his own and allow her to get her water. When he didn't, she eventually cleared her throat to get his attention. His head jerked up in response, managing to smack into the well's wooden roof. He let out an "OW!" and staggered backwards, holding his head with his hands. Guinevere immediately felt bad.

"I'm sorry!" she cried, biting her lower lip. "I didn't mean to startle you."

The boy managed to straighten, then shook himself. He looked up at her. "It's all right," he said. "My fault, really."

"What were you doing?" she asked.

"I was just thinking about being a fish," he replied. As

if this weren't a strange thing to say to someone, especially someone you just met.

"Hm. I don't think there are any fish in this well," she couldn't help teasing. "I mean, I hope not, at least. It wouldn't be very pleasant for them. Or us, for that matter." She grinned.

He laughed. It was a nice laugh, full and rich and hearty, unlike Mim's giggles. "You're probably right," he agreed, leaning against a nearby tree. "Perhaps a bird would be better." He looked up into the sky. Guinevere noticed his eyes were very blue.

"I don't know about that," she replied before she could help herself, remembering the time Mim had zapped her into a bird during a lesson on shapeshifting magic. Guin still remembered how terrifying it had been to feel her body shrink in size and her bones reshape themselves. And if that wasn't bad enough, Mim had found it hilarious to pick her up and toss her high into the air, assuming she'd learn to fly before colliding back with the ground.

She hadn't, it turned out. And if Mim hadn't caught her at the last moment in a magical bubble of air, she probably wouldn't even be there talking to the boy now.

"Where would you go if you were a bird?" she asked as she grabbed the well's rope and started pulling up its bucket.

"I don't know," the boy mused, seeming to take the question more seriously than she'd meant it. "But wherever it was, it would be far away from here. Where no one could find me."

The tone in his voice sounded both sad and a little lonely. Guinevere watched as he stubbed his toe into the dirt. "Is that why you're out here?" she asked kindly. "Because you don't want to be found?"

"Most definitely," he agreed with a long sigh. "Life has become... well, complicated lately. I just wanted a few moments to myself. You can imagine, right?" He gave a half laugh and looked at her as if she would understand.

And she did, actually. As much as she loved her foster mother and their simple life in the forest, sometimes Guin found herself longing for some freedom or a chance for adventure. Mim was a lot of wonderful things, but she was also very protective of her daughter, insisting she always stay close for her own safety. The world was a dangerous place, Mim would say. With evil wizards like Merlin always lurking about in the shadows. You couldn't be too careful.

Guin was appreciative of her mother caring about her so much and protecting her from harm. But still, sometimes she couldn't help wishing for more...

"Do you live in the village?" she asked the boy,

deciding to change the subject. "I don't think I've seen you here before."

For a moment he looked startled at the question. Almost as if he had expected her to know this already. But then a small smile crept over his face.

"Yes," he said. "I, uh, live in the village. My name's, uh, Wart."

"Wart?" she repeated, raising an eyebrow. "What a peculiar name."

His face turned bright red. "It's a… nickname," he confessed. "Perhaps not the most flattering…"

Guinevere immediately felt bad. "I like it, actually," she pronounced. "It's very unique. I mean, everyone and their brother these days is a Gawain or a Galahad or a Gaheris. But I don't know a single other Wart." She smiled at him. He smiled back, clearly relieved.

"What's your name?" he asked.

"Oh! Well, I'm Guinevere," she replied. "I live just down the path with my mother in a small cottage in the woods. We come here to get well water because our well ran dry."

That wasn't exactly what had happened. In truth, one of Mim's spells had backfired when they'd first arrived and left the entire well filled with green slimy goo. The wizard was still trying to work on a reverse spell, but so far had only managed to change the goo's colour to purple, which Guin didn't feel was much of an improvement, at least when it came to drinking it.

But, of course, she wasn't to speak of such things to strangers. That was Mim's number one rule. Never talk about magic to mortals. They might think you dangerous. Like Merlin was. They might even try to lock you up and throw away the key. In fact, they'd tried to do that with Mim once. Guinevere would never forget the day she came home to find her mother gone. Thank goodness Mim had outsmarted her captors in the end. She'd turned them all into toads and poofed herself back home.

Can't keep a good wizard down! she'd declared. And Guin had nearly collapsed in relief. After all, her mother was all she had. And as much as she feared magic, she feared losing Mim most of all.

"It's nice to meet you," Wart said, interrupting her thoughts. He held out his hand and Guinevere took it in her own, surprised at how strong his grip was. She had assumed from his thin, gangly arms and legs he would have a softer touch.

"Nice to meet you, too," she said. Then she glanced up at the sky. "Though I really must be getting my water and heading home. It is starting to get dark, and I don't want to run into any wolves on the way back."

"I'll walk you back," Wart proposed. "They'll be less likely to attack if there's two of us. And I do have a sword," he added with a small blush, gesturing to his side. The sheathed weapon hanging there had a rather ornate hilt – the kind of hilt that likely meant the sword was quite expensive. She wondered how a commoner like him could have come into possession of such a prize. She hoped he hadn't stolen it…

"It's really not necessary," she hedged, knowing Mim wouldn't be pleased about her leading a stranger to their home.

"It's a knight's duty to serve a damsel in distress!" Wart declared, puffing out his skinny chest. Guinevere couldn't help a giggle.

"First, I'm no damsel in distress," she scolded playfully. "And second, I'm willing to wager you're not a knight."

His chest drooped. He looked so forlorn that for a moment she felt bad.

"But I *would* like the company," she added hastily as she worked to fill her buckets with well water. After she said it, she realised it was true. It was a long walk, and it would be lovely to have someone to talk to along the way. Especially someone as pleasant as Wart. They could get to know one another better on the journey, and then she could say goodbye to him well before the cottage came into view.

Mim would never be the wiser. "So what do you say?" she asked.

Wart's blue eyes lit up. He took one of her now-filled buckets with one hand, then made a sweeping gesture towards the path with his other. "Lead the way, m'lady," he said grandly. Which made her giggle all over again. "Our quest begins!"

CHAPTER FIVE
ARTHUR

What do you think you're doing? Arthur scolded himself as he followed Guinevere down the windy forest path in the direction of her home. *This is pure foolishness.*

And it was. As king, he wasn't even supposed to leave the castle, at least not without a full complement of knights at his side. And even then, he certainly was not supposed to talk to strangers he met along the side of the road. It was too dangerous, Sir Pellinore had lectured when Arthur had first tried to set out for a stroll shortly after his coronation. After all, he was England's only hope. The country's entire future rested on his admittedly scrawny shoulders. Which meant those shoulders needed to be protected. If anything happened to him, the land could fall back into a dark age. And no one wanted that.

Arthur didn't want that either, but still! It was so stifling being king. To be stuck inside all day long, listening to adults drone on and on about this problem or that. Sometimes he even longed for his old life back in Sir Ector's crumbling castle. At least there he had honest hard work to keep him busy, and he could go outside anytime he wanted without even having to tell anyone first. In a moment of desperation, Arthur had tried to sneak down to the Camelot kitchen to wash some dishes like he used to back then, but he was quickly discovered and sent back to the throne room. A king, it seemed, did not dirty his hands with menial labour.

So when Pellinore and his knights had left the castle that afternoon to go follow Arthur's orders and invite the invading Saxons to dinner, Arthur had found himself in a rare position of not being watched like a hawk for once. And when he'd discovered a servant's door left ajar, he couldn't resist taking full advantage, slipping out of the castle and wandering into the woods.

Just for a few minutes, he'd told himself. And he'd go right back.

But then he'd met her.

His eyes rose to the girl dancing down the path in front of him. She wore a plain peasant dress, un-cinched at the waist, and her long golden curls tumbled messily down her back in waves, free of all the severe braids and bindings so in fashion at the castle. It was almost as if she were a wild thing, untamed by civilised life. He couldn't imagine the ladies in court ever dancing so freely, as if they didn't have a care in the world.

And the best part was? She had no idea who he was. Which had shocked him at first – after all, he was currently the most famous person in all the land. And so many had attended his coronation. But then, she'd said she and her mother lived deep in the woods and didn't get out much. So it made sense she wouldn't recognise him. She hadn't even recognised the sword Excalibur at his side.

Which meant, for a moment, he could be his old self again. Not the long-destined king of legends, pledged to save the realm, but a simple boy out for a walk in the woods with a nice girl by his side. In fact, it had felt so good to be Wart again that he hadn't wanted the moment to end. And so he'd blurted out his offer to walk Guinevere back home. Just to spend a few more minutes feeling normal.

What if it's a trap? an annoying voice in his head nagged. *Maybe she knows exactly who you are and it's all part of her ruse. What if she is leading you into an ambush of your enemies? After all, not everyone in the land is pleased to have a young boy as their king. And they would be thrilled to get their hands on you, all alone, unprotected in a dark wood…*

"Ooh! Are those violets?" Guinevere asked, interrupting his worried thoughts. She leant down and plucked a handful of small purple flowers, then slipped them into a small pouch tied to her belt. "I haven't found any since we moved here, and they're so great for easing one's coughs when mixed with yarrow flowers."

"You make medicines?" Arthur asked, curious.

"Oh, yes. It's sort of a hobby of mine." Guin's cheeks coloured slightly. "Nature provides us with so many natural gifts. You just have to know what to look for. Back home I had a whole garden filled with herbs that I used to make potions with to help those in the nearby village."

"Home?" Arthur queried. "Are you not from around here, then?"

"We just moved here recently," she explained. "Around the same time they crowned the new king. We used to live miles away from here, in the Forest Sauvage. It's a wild place, but just as beautiful."

Arthur stopped short. "The Forest Sauvage?" he repeated incredulously.

"Yes." Guinevere stopped and turned to look at him quizzically. "Have you heard of it?"

"I used to live there!" he exclaimed before he could stop himself. "Until…" His voice trailed off. "Until… I came here," he stammered. He had to be careful not to give out too much personal information, just in case.

But Guinevere didn't seem to notice his stammer. She was shaking her head in wonder. "Wow! What a small world!" she whispered, an excited gleam in her dark eyes. "I wonder if we ever ran into each other back then and never realised it!"

"I don't think so," Arthur replied. "I would have remembered you."

As soon as the words left his mouth, he felt his face heat into a blush. *Imbecile! Why would you say something like that?* But then he caught her glancing at him with a shy smile on her lips, and something inside him made him glad he'd said it after all.

"It's getting rather dark," she pointed out, fortunately changing the subject. She looked up at the sky, still painted in bands of orange and gold from the setting sun. "I hope Mother isn't too worried. She doesn't like me being out at night by myself."

Arthur nodded absently, a little worried himself. He'd never meant to stray from the castle for so long. By now someone surely had noticed he was gone. Would they send out a search party for him?

Maybe it was time to say his goodbyes.

"Look, I…" he started, but trailed off as he heard a horn blowing in the distance. Along with a few shouts of "Arthur! Arthur!"

Oh, no. There *was* a search party. And they weren't far away, either, from the sound of it.

"Come on," he said, grabbing Guinevere's hand and urging her forwards. "Let's go!"

She gave him a puzzled look but complied, picking up the pace and dashing down the wooded trail. Arthur could hear the heavy clomping of hooves behind them, sounding as if they were getting closer by the second. This was not good.

"What's wrong?" Guinevere asked breathlessly. "Why are we running?"

He swallowed hard. Maybe it was time to come clean "Look, there's something I should tell you—" he began. But he was cut off by the horn blowing again, so close this time he had to put his hands over his ears to block out the sound. It was then that he realised Guinevere had stopped running. She turned to face him, putting her hands on her hips.

"So you *did* steal that sword, didn't you?" she accused, glancing down at Excalibur. "I knew it. It's far too grand for a peasant boy like yourself. And now they're looking for you! They want to arrest you for grand theft!"

"What?" Arthur's eyes bulged. "Wait, Guinevere – no!" He reached for her hand, but she ripped it away.

"I don't associate with thieves," she spit out. Then she turned in the direction of the search party. "He's over here!" she called.

Arthur's face went pale. "Shhh!" he cried. "Please! Don't attract their attention. I didn't steal the sword, I swear! I just… they can't find me!"

"Why not?" Guinevere demanded, looking very displeased. The sounds of horses were getting closer and closer. They must have been almost on top of them.

Arthur felt his knees practically give out. This had all been such a terrible mistake. "Look, Guinevere…" he tried.

But he got no further. At that moment, they were surrounded by a group of knights, led by none other than Sir Kay, Arthur's foster brother himself. Kay smirked as he looked down from his horse at Arthur and the girl standing in the middle of their circle.

"Well, well. Now I think I understand," he joked.

Arthur felt his hackles rise. Of all people to find him, it had to be Kay. There was no one who resented his rise to the throne more than his foster brother. And Kay was constantly letting him know it.

"Understand what? What did this boy do?" Guinevere demanded, looking fiercely from knight to knight. It was funny; here Arthur was terrified, and yet she didn't look one bit afraid to face off with a band of knights. "Did he truly steal the sword he wears on his belt?"

The knights looked at her incredulously, then broke out into laughter. Arthur cringed. Guinevere's scowl deepened.

"What's so funny?" she demanded.

"Sorry, m'lady," Sir Bors said, choking back his laughter. "It's just… do you not know who this young lad is?"

Guinevere looked over at Arthur, confusion clouding her face. "Who is he?" she asked, her voice suddenly a little wobbly.

"Why, m'lady, this is King Arthur, ruler of all England. And that sword he wears? He pulled it from the stone."

CHAPTER SIX
GUINEVERE

Guinevere stared at Wart – no, Arthur! – in shock. She couldn't have been more surprised if he'd suddenly sprouted wings and turned into a bird right then and there. *This* was Arthur? The one who had stolen the throne of England?

And she had somehow *befriended* him?

"Is it true?" she managed to sputter, wanting to hear the confession spill from his own lips. She realised a part of her still held out hope that maybe it was some ridiculous joke. That the knights were putting her on for their own amusement. Because surely this boy – this skinny young boy who dreamt about being a bird and flying away – couldn't be the usurper out to destroy England.

Could he?

Wart's face turned bright red, confirming her worst fears. Anger rose inside her, mixed with burning shame. What would Mim think if she could see her now, already falling for the charms of Merlin's pawn? Why, she was supposed to be the one tricking *him,* not the other way round! Her mother would be so ashamed.

"I have to go," she muttered. This was clearly why Mim never let her do anything on her own. She was the worst judge of character ever. She'd taken him at his word, and he'd lied to her. And of course he had – he'd lied to the entire kingdom, pretending to be their rightful monarch. And worse, she'd believed him without question.

"Guin!" Arthur cried. He sounded upset. "Please! I can explain!"

"I'm sure you can," she managed to say, trying to keep her voice thick and haughty. As if his deception meant absolutely nothing to her. "But I'm not interested in hearing it."

And with that, she turned and walked down the path, keeping her shoulders squared and her head held high. She could hear him calling for her, but she refused to give him the satisfaction of turning around to look. Only when she heard the sounds of the knights' horses galloping away, presumably with Arthur in tow, did she allow herself to run. Down the path, through the woods, not stopping for a moment until she reached the cottage.

She burst through the door, out of breath, her hair windswept and her face stained with tears and dirt. She leant over, hands on her knees, trying to catch her breath.

Mim looked up from her card game, raising a bushy eyebrow. "Where's the water?" she asked.

Oh, no! The water! Guinevere looked down at her bucket to find it nearly empty. And, she realised miserably, she had never grabbed the second bucket back from Arthur when she fled.

"I'm sorry," she said. "I, uh, ran into some wolves. I had to run home. I must have dropped one of the buckets on the way."

She felt a little guilty lying to her mother, but what else could she say? That she'd lost their precious water because she'd accidentally befriended the kingdom's number one enemy? If she confessed to Mim that she'd fallen for Arthur's charms even before she got to the castle, Mim would think her a silly girl who wasn't ready to undertake such an important quest. And Guinevere *needed* this quest – now more than ever. If for nothing else than to teach that cowardly king a lesson in manners. He shouldn't be able to get away with lying to people. And she was going to make him pay for tricking her, whatever it took.

Mim sighed deeply. "You know, you could have just poofed yourself home. Or shapeshifted into a bird or a mouse to get away." She shook her head. "You always make things so hard for yourself, my dear."

Guinevere hung her head. Of course her mother would go right to magic. Magic was Mim's solution to every problem. And she couldn't understand Guin's reluctance to use it.

"In any case, I'm fine," Guin pointed out. Though she didn't feel very fine at all. In fact, if she was being honest with herself, she felt downright miserable. She was still furious at Arthur. But also kind of sad. Like she'd lost a friend just as she'd made one.

"Of course you are!" Mim agreed. "And don't worry. I'll conjure us up a bountiful feast – just for tonight." She gave Guin a scolding look. "Surely you can stomach a little magic if it means a full stomach. I'm thinking… slug à la mode! What do you say?"

Guinevere nodded reluctantly. Slugs with ice cream sounded pretty horrific, but then it was her fault they wouldn't have their stew. And she didn't want to appear ungrateful when her mother was acting so understanding.

"Now sit down, my pet, before you pass out on me," Mim instructed, pulling a chair close to her own. Guinevere gratefully collapsed into it, and Mim took her hand, squeezing it lightly. Guin let out a shuddering breath and closed her eyes.

"Wow. You were really upset," Mim noted with surprise. "And all over a silly little wolf? That's not like you, my dear."

Guinevere opened her eyes a crack. Her mother was staring at her suspiciously.

"I… thought it was a dog," she stammered. "Until I got close to it. It… surprised me."

Mim's grip tightened, just a little, but enough to tell Guinevere she didn't quite believe her. Which made sense, of course, since it was a blatant lie. Luckily, however, there was no way for her mother to guess the truth. Mim might have been magical, but she wasn't a mind reader. And eventually Mim's hand relaxed again.

"Poor child," she soothed, stroking Guin's palm. "So frightened of the world. I suppose that's partially my fault, keeping you so close to me all these years." She paused, then added, "Maybe sending you to the castle isn't such a good idea after all…"

"No!" Guinevere cried, her eyes flying open. She jerked her hand away. "I want to go! I'll be fine, I promise. You don't have to worry about me!"

Mim held up her hands in protest. "All right, all right!" she cried with a giggle. "No need to beg! I'm sure it'll all be simply marvellous! I can't wait to see!" She paused, then added, "There's one thing, however..."

"What's that?" Guinevere asked warily, noting the change in her mother's voice. No longer laughing – but dead serious. Which was unusual for Mim, to say the least.

Mim's eyes rested on her daughter. "When you get to the castle, whatever you do, whatever you say, do not let Arthur know you are related to me in any way. No matter what happens. If he learns that I sent you, there's no telling what he'll do to you... or me, for that matter." She gave Guin a strong look. "Arthur may only be a boy – but at the end of the day, he serves Merlin. You'd do best to remember that."

"I understand," Guin said softly, feeling a shiver trip down her spine. "You can trust me. I won't let you down."

"That's my girl!" Mim cried, her demeanour changing again. She leapt to her feet. "Now let's eat! Can't save a kingdom on an empty stomach, can we?" She waved her arms wildly in the air. "Bring on the slugs!"

CHAPTER SEVEN
ARTHUR

"Sire, we've gone over this a hundred times. You cannot leave the castle unattended," Sir Morien scolded. The brawny, bearded dark-skinned knight paced the throne room, his long steps eating up the distance between stone walls.

Arthur slumped in his throne. "I said I was sorry," he muttered, a little sulkily. But who could blame him? After all, he hadn't asked for this. All he ever aimed for in life was to maybe become a squire to a famous knight and go questing throughout the land – facing dangers untold and maybe, if they were lucky, a few dragons. Instead, he was stuck in a musty old castle, deciding the fates of random chickens and hoping he didn't accidentally start a war.

It was *not* good to be the king.

He sighed deeply, thinking back to his fleeting moment of freedom in the forest earlier that day. It had felt so good to be his old self again. The orphan Wart, who hadn't had a care in the world. Back when he lived that life, he hadn't fully appreciated it. Now, he'd give anything at all just to have it back.

To see Guinevere again.

His mind flashed to the girl he'd met in the forest. She'd been so nice to him – not caring about his social status or who his parents might be. In fact, it hadn't mattered one bit to her that he was a nobody. Which, in a strange way, made him feel like a somebody. Somebody worth talking to. Somebody worth becoming friends with.

Well, until she realised the truth. He winced as he remembered the look of shock that crossed her face when she realised he had lied to her, followed by the crushing look of betrayal. At that moment, his greatest wish on earth would have been to climb down into that deep dark well and never come out again.

He resisted the urge to slap his hand to his forehead. Oh, why had he lied to her? It was so stupid and shortsighted! Not to mention completely disrespectful to her. This was not how Merlin had taught him to be!

But it didn't matter now, he supposed sadly. For he

would likely never see her again. At least not without a full accompaniment of knights, which would spoil any chance of fun. Not to mention the fact that he was pretty sure she had no interest in running into him again – knights or no. His stupid lie had ruined their chance of friendship. Probably forever.

There was a knock at the door. Arthur rose to his feet. "Come in," he commanded, after throwing a quick look at Morien, thankful for a distraction to his scolding. The knight sighed deeply, shaking his head.

As the door swung open, for a brief moment Arthur allowed himself to indulge in the fantasy that it would be Guinevere on the other side of it, come to the castle to give him a chance to apologise.

But, of course, it was not Guinevere. It was the castle steward.

"Your Majesty." The steward bowed low. "Sir Pellinore and his men have returned from their meeting with the Saxons. They are requesting an audience with you."

Arthur's heart quickened, relegating all thoughts of Guinevere to the back of his brain. "Send them in," he declared.

The steward bowed again and disappeared out the door. A moment later, he returned, accompanied by Pellinore, Kay, and a tall knight with broad shoulders and a shock of jet-black hair whom Pellinore introduced as Gawain. All three bowed low to Arthur.

"So?" Arthur asked impatiently. "What did they say?"

Pellinore straightened. His face broke into an excited smile. "Your Majesty," he said, "I can barely believe I'm sharing this news with you. But somehow the Saxons have agreed to your request. They are planning a trip to Camelot to attend your promised feast."

"Really?" Arthur stared at the knights. It had worked? His plan for peace had worked? Well, not completely – not yet, anyway. But they'd agreed to come. That was a big step.

"Really," Gawain agreed with a toothy grin. Arthur liked him immediately. "They're packing up now and plan to arrive at the castle in a week's time. Their king seems very eager to meet you."

"This is amazing," Arthur cried, overjoyed. "I knew this would work—"

"Bah!" Kay interrupted, shaking his head. "I don't like it. I don't like it at all. Inviting these barbarians to our banquet halls – to sup like they're civilised people?" He scowled. "It's just not done."

"Maybe not, but it's *being* done now," Arthur corrected, a little cross at being challenged. Especially by his foster brother, who had always made it clear he thought he knew better – even when he clearly didn't. "And who knows? Maybe they'll surprise you."

"Or maybe they'll surprise *you*," Kay shot back, not missing a beat. "Ever think of that? Maybe it's a trick to breach our castle walls. To learn our ways and the depths of our forces, so they can gain the upper hand when they come back to attack us at a later date."

Arthur swallowed hard, his earlier enthusiasm deflating. He didn't want to admit it, but Kay did have a point. What if opening their gates in peace led to nothing but war? And worse – gave their enemies an advantage?

It would be all his fault.

"Oh, Kay," Gawain broke in, smacking Arthur's foster brother so hard on the back that Kay almost fell over. "You worry too much. By the gods, they're invited to dinner, not a behind-the-tapestries tour of the inner workings of Camelot Castle. We knights can keep an eye on a few barbarians, don't you think? Make sure they mind their manners."

"Exactly," Arthur agreed, thankful to Gawain for sticking up for him. "We'll show them we're kind. But not stupid."

Kay opened his mouth as if to speak, but a stern look from Gawain made him close it again. Instead, he crossed his meaty arms over his chest and stuck out his lower lip in a pout. Arthur resisted the urge to snicker. It wasn't often he'd got to see Kay put in his place. But he was a king, he reminded himself; he couldn't afford to be petty.

Sir Pellinore turned to Arthur, clapping his hands.

"Very good, Your Majesty," he said. "What would you like us to do in the meantime?"

"Let's have the cooks start working on the menus," Arthur said. "And the staff need to be cleaning out the halls and guest rooms, and making sure there's enough room in the stables for their horses." He listed off the various tasks, the kinds of preparations he himself was quite familiar with from when guests arrived at Sir Ector's castle back when he had worked in the kitchens.

"Oh, yes! We'll be sure to get right on all of that, *m'lord*," Kay jeered, making a mocking bow in Arthur's direction. Gawain sighed and gave Arthur an apologetic look before he and Pellinore led the other knight out of the throne room. Morien followed close behind. Arthur let out a breath of relief. It seemed his lecture for leaving the castle was over.

And the day was finally starting to look up.

He sat back in his throne, feeling rather pleased. A moment later, Archimedes flew down from his perch on the rafters above and landed on his throne's armrest.

"Well done, lad!" the owl chirped. "Your first act as king, and it seems to be turning into a smashing success."

Arthur smiled goofily, feeling better now that they were

alone. "I wasn't sure it was going to work," he confessed. "I mean, when I first decided on it, everyone seemed to think I was mad. Some still do, I suppose," he added, thinking of Kay's sneer.

"It's not mad, it's civilised," the owl corrected haughtily. "And I'm sorry, but a knight like Kay has no room to complain about barbarians. Not when he's only one step above one himself."

Arthur smirked. "You said it, not me."

"I'm proud of you, boy," the owl continued. "Perhaps you will make a fine king yet."

"Thank you," Arthur said. "That means a lot coming from you." He leant back in his throne, staring up at the ceiling thoughtfully. "Do you think this was all part of Merlin's plan from the start? Do you think he knew my destiny? Was that why he agreed to teach me in the first place? So I'd know how to do this?"

The owl shrugged. "He did say something about leading you to your rightful place," he told Arthur. "Perhaps this is what he was talking about?" He fluffed his feathers. "I just assumed he meant to have you become his apprentice – maybe take over for him someday. But perhaps it was more than that."

"I wish he were here now." Arthur sighed. "It would be nice to have his advice."

"I know, boy," Archimedes agreed. "I miss him, too." He scowled. "Though you better never tell him I said that."

Arthur laughed. "Your secret is safe with me."

Archimedes took flight, making small circles around the throne. "I have to admit, I am getting worried about him. He's been gone a very long time. Longer than I can ever remember his being gone before. Sure, he'll sometimes time travel when he's angry. But he always comes back. So where is he now?"

"Morgan said he was on something called a *holiday*," Arthur told him.

The owl stopped in midair, almost falling to the ground in the process. "Morgan?" he repeated. "Who's Morgan?'

"Morgan le Fay?" Arthur tried to remember. "She's a wizard like Merlin. She came here the day I had to rule about the chicken. She told me Merlin sent her." He wrinkled his nose. "But something was very strange about her. And her advice seemed very odd. Very un-Merlin-like."

"Morgan le Fay?" Archimedes landed back on the throne, shaking his head. "Why does that name sound so familiar?"

"I don't know." Arthur shrugged. "Should we track her down again and see if she knows more about Merlin? Maybe she knows where he is."

"Maybe. Or maybe she's the reason he's not back

yet," Archimedes suggested worriedly. "After all, it seems quite a coincidence that she shows up right after Merlin's disappearance. What if she did something to him?"

Arthur frowned. He hadn't thought of that possibility. But she *was* a wizard, which meant she had magic…

"What should we do?" he asked the owl.

Archimedes seemed to consider the question for a moment. Then he shook out his feathers. "Let me fly back to Sir Ector's castle," he said. "Merlin's books are probably all still in the tower where he left them. Maybe I can learn something from them about this Morgan le Fay character. Then we'll know if we can trust her… or not."

Arthur shuddered at the thought. "Do you really think she might have done something to Merlin?" he asked nervously, thinking back to his poor teacher. If anything had happened to him…

"I don't know," Archimedes admitted. "But I plan to find out."

CHAPTER EIGHT
GUINEVERE

"You call that washed? What's that smudge on the side? You're washing for a king now, girl! Kings don't tolerate smudged plates!"

Guinevere groaned as she attempted to take back the plate from the castle cook, Mistress McCready, and balance it on the top of the already towering pile of dishes she was carrying into the kitchen after clearing the banquet hall from breakfast. Unfortunately, the plate missed its mark and fell. When she instinctively dived to catch it, she lost her balance, and her entire stack of dinnerware came crashing to the ground.

"Now look what you've done!" screeched the cook. "Stupid, clumsy girl! You've managed to break them all!"

"At least you don't have to worry about them being

smudged now," Guinevere retorted under her breath as she knelt down to pick up the pieces.

The cook wrung her hands together in annoyance. "It is truly impossible to get good help these days," she muttered as she stormed back into the kitchen, leaving Guinevere alone to pick up the mess.

Guinevere sighed, looking over the damage she'd done. Not a single plate or bowl appeared to have escaped its fate. Wonderful. Reluctantly, she started gathering up the bits of broken earthenware in her hands and taking them over to a nearby bin.

So much for saving the kingdom. She couldn't even save a pile of plates.

Could this quest of hers possibly be going worse? It was bad enough she'd had that embarrassing encounter with Arthur in the forest. But at the very least they'd been face to face and talking. Since she'd arrived at the castle, she'd been stuck down in the kitchen, washing dishes; she hadn't had the chance to talk to Arthur at all. In fact, she'd only ever even got a brief glimpse of the king one time since she'd arrived – and then only from a distance. How was she supposed to keep an eye on him when she literally never saw him?

She shook her head. Her mother was going to be so disappointed in her.

"Oh, wow! I remember those days!"

Guin looked up, startled at the sound of a new voice approaching. Her eyes widened in shock as she realised who it belonged to. None other than King Arthur himself, stopping at the bottom of the stairs, looking down at the mess, a strange look in his eyes.

He was dressed quite differently than when she'd first met him in the forest, where he'd worn typical peasant attire: a plain, undyed tunic and tights. He was now garbed in a rich red velvet doublet over a billowy white shirt. A heavy golden chain hung across his shoulders, and an ornate crown that looked a bit too large for him perched on his head. She watched as he shoved the crown back up his forehead, almost absently, as if he had to do so often.

Before she could say anything, he knelt beside her, checking out the mess. He picked up a piece of pottery and tossed it in the bin. Guinevere felt her cheeks heat.

"What are you doing?" she demanded before she could stop herself.

"Helping, I think," he replied, grabbing another plate. "Unless you meant for them to stay on the floor?"

"Of course not," she snapped, feeling hot and embarrassed. Here she'd been waiting all week for her chance to get close to the king, and this was how she finally ran into him? On the floor, surrounded by broken dishes, looking a sight? Pathetic. Truly pathetic.

"Look," she tried, "you don't have to—"

She was interrupted by a cry of surprise. She frowned, looking up to find Arthur staring at her, a look of astonishment on his face.

"Why, it's *you*!" he declared in a voice rich with wonder. "Guinevere, right? From the forest?" He couldn't have sounded more surprised than if she'd been a purple dragon he had spotted wandering the halls. Which she supposed made sense, seeing as they'd met under such different circumstances the first time round.

For a split second, she considered lying – saying he was mistaken. That her name was Mary or Martha or Elaine. Maybe it would have been a good idea. She was trying to keep a low profile, after all. But then again, this was the first conversation she'd been able to have with him since she'd arrived at to the castle, and she didn't want him to just walk away.

"I suppose I am," she choked out, trying to keep her voice light. "Nice to see you again, *Wart*."

Now it was his turn to look embarrassed. He hung his head, causing his crown to tumble to the floor. He grabbed it and shoved it back on, looking unhappy.

"About that," he said. "I suppose I should explain."

Guinevere shrugged, going back to the broken dishes. "No need," she replied airily. "You're the king. I suppose you can do whatever you want." She reached out for a dish.

Arthur grabbed the dish from her hands, causing her to look up at him in surprise. He met her eyes with his own, and she was astonished to see they were practically radiating with apology.

"I shouldn't have lied to you," he said solemnly. "It was wrong, and I knew it. It was just… well, the way you were treating me. Like I was a normal, everyday person – not some fancy king. Let's just say I don't get that a lot any more." He sighed deeply.

"I imagine you don't," she muttered, trying to ignore the sudden tug at her heart as she caught the forlorn expression on his face. Ugh. The last thing she needed was to start feeling sorry for him. He had stolen the throne of England, she reminded herself. He wasn't some innocent victim.

"Besides," he added, smiling, "if you had known who I really was, would you have let me walk you home?"

"Probably not," she admitted.

His eyes sparkled. "So you see the need for my deception, then."

Guinevere felt herself blushing again as she forced her eyes back to her task. He was certainly charming – she'd give him that. A lot more charming than she'd imagined someone like him would be. Still, she couldn't allow herself to let down her guard. To forget who he really was. And whom he served.

She had to be careful. But at the same time, she had to play nice. To get him to trust her, to open up to her, so she and Mim could find a way to take him down.

She realised he was looking at her expectantly.

"It's really all right," she assured him, giving him a bland smile. "I'm not angry with you."

Hope flushed on his face. "So you… forgive me?"

"It's already forgotten."

The lie tasted like sawdust on her tongue, but she swallowed it down, knowing it was necessary. Still, she couldn't help feeling a little guilty when she caught the relief on his face. *Now who's the liar?*

Arthur grabbed another piece of broken pottery and tossed it expertly into the bin. "So what are you doing here, anyway?" he asked. "You never told me you worked in the castle."

"I didn't until last week," she confessed. "My mother thought it might be nice for me to get a job to pass the time and help pay our expenses." The lie rolled easily off her tongue, surprising her. She tried to imagine herself as a spy, deep undercover – a notion that pleased her quite a bit.

Especially when she caught the look on Arthur's face and realised he believed every word.

"Well, I'm glad you did," he said. "I've been feeling terrible about what happened and wanted to apologise to you. But they won't let me out of the castle any more. They say it's too dangerous." He scowled, telling her exactly what he thought of that notion.

"I'm glad to see you again, too," she replied. "Though I wish it were under better circumstances than a pile of broken dishes. I promise I'll pay for them," she added quickly. "They can take it out of my wages."

Arthur looked shocked at the idea. "Certainly not," he said, scooping up an armful of broken pottery. "Do you know how many dishes they have in this castle?" He paused, then grinned. "No, of course you don't. No one does. And no one's ever going to count them, either."

She couldn't help a laugh at this. "I suppose not."

"Trust me, I broke more than my share of dishes back in the day," he told her, tossing his load of pottery into the bin.

"You used to work in a kitchen?" she asked, surprised.

"Oh, yes – for years, actually. What I told you out in the forest – it wasn't altogether a lie. I was Wart before I was Arthur. Just an orphan boy, lucky enough to be taken in by an old knight and his son and given a job."

She bit her lower lip, dropping her head to concentrate on her task again. It seemed the two of them had more in common than she had thought. They were both orphans, both raised by foster parents, both trained by wizards. But now one of them was sitting on the throne of England. And one was washing dishes in a castle basement.

No, she scolded herself. That was just his cover. He didn't belong on the throne at all. He'd taken it from the rightful king.

She wondered suddenly if he knew this. Had Merlin let him in on the plan from the start? Or did he really think this was his destiny? Was he a mastermind, deceiving them all? Or was he just a puppet for Merlin – having no idea what he was doing?

Arthur threw the last piece of pottery in the trash. "There!" he declared. "Much easier when you have help, am I right?"

"Much," she found herself agreeing.

"And now look!" he added. "You've got time for me to give you a tour of the castle." He held out his arm gallantly.

She stared at it, not taking it. "A tour?" she asked, surprised.

His confidence fled his face. "I mean, if you wanted one, that is. If you have other things to do..."

She swallowed hard. She certainly did have other things

to do – a pile of chores in the kitchen that would take her all day. But how could she turn down her first chance to spend one-on-one time with Arthur? That was the true reason she'd come here, after all.

"Actually, a tour sounds lovely," she declared, giving him what she hoped looked like a sweet smile. She hooked her arm in his. "Lead the way."

CHAPTER NINE
GUINEVERE

The tour took almost an hour. Camelot Castle was huge, with perhaps a hundred rooms. Arthur took his time showing Guinevere each and every one, and she forced herself to ooh and aah over the rich purple drapes and golden ornamentations in each one, as if they were visions of her greatest dreams come to life. In truth, however, she found the whole thing a bit shocking – to see so much luxury and riches go to waste. Rooms that were not even used, containing enough wealth for a peasant to live on for a lifetime. It didn't seem quite fair. But she kept her mouth shut and played the good servant girl as the tour progressed, knowing it was more important to gain Arthur's trust than criticise his lifestyle.

"And this is the final bedroom," Arthur announced as they stepped into yet another room, this one with a giant stone hearth in the corner and a window with real leaded glass that looked out over the castle gardens. There were thick animal-skin rugs on the floor and a massive canopy bed in the centre, covered with at least a dozen pillows and draped in heavy crimson curtains. "At least I think so," he added with a bashful grin. "I've lost count at this point."

She snorted and walked over to the bed. Feeling a little mischievous, she climbed onto it and began dancing on it to see if it was as soft as it looked.

Turned out it was even softer.

Arthur stared up at her as if shocked by her brazen move. She grinned, beckoning him with her hand, suddenly feeling silly and free. "Don't tell me you've never tried jumping on one of these beds?" she teased. When he shook his head doubtfully, she laughed. "Well, it's no wonder you think this place is boring, then."

For a moment, he stood there as if warring with his own indecision. But at last he shook his head and scrambled onto the bed. Soon the two of them were jumping up and down so high they almost smacked their heads on the ceiling twice. The third time, Guinevere managed to lose her footing on the way down and tumbled into the pile of pillows. Arthur laughed as she struggled to right herself, tangled in their silk covers.

"Need some help, m'lady?" he asked in a mocking voice.

"Please," she scoffed, grabbing a pillow and throwing it in his direction. It hit him square in the chest, and he too lost his balance, tumbling off the bed altogether and landing on the floor with a heavy thump. Guinevere gasped.

"Are you all right?" she asked, leaning off the bed to check on him.

"I'm fine," he said with a sly grin as he picked up two pillows off the floor. "But you… you are dead!"

He lunged at her. She leapt off the bed, screaming, dashing to the other corner of the room. He gave chase, but it was hard to run with an armful of pillows, allowing Guin an easy escape. She leapt back onto the bed and grabbed her own stash, throwing them at Arthur one after another while using her own pillow as a shield.

"You shalt not win, evil knight!" she cried out. "I will be the victor!"

"We'll see about that," Arthur shot back, leaping up on the bed and diving in her direction. She lost her balance again, and this time they both tumbled to the floor together, tangling up in a pile of limbs. They were laughing so hard at this point, they could barely speak.

"Do you yield?" Arthur asked with a sly smile.

"Never!" she declared, struggling to sit up. "As long as there be breath in my body, I shall never—"

The door burst open. Two guards rushed in, grabbed Guinevere, and yanked her backwards. She cried out in alarm as her arms were pinned behind her painfully and a rough hand grabbed at her throat.

"Leave me alone!" she cried, trying to fight them off. But they were grown men. Far too strong. For a split second she actually considered using magic – that's what Mim would have done in a situation like this. But she realised it would destroy her cover and probably get her banned from the castle. So instead, she stopped struggling and submitted.

"Who are you?" the first guard demanded, once he had her under control.

"And what are you doing to the king?" added the second.

"It's okay, Brutus," Arthur broke in. Guin turned to see he'd managed to get up off the floor and was approaching the guards. "We were just playing."

"Playing, Your Majesty?" the guard – Brutus – exclaimed, spitting out the word as if it were poison. "But we thought…"

"We heard screams," added his partner, looking personally offended. "We thought you were being attacked."

"It was just a game," Arthur explained with a heavy

sigh. "I'm sorry I worried you." He pressed his lips together. "So… can you please let her go?"

The guards reluctantly released Guinevere. She shook out her arms, giving them a sour look. Inside, her heart was pumping a thousand beats a minute. She glanced over at Arthur. He shot her an apologetic smile.

"I should get back to the kitchen," she mumbled, feeling incredibly awkward all of a sudden. Not to mention more than a little ashamed. What had she been thinking, jumping on royal beds and pillow fighting with the king of England, as if she were an unruly child who didn't know any better? What if they told her mistress – the cook – about her bad behaviour and she lost her job because of it? What if they banished her from the castle altogether? Arthur wouldn't order it, she was pretty sure, but from what he'd said, he didn't always get to make the rules. If she lost her chance to complete her quest, Mim would be so disappointed.

Also, England would be doomed. Which was almost as bad.

"Are you all right?" Arthur asked, catching the look on her face.

"I'm f-fine," she stammered, feeling the eyes of the guards on her. "Um, thank you for the tour."

The corner of Arthur's mouth lifted. "Thank *you* for making my afternoon a lot more interesting than usual," he said, bowing grandly in her direction. She noticed he had a small bruise on the side of his face, probably from hitting the floor so hard. Hopefully no one would ask him how he got it.

Brutus cleared his throat, nodding to the door. She realised it was her invitation to vacate. She gave Arthur one last rueful look, then scurried towards the exit, hoping she'd be able to remember her way through the twisty passages back to the kitchen and that no one had noticed she'd been gone.

She was almost to the door when she heard his voice again.

"Wait."

She stopped in her tracks. "Yes?" she asked, turning, her pulse beating fast at her wrists.

For a moment Arthur just stood there. Then his mouth opened. "Would you like to have dinner with me tonight?" he asked, his voice wobbling a bit on the words, as if it took an effort to speak them. "It's a bit of a special night. The Saxons are coming to visit, and we're holding a grand feast in their honour."

She raised her eyebrows. He was inviting her to dinner? Dinner with the Saxons?

"Aren't the Saxons our enemies?" she blurted out before she could stop herself.

But Arthur only smiled. "Not for long," he said mysteriously. He paused, then added, "So what do you say? Will you join me? Eat by my side?"

Guinevere shuffled from foot to foot, indecision whirling through her. This was the opportunity she'd been waiting for, the reason she'd been sent to the castle to begin with: to observe courtly matters and report them back to Mim.

So why did she suddenly feel so conflicted?

She glanced up at Arthur. His face was awash with what could be described only as hope.

"Of course," she mumbled, forcing herself to curtsy to him. "If you want me there, I will come."

Arthur smiled. "There is nothing I would want more."

CHAPTER TEN
ARTHUR

Arthur was only halfway dressed for the banquet when he heard a rapping at his window. Puzzled, he ran over to see what it could be and was surprised to find none other than Archimedes flapping on the other side, pecking the glass with his beak. Excited, Arthur yanked the window open to let the bird in.

"You're back!" he exclaimed. "Did you make it to Sir Ector's castle? Were Merlin's books still there? Did you find something in them? Did you discover what happened to Merlin? Who's Morgan le Fay?"

The owl flew to his perch by Arthur's bed, settling in and carefully picking at his wing feathers before answering. Arthur hopped from foot to foot impatiently.

The owl had always had a flair for the dramatic. But this was ridiculous.

"Come on!" he cried. "I don't have a lot of time before the banquet starts. I need to know what you found out."

Archimedes had been gone a week, and Arthur had started worrying something might have happened to him. Which would have been horrible – Arthur had admittedly grown pretty fond of him over the last months. Of course he would never admit this to the grumpy old bird, knowing full well Archimedes would never, in turn, admit to appreciating this kind of concern on his behalf.

Archimedes spat out a feather. "Yes, I am back," he said grandly. "And let me tell you, I'm very happy to be so. That horrible tower that your foster father had Merlin stay in is so damp and cold and dreary – I don't know how we ever put up with it back in the day."

"Yes, yes, it's terrible," Arthur agreed peevishly. "But were Merlin's books still there? Were you able to read them?"

"Of course I was able to read them," the owl clucked. "What do you think I am? A bumbling medieval idiot? I'm the one who taught you your ABCs, and don't you forget it."

Arthur groaned, plopping down on his bed. Clearly the owl refused to be rushed.

Archimedes flew over to join him. "Yes, my impatient

boy," he said patronisingly, "I was able to go through Merlin's books. He has quite a lot of them, as you know, which was what made it take so long. But in the end, I did manage to find out quite a bit about your Morgan le Fay."

Arthur sat up in bed. "You did? What did you learn?"

The owl frowned. "Unfortunately, it's much worse than we thought. It turns out Morgan le Fay is a very powerful wizard who practises sorcery of the worst kind. Sorcery you've actually witnessed first hand – though at the time she was going by another name."

Arthur stared at the bird for a moment. Then something suddenly dawned on him. The purple eyes. The purple dress. The purple fingernails.

"Madam Mim!" he exclaimed, horrified. "Morgan le Fay is Madam Mim?"

"Give the boy a gold star," Archimedes proclaimed. Then he huffed. "Of course it would have been better had you figured that out when she first showed up at the castle. Would have saved me a lot of draughty nights in that leaky tower."

"Sorry," Arthur said. "But she didn't look anything like herself at the time. Except for all the purple. She probably shapeshifted – like she did during the wizard duel between her and Merlin."

"Yes. Quite likely," Archimedes agreed. "She is a master at shapeshifting. The only way to truly tell it's her is by all the purple. She can't quite manage to get rid of that in any shape or form."

Arthur shook his head, thinking back to their encounter. If only he'd put two and two together. He could have had her arrested or something. Though if she was truly as powerful as Archimedes said, that might not have done any good.

"Why do you think she wanted me to go to war with the Saxons?" he asked. "She was very insistent about that."

"Right." Archimedes nodded. "Well, from what I've read, Mim or Morgan – whatever she wants to call herself – is a big fan of the gruesome and grim. And she loves to cause trouble. The more chaotic things become, the more she enjoys them."

Arthur considered this. "I guess that makes sense," he said. "She probably thinks a peaceful England is a boring England."

"Indeed. And don't think this will be her last attempt to interfere with your rule. As long as Merlin is away, there's no one to stop her from trying her worst. You must keep on guard and be ready for when she strikes again. Likely in a way you least expect it."

"Please. She's not going to get by me," Arthur declared.

"I know her tricks now. Her purple colour. I'll be ready for her next time she shows up." He jumped off the bed, launching into a few knightly poses to back his claim. Archimedes rolled his eyes.

"Very scary," he deadpanned. "I'm sure she'll be quaking in her purple boots when she sees you coming."

"She'd better!" Arthur declared, grabbing Excalibur and waving it in the air. "Or else I'll— I'll—"

Suddenly, there was a loud knock at the door, causing Arthur to practically leap out of his skin. Excalibur slipped from his hands and went crashing to the floor. Archimedes snorted.

"You were saying…?" he replied drolly.

Arthur ignored him, pulling the door open and revealing the castle steward standing on the other side. "Oh. It's you," Arthur said, blushing. "What is it?"

"Your Majesty, everyone has gathered in the great hall," the steward informed him, giving him a doubtful once-over. It was then that Arthur realised he was still only half-dressed. "Including the Saxon king and his men. They are awaiting you to start the feast."

Arthur slapped his hand to his forehead. "Oh, no! I'm late. All right. Thank you! I'll be right there."

"Very good, sir," the castle steward replied, bowing low before closing the door behind him. Once he was gone, Arthur turned to Archimedes.

"What do I wear?" he asked. "I want to look kingly for the Saxons."

Archimedes groaned loudly but flew over to Arthur's wardrobe and used his beak to open it. He plucked out a red robe with a golden belt.

"However did you manage while I was gone?" he asked, shaking his head.

Arthur excitedly grabbed the robe and slipped it over his head. "I did great while you were gone, actually," he said haughtily, cinching the robe with the belt. "I made laws. I found a nice round table for my knights to sit at during meetings. Oh, and I even met a girl. I invited her to dinner tonight, too."

Archimedes stopped mid-flight, but managed to recover quickly enough to land on his perch instead of the ground. His eyes locked on Arthur. "You *what*?"

Arthur blushed. Maybe he shouldn't have mentioned that last part. But truth be told, he hadn't been able to concentrate on much else since inviting her earlier that day. Every time he'd try to focus on courtly politics, he ended up getting lost in thought, his mind whirring with memories of her dark brown eyes.

"She works in the kitchen," he explained as he grabbed his boots and put them on one at a time, not meeting the owl's eyes. "Her name is Guinevere. She's really nice."

"Really nice?" Archimedes repeated. "Really nice? Is that what they're calling it these days? And you invited her to dinner? Your very important Saxon peace treaty dinner?"

"Um… yes?"

The owl shook himself, feathers flying everywhere. "This is why I should have never left. You're perfectly incapable of handling yourself alone." He shook a wing at Arthur. "Don't tell me you're in love with her. You can't afford to be in love with anyone. You're far too young. Also, you have an entire kingdom to run. Which leaves no room for romance."

"Don't be ridiculous," Arthur shot back, perhaps with a tad too much defensiveness. "I'm not in love with anyone. I just invited her to dinner because she's kind and fun. And I don't have any other friends in this boring old place."

Archimedes huffed, ruffling his feathers. "No friends?"

Arthur groaned. "You know what I mean!" he protested. "Human friends! My own age!"

The owl sighed. "I understand. I really do. But, Arthur, you can't allow yourself to be distracted. Especially now with the Saxons coming tonight for your peace treaty feast. This event must go off without a hitch. Without one tiny snag. If these men leave without signing your treaty, your people will see it as a failure on your part. They'll think you don't know how to be king."

"Well, they wouldn't be entirely wrong," Arthur muttered.

"Now, now, boy! What kind of attitude is that? What if Merlin heard you right now? Do you think he'd approve of you putting yourself down? Now buck up and get down to that feast like the king you are."

And with that scolding, the owl took flight, straight out the window and into the night. Arthur sighed, watching him go. He knew Archimedes was right. He was getting distracted. Still, it was nice to have one thing in his life that wasn't a total disaster. Between being stuck in the castle, Merlin being missing, and now Madam Mim trying to cause trouble, he had a lot of negatives to deal with.

But Guinevere – she was the one shining light in his life. And it would take a lot more than a grumpy, highly educated owl to convince him to smother it.

CHAPTER ELEVEN
SIR ECTOR

"Look at 'em over there, making themselves right at home. Why, I bet not a one of them has had a bath in the last three years. Maybe longer. Have you smelt them yet? I've had pigs that smelt better." Sir Ector grunted disapprovingly, elbowing his son Kay to get his attention. Kay was sitting beside him in the banquet hall, gnawing on a turkey leg. He rolled his eyes at his dad.

"Whatever," he said, his mouth full.

"Whatever!" Sir Ector snorted. "I'll show you whatever. This isn't right, I tell you. And the Wart should know it! Did we teach him nothing at all during his time at our castle?"

"He doesn't even know how to properly wash dishes," Kay muttered. "How can you expect him to run a country?"

Sir Ector sighed loudly, his eyes scanning the castle's great hall, which was decked out to within an inch of its life and packed to the gills with nobles and knights from around England, sitting at long tables lined up in rows across the room. Each table was covered in mountains of food – choice meats and fine cheeses and delectable roast pheasant – piled high and almost overflowing their platters. They had even put out some sugared dates and almonds – rare delicacies, usually saved for very important guests.

Instead, they were serving the Saxons. Barbarians from across the sea who had been nothing but trouble for England ever since Rome had left and taken their armies with them, leaving the country basically defenceless. War chiefs from different regions had tried to take on the problem, but could never seem to stop fighting one another in order to unite against their common enemy. At the time, it seemed England would be destined to fall to foreign rule.

Then King Uther had come – a vicious war chief who had never lost on the battlefield and yet was charismatic enough to convince the smaller lords to join his realm. Once he'd united England, he'd taken on the Saxons with brutal force – letting them know, in no uncertain terms, how unwelcome they were in his country. Let's just say they hadn't been a problem since.

Until now.

Until England decided to put a child on the throne.

Sir Ector huffed, infuriated all over again. This was all Hobbs's fault. If only the man had not suddenly come down with the mumps, Ector would have never been forced to take the scrawny little orphan to London instead, to serve as Kay's squire. And if the Wart hadn't been in London, he'd never have even seen the sword in the stone, never mind have had a chance to pull it out. The tournament would have been held as promised – with the strongest knight being awarded the throne. Why, at this very moment, Kay could have been their king.

Instead, it was the insufferable Wart wearing the crown – which didn't even fit him properly!

Sure, at first Ector had believed the whole thing was some kind of a miracle, just like everyone else. A gift from the heavens – the promised king, delivered to them at long last. He'd even bowed before Wart as if he were some long-lost hero, come to save them all. But ever since that day, he'd started to have his doubts on the whole matter. Especially since it was clear Wart had no idea what he was doing. The heavens must have made a mistake.

And now Wart was making a much worse one, trying to befriend England's enemies.

Luckily, Ector had a plan. A good plan.

A plan to show everyone here – especially those filthy Saxons – that while Wart might have been able to pull a sword from a stone, he had no idea how to use it.

He turned to Kay. "Are you ready for this?" he asked, grabbing the turkey leg from his son's hand and tossing it back on his plate.

Kay gave his father a sulky look. "I said I was, didn't I?"

Sir Ector slapped Kay on the back. "Of course you did, my son! And it's going to be great. A historic event the bards will sing of for years to come!" He smiled widely, chuckling to himself as he tried to imagine the Wart's face when it all went down. When *he* went down.

And Ector would become father to the king of England.

CHAPTER TWELVE
ARTHUR

"Presenting His Majesty! Arthur, king of England!"

Arthur squirmed a little as the herald called out his name, his voice ringing through the great hall, as loud as a trumpet. As Arthur stepped into the room, his ears were further assaulted by spontaneous cheering from his guests. Shouts of "Hail King Arthur!" and "Long live the king!" resounded through the large space as he made his way through the room to the king's table, which had been set on a raised platform at the very front. He'd never understand why they forced kings to sit on a stage to eat, as if they were part of an actor's show. But the constant scrutiny did remind him to always chew with his mouth closed.

He climbed up on the platform, scanning the room. All eyes seemed to be on him, their expressions expectant. At first he wasn't sure if they wanted him to make some kind of speech – something he was not exactly prepared to do. But then he noticed none of the food on the tables had been touched. In fact, the only person he could see eating was Kay, who was gnawing on a huge turkey leg, chewing with his mouth wide open. Everyone else was sitting patiently in front of empty plates.

Had they all been sitting waiting for him to start eating? Ugh.

"So… sorry I'm late!" he stammered. "Please help yourself to the food. There's, uh, plenty to go round!"

Fortunately that seemed to serve as speech enough, and everyone turned excitedly to the bounty before them. Soon the room was filled with a cacophony of banging plates and animated conversation, everyone eating and drinking and chatting among themselves. Arthur sat down at his table, relieved to no longer be the focus of everyone's attention.

It was then that he wondered where Guinevere was. A quick scan of the hall told him she was not present. Had she decided against coming after all? A wave of disappointment washed over him, even as he tried to push it away. He tried to remind himself of Archimedes's warning – this was an important dinner; he couldn't be distracted. But still, he had to admit, he had been looking forward to seeing her again.

He had just started to help himself to food when the door at the back of the great hall opened. A lone figure stepped shyly into the room. It took Arthur a moment to realise it was Guinevere, she was dressed so differently than when he'd seen her earlier that day – or in the forest by the well. Now she wore a long sky-blue gown with bell sleeves and a simple silver sash. Her once flowing blonde hair had been tied up in a series of complicated braids, framing her head like a crown.

Excitedly, Arthur stood up and waved from his platform. She met his eyes, her own widening in disbelief as he beckoned her forwards. As she took a few cautious steps in his direction, it seemed like everyone in the room turned to stare, wondering what had captured the king's attention. But when Guin noticed their eyes, instead of cowering in embarrassment, a mischievous grin spread across her face and she began to dance wildly down the aisle, as if to lively music. When she reached the stage, she leapt up onto the platform, then turned to the guests, giving them a saucy bow. The room broke out into whoops and cheers.

Guin turned to Arthur, giving him an impish smile. He laughed and clapped along with the other guests.

"You're a pretty good dancer," he remarked as she settled down in the chair next to him. "I wish I could make an entrance like that."

"It's not hard. I'll teach you," she told him, grabbing a plate and helping herself to some of the meat. All eyes were still on her, but she was looking only at Arthur. "This is quite a feast," she remarked as she sampled a sugared date. "I don't think I've ever seen so much food in one place in my entire life."

"It is a bit much, honestly," Arthur confessed. "I had no idea when I asked them to prepare it that this is what they'd come up with. At least there will be a lot of leftover food to share with the people in town tomorrow."

"You're going to share your food with the people?" Guinevere looked surprised.

"Well, yes. It's better than having it go to waste, isn't it?" Arthur replied with a shrug. "And why shouldn't they enjoy it? They're part of our kingdom, too. I want them to know that they matter."

Guinevere's face took on a peculiar look. She dropped her eyes, concentrating on her food. Arthur wondered if he'd said something wrong. But then, what would she want him to do? Hoard the good food in the castle and allow the people to go without? That didn't seem very kingly to him.

"By the way, you look really nice," he blurted out, feeling the need for a subject change.

She looked up, her cheeks flushing. "When I told Mistress McCready I'd been invited to dinner, she insisted on finding me something *proper* to wear – seems my everyday kitchen rags don't cut it in court. This monstrosity of a dress once evidently belonged to the great and lovely Lady Igraine, who lived here many years before." She made a gesture of putting on the airs of a grand lady. Then she laughed. "To be honest, it's dreadfully itchy, and I can't wait to be rid of it."

Arthur nodded knowingly. "I know exactly how you feel," he confessed. "And I'll never understand it. Why, these clothes cost so much, you would think they'd be required to make them comfortable to wear."

"Exactly! There ought to be a law. Hey! Maybe you could make one," she joked. "You are the king, after all. Might as well get something out of the job."

"That's a good idea." Arthur squared his shoulders, shooting her a look of mock authority. "I declare, from this day henceforth, all clothes in the kingdom must be made comfortable – on penalty of death!"

Guinevere clapped her hands. Arthur made a short bow. He was already glad he'd invited Guinevere to dinner. She brought a spark of life to the dreadfully boring court.

He opened his mouth to say something more, but at that moment, they were approached by Sir Pellinore and a man in chain mail whom Arthur didn't recognise. The knight bowed before his king, then straightened.

"M'lord, I'd like to introduce you to King Baldomar," Pellinore said, gesturing to the visitor. "He is king of the Saxons and was the one who agreed to come and join your feast this eve."

Oh. Arthur swallowed hard. So this was the invading king. He looked… tall. And pretty muscular, too. He had curly black hair on his head and a thick, ugly scar cutting across his left cheek – the mark of a true warrior. Arthur glanced down at his own skinny, gangly body and felt suddenly awkward. Like a child playing dress-up in his father's clothes.

No. He couldn't think like that. He had to play the part, or this wasn't going to work. He had to act like he had been born into this role, with full confidence. He could not let King Baldomar see a hint of weakness or fear. Or else that chaos Mim wanted so badly? It would become inevitable.

"You are most welcome, Your Grace," he said, giving a small bow of respect to the other king. "I am pleased to make your acquaintance and delighted to welcome you to my kingdom. Thank you for accepting my invitation."

Wow. That sounded pretty good, actually, he thought after he had spoken. Maybe he could make this work.

The burly king gave him a crooked smile. "How could I not come?" he asked with a wink. "Everyone in the land is talking about the miracle boy king. Of course I had to see him for myself!"

Arthur felt his cheeks heat at this, but forced himself to keep his eyes on the man and not look away. "And now you've seen me. And my court. What do you think?"

"I think it's quite a merry place, Your Grace," Baldomar replied with a smile. "I will be honest, most of my men didn't agree with my decision to come here. They thought it might be a trap. We came fully expecting we could be met by swords and arrows." He gestured out to the room. "Instead, you feed us and give us respect. It's not something we're used to from the English, if you pardon my saying."

"Of course," Arthur replied, feeling secretly pleased. His plan was working! "I have no quarrel with you. As long as you keep to your own lands, I think we can agree to live in peace." He paused, then added, "And perhaps even take things a step further, if you're willing."

"What are you proposing?" Baldomar looked interested.

"We agree to become allies. Meaning we help one another out. If you need food or medicine, you can call on us and we will give it to you. Or if we need an army to protect our shores, you will send your vast fleet of ships to lend us aid."

King Baldomar looked surprised. For a moment he said nothing. Then he nodded slowly. "This is an interesting proposal," he said. "I will think on it this eve. If it pleases you, I will give you my answer tomorrow morning, after I speak with my men."

"That's fair," Arthur said, just happy Baldomar hadn't laughed in his face at his idea. Kay had claimed the Saxons were barbarians, but they actually seemed quite reasonable. "I will eagerly await your response," he added, then waved his hand. "But for now, please enjoy yourself and the feast. Sit by my side, if you like. You are my personal guest, after all." He gestured to the empty place at his left.

"I thank you, Your Majesty, but I prefer, I think, to sit with my men. If that's all right with you. They might not like me putting on airs, sitting on stages." He laughed good-naturedly.

"Oh. Yes, of course," Arthur replied with a grin. "Believe me, I don't like sitting up here much, either. I feel like I should be putting on a show."

The king laughed again, slapping Arthur on the shoulder. "I like you, boy king," he said. "I think you and I may be able to work something out."

The king returned to his men at the table, and Arthur turned back to his plate, feeling flushed with pleasure. This had gone better than he'd imagined. And in front of the whole court, too. Now everyone could see his plan wasn't as mad as some of them had wanted to make it out to be.

As he lifted a slice of pheasant to his mouth, he felt eyes at his side. He turned to see Guinevere watching him, another strange expression on her face. He cocked his head in question.

"What?" he asked. "Don't tell me I just did all that with food in my teeth."

"No." She smiled and shook her head. "No. Your teeth are fine."

"Then… what is it?"

She shrugged. "Oh, nothing. I'm just… surprised, I guess. Most kings would not be as generous as you were just now."

Arthur considered this for a moment. "I suppose not. But then, none of them studied under Merlin."

Guinevere's smile faded, just for a moment. Arthur wondered why.

"Do you know Merlin?" he asked.

"No," she said quickly. Maybe too quickly. "I mean, I've heard of him, obviously. Everyone has. But I've never… had the pleasure… to meet him." Her face looked pinched all of a sudden, as if she smelt something bad.

"Well, if he ever comes back, I'll introduce you!" Arthur declared. "You'll love him, I promise. He's so smart. And he's an amazing wizard, too. He's taught me everything I know."

"Does he tell you what to do?" Guinevere asked, suddenly looking very interested. "Like, how to run the land? Does he give you advice? Orders?"

Arthur frowned, confused at her questioning. "Well, no," he said. "To be honest, I haven't seen or heard from him in ages. Not since before I came to London and pulled the sword from the stone." He hung his head, remembering. "We had a fight, you see. And he flew off to someplace called Bermuda. I wish he'd come back. I don't like doing all this without him. I feel like I'll make a wrong choice or something. And someone will get hurt."

Guinevere pursed her lips for a moment. "You seem to be doing pretty well without him," she ventured, her voice hesitant. "I mean, all of this" – she gestured to the room – "this was all you, right? Not anything to do with Merlin."

"I suppose. But—"

Arthur was interrupted by a sudden commotion in the hall. When he looked out to see what it could be, his jaw dropped in surprise as his eyes fell on Kay, storming up to the stage. His foster brother's eyes were narrowed. And his hands were clenched into fists.

Arthur's heart quickened, though he wasn't quite sure why. Was his foster brother going to complain about his treaty with the Saxons again? If so, he was choosing a very poor time to do it.

"Um, Kay?" Arthur tried as his foster brother stepped up to the table, glaring down at him. If looks could kill, Arthur was quite sure he'd be on the floor. "Is something wrong?"

Kay scowled. He glanced back at his father, who was watching with far too much interest for Arthur's comfort. Sir Ector waved his hands at his son, urging him on. Kay huffed, then turned back to Arthur.

"Is something wrong?" Kay growled. "I'll tell you what's wrong. This farce has gone on long enough. You were never meant to be our king."

CHAPTER THIRTEEN
ARTHUR

Arthur stared at Kay in shock. Of all the things he'd expected his foster brother to say, this was definitely not one of them.

"What did you just say?" he asked, trying to keep the tremble from his voice. This was not a time to show weakness. Not with everyone in the kingdom watching. Not to mention the Saxons.

"I think you heard me, *Wart*," Kay snarled, spitting out Arthur's nickname as if it were a bad joke. "You don't deserve to be up here. And you certainly shouldn't be running the kingdom."

Arthur paled. Oh, no. Not now. Not in front of the Saxons, not when he'd just proposed an alliance.

He'd known from the start it was possible there would be someone someday who felt the need to challenge his kingship. He was only a child, after all. Untrained in just about everything to do with being a king. It made sense that someone would eventually rise up and try to take him down.

He just hadn't expected it to be his own brother.

He stole a glance over to the table where the Saxons were sitting. King Baldomar was watching the scene with steely eyes. He did not look pleased. Wonderful.

"What are you doing?" Arthur asked through clenched teeth, trying to keep his voice as low as possible so no one else could hear. "If you have a problem with me, can we just talk about it later? Privately? At least not in front of the entire kingdom and our invited guests?"

Kay shook his head. "No!" he said loudly. "For this concerns your entire court." He beckoned to the crowded room with his hand. "No one wants to say it, so I will. You are too young to be our king. Why, you haven't even grown your first whiskers yet!" he jeered. As if he himself had some kind of grizzly beard.

Arthur heard a few nervous laughs from the crowd. It made him want to crawl under the table. Why was Kay doing this? And why now of all times?

He could feel Guinevere's eyes on him from the side, but couldn't bring himself to look at her. Whatever he said next might change the course of history. And he would be responsible for the outcome.

"I hate to inform you, *brother*," he said stiffly, "but whiskers don't make a king. I may be young, but I pulled the sword from the stone. And as the prophecy says—"

His words were cut off by Kay's mocking laugh. "The prophecy," he spit out. "England's king was *meant* to be decided by a tournament. And because you pulled some sword from some stone, I never got my chance to compete. Does that seem fair to anyone?" He turned to the crowd, who was still watching the whole thing as if it were some kind of riveting play.

Sir Ector rose from his seat. "Well, I certainly don't think so!" he bellowed, and Arthur cringed as he noticed a few people nodding in agreement. *And why not?* he thought. To be honest, he himself had never thought it was quite fair. And he'd never asked for it, either. In fact, the last thing he'd wanted was to become king of England. Though he wasn't quite sure dim-witted Kay would fare any better.

He realised Kay was waiting for an answer.

"What do you want from me?" he asked, not knowing what else to say.

"I came to London for a tournament," Kay replied. "And I'm still waiting for my chance to fight." He sneered at Arthur.

"Face me in single combat. We'll see, once and for all, who's *really* meant to be king."

Arthur swallowed hard. He could feel his forehead break out into a cold sweat. Kay wanted to fight him? His brother was ten times bigger than Arthur and probably twenty times stronger. Not to mention he had years of training, whereas Arthur had none.

Heavenly prophecy or no, if he fought Kay, Arthur would not stand a chance.

He could feel Guinevere's hand on his arm. "You don't have to do this," she whispered. "Just call your guards. Have them take him away."

It was a good idea, but Arthur knew it would serve as only a temporary reprieve. Kay would be back, or others would take his place. The gauntlet had been thrown, and he had to prove himself worthy of the throne – or everyone would remain in doubt. The Saxons would think him a coward. They might start thinking twice about the treaty.

And so Arthur squared his shoulders. Lifted his chin. "Name your time and place," he said simply. "I will answer your challenge."

There were gasps from the crowd. Kay's smile widened.

"Excellent," he said. "I knew you'd see reason." He pressed his fists against the table, leaning forwards. So close Arthur could smell his foul breath. "Meet me in the courtyard tomorrow morning and we shall battle. And to the victor goes the kingdom."

"I will be there," Arthur replied, hoping he sounded brave. In reality, he was shaking like a leaf.

Kay smirked, then turned and stormed out of the great hall. As the heavy door swung shut behind him, the court erupted into conversation. Arthur guessed they would probably be making wagers on the battle – and he assumed most of them would not be in his favour. Not that he blamed them. His odds of beating a trained warrior in hand-to-hand combat were next to nothing.

"What were you thinking?" Guinevere demanded, grabbing his arm. He turned to look at her and realised her face was ashen with fear. "You're never going to win against a man like that!"

He grimaced. "Thanks for your support."

"I'm sorry." She hung her hand. "I'm just trying to be sensible." Arthur watched as she inhaled a long breath through her teeth. "Look, maybe..." she began hesitantly. "Maybe you should just give him what he wants."

"What?" Arthur looked shocked.

"Do you really like being king? Being trapped here in this castle, under guard? I saw you out in the forest. You seemed happier there. You... could go back to that."

Arthur stared at her. She wasn't wrong – and it was a

tempting thought, to say the least. To just walk away from it all. Get a second chance at a simple life. One where he didn't have to make rules or avoid wars or be responsible for the well-being of people he had never met.

And all he would have to do was give up his crown. Which didn't even fit.

But then his eyes travelled to the Saxon table. They were all watching closely, their faces guarded, but clearly concerned. Arthur remembered his conversation with Kay the week before. His foster brother had called Saxons barbarians. He said they deserved to be destroyed.

If he backed down now – abdicated the throne – these men, who had come here under his protection and promise of peace, would likely be arrested where they sat. Taken to a dungeon. Maybe even killed.

All talks of peace would be over.

The kingdom would erupt into war.

"I can't," he said sadly. "As much as I might want to. There's too much at stake." He gestured to the Saxons. Guinevere nodded unhappily, as if she'd known this would be his answer all along.

"You can't sign a peace treaty if you're dead," she said in a low voice.

He bit his lower lip. "Well, then, I'm just going to have to figure out a way to stay alive."

CHAPTER FOURTEEN
GUINEVERE

The feast went late into the night, and by the end of it, the Saxons and Englishmen were making merry with one another, dancing and laughing, as if they were long-lost friends. In fact, the only person who didn't look like he was having fun was Arthur himself. Sure, he tried to keep a brave face, but Guinevere could see the traces of fear in his eyes that he couldn't quite hide. And she couldn't help feeling sorry for him. She was convinced, at this point, he didn't know about the evil Merlin had done; he'd been tricked into thinking he was meant to be king. Which made her quest a lot more difficult. She knew he still needed to be brought down, but she didn't want him to get hurt in the process. If only he'd just given up the throne – walked away from it all when he had the chance…

But he wouldn't, she realised. He felt responsible for the people of England. He hadn't been king long, but he cared about the realm and his chance at peace. He had all the instincts of a good leader, even if he wasn't meant to sit on the throne.

Eventually she left the feast to retire to her humble little bedroom down the hall from the kitchens. She was just about to take off her itchy gown and replace it with a soft night garment when she heard a scratching at her window. She pulled open the wooden shutters (servants, of course, didn't get real glass windows like kings did) and found a little purple squirrel on the other side, twitching its nose at her.

She raised an eyebrow. "Mother?" she whispered. "Is that you?"

Not that she had much doubt in the matter. The purple rather gave it away.

As the squirrel hopped up onto the windowsill, Guinevere ran to lock her door. Then she headed back to the window, scooped up the squirrel in her arms, and took it over to her bed. A moment later there was a quick *poof*, and the squirrel disappeared, replaced by Mim.

"Ugh. I hate squirrels," Mim grumped, brushing off her

muddy dress with her hands. "They're so dirty and smelly. Rats with bushy tails, that's all they are."

Guinevere nodded dutifully, even though she was quite fond of squirrels herself.

"What are you doing here, Mother?" she asked, trying not to notice all the dirt and mud flakes landing on her bed as her mother continued to shake out her dress. Why had Mim felt the need to use magic instead of just coming through the front door like a normal person?

"Why, I'm here to see you, of course! I missed you, my dear! It's so dreadfully boring in the cottage without you dancing around all the time! I even had to play card games by myself! Which I won, of course! You do get such a better chance of winning when you play both sides of the table!" She giggled.

Guinevere couldn't help a small smile. She hadn't realised how much she'd missed her mother's silly banter. "I'm glad you're here," she assured her. "Only it's very late at night. I would think you would want to wait till morning."

Mim waved her off. "Sleep is for the weak. And I couldn't wait. Not when I heard the news!"

"The… news?" So much had happened that night, Guinevere was at a loss as to what her mother might be referring to. Did she mean the Saxon treaty? Sir Kay's challenge to Arthur?

"The whole town is buzzing about it," Mim clucked. "The mysterious blonde girl in the blue dress who danced through court like an angel and dined like royalty with the king himself." She gave Guinevere a meaningful look. "It seems you've been enjoying yourself, my dear."

"Oh. That." Guinevere stared down at her feet, feeling sheepish. "Yes, Arthur invited me to dinner tonight. I, uh, thought it would be a good chance for me to spy on him, as you asked me to."

"Indeed, my pet!" Mim looked positively gleeful. "Earn his trust and friendship, and then – pow! Off with his head!" She cackled loudly. "I mean, not literally, of course," she added as she caught Guin's horrified look. She leant in closer. Her eyebrows waggled. "So tell dear Mother, what have you learnt about our boy king? Anything useful we can use against him?"

Guinevere opened her mouth to speak, but strangely nothing came out. Instead, she felt a weird shimmer of unease waft through her stomach. She had plenty to tell Mim from her day with Arthur. So why was she suddenly feeling reluctant to share it?

"Well, come on, girl!" Mim scolded. "We don't have all night!" She puffed up her wild purple hair with her hands. "I need my beauty sleep, you know! I mean, not that I'm not perfectly lovely as I am..." she added, preening at her reflection in Guinevere's water basin.

"Sorry," Guinevere mumbled. She forced herself to straighten her shoulders and draw in a deep breath before giving her report. "The Saxons arrived tonight and dined with the king. Arthur presented his idea of a peace treaty, and they're going to tell him tomorrow whether they want to sign it."

"Bah!" Mim spit on the floor. "This was exactly what I was afraid of."

Guinevere bit her lower lip. "But... why?"

"What do you mean, why?" Mim looked at her, puzzled.

"I don't know. It's just..." Guin shrugged. "Why don't we want peace? I mean, wouldn't that be a good thing?"

"Well, y-yes. I mean, of course it would," Mim stammered, looking a little taken aback by the question. "Peace would be wonderful! Just peachy! We all want peace. Of course we do! It's just that – well, how do we know it's not a trick? Maybe they're pretending to want peace – just to get us to let our guard down. After all, you know how *Saxons* can be!" She gave Guinevere a pointed look, as if daring her to argue. Then she waved a hand dismissively. "Anyway, what else did you learn?"

Guinevere gnawed on her lower lip. "Well, Arthur's foster brother, Sir Kay, has challenged his right to the throne."

She had a feeling her mother was going to appreciate this piece of news more than the first. "They're set to fight first thing tomorrow morning. Arthur had to agree to it, or he risked looking weak in front of the Saxons. But I'm afraid he's not going to be up for the challenge. He's just a boy. And this knight is an experienced warrior."

Mim rubbed her hands together in glee. "Now that's more like it! If we're lucky, maybe he'll manage to ruin everything on his own!"

"But then Kay would be king," Guinevere protested. "And he's not the rightful ruler, either."

Mim shrugged. "Well, we can't have everything, now can we, my dear?"

"But that seems kind of like a *big* thing," Guinevere insisted. She was starting to get really confused. "I mean, Arthur's actually a good king. He's young, but he's smart. And he seems to care about people."

Mim pinched Guinevere's cheeks hard. "Oh, my dear, sweet girl," she cooed. "Do not tell me that you're falling for this usurper's lies!" She released Guinevere's cheeks and danced to the other side of the room. "He may seem innocent enough. But never forget what master he serves."

Guinevere flinched. "Merlin," she said softly.

"Merlin," Mim affirmed. "You know, *he* seemed quite lovely once upon a time, too. Just a dear old doddering fool.

Until he slaughtered your parents in cold blood, that is." She gave Guin a hard look. "And the apple, my dear, never falls far from the tree."

Guin swallowed hard, her mind racing. She thought back to Arthur at the banquet, talking so lovingly about his teacher. Something wasn't adding up.

"Why did Merlin kill my parents?" she blurted out before she could stop herself.

For a moment, Mim froze. Then she laughed. "I've told you this story a thousand times," she reminded Guin.

"Yes," Guinevere agreed. "But you never told me why. *Why* did he want to kill my parents? I mean, he must have had a reason."

"Because he's evil! Obviously!" Mim replied. "And evil people do evil things. There's no sense in looking any deeper than that, my darling. You'll only drive yourself mad."

"Right." Guinevere sighed. Clearly she wasn't going to get any more information out of her mother tonight. But there *had* to be more to this than she'd been told. After all, the Merlin of Mim's stories was so unlike the Merlin of Arthur's. So which was the true Merlin?

And what did he really want from Camelot?

CHAPTER FIFTEEN
ARTHUR

"This is pure foolishness, boy! Pure foolishness, I say!"

Archimedes flew from one end of Arthur's bedroom to the other, his wings flapping furiously. It was still early in the morning, and Arthur wondered if the owl had slept at all the night before. Merlin used to joke that Archimedes was especially grumpy when he stayed out all night. Or maybe it was just the situation that had him all riled up.

"What am I supposed to do?" Arthur asked with a shrug. "It's not like I want to fight him. But I have no choice."

"You always have a choice. In fact, you could have chosen to put that sword back where you found it, for that matter – like I told you to. Then you wouldn't be in this mess."

"Well, it's too late for that now. And a lot of people are depending on me. I can't let them down by being a coward."

"Being a coward! How about being stupid and getting yourself killed? I'd imagine *that* would also let a few people down. First and foremost, me."

"Aw, Archimedes. I didn't know you cared," Arthur couldn't help teasing.

The owl huffed, offended. "Please! I could care less what you do with your own skin. I just don't want to have to deal with Merlin coming back and learning I let his favourite pupil be pounded into a pancake while he was gone," Archimedes grumbled. "I don't need that kind of pressure on my handsome feathered shoulders, thank you very much."

"Come on, Archimedes," Arthur begged. "A little faith?"

"Faith, trust and pixie dust!" Archimedes spat. "And we're all out of pixie dust."

"What's pixie dust?" Arthur asked, cocking his head. "And why would we need that?"

The owl rolled his eyes. "It's just an expression. Something Merlin used to say. The point is, having faith is one thing. Having smarts is quite another. And you clearly don't have any of those."

Arthur sighed. "Look, I'm not going to let myself get pounded, all right? I've been in dangerous situations before. Like when Merlin turned me into a fish? And a squirrel? And a bird?"

"Yes, yes. Give the boy a medal for his marvellous near misses. Believe me, I was there to witness them. But this time I can't fly in and save you if you get yourself in a jam."

"No. But I can use the lessons I learnt from those experiences. Like the one about brains being just as good as brawn. I may not be as strong as Kay, but I'm pretty sure I'm smarter."

"That big rock out on the courtyard is likely smarter than your foster brother," Archimedes admitted reluctantly.

"Exactly. And I know Kay's fighting style. I helped him train for years, remember. I know he's weaker on his left side. And when he feints right, he leaves his neck exposed. It used to drive Sir Ector mad."

"I suppose knowledge like that *could* be useful," the owl hedged.

"Exactly. Knowledge. That was what Merlin always tried to teach me. That knowledge is just as powerful as a sword. I can do this, Archimedes," he added, feeling excitement well inside of him for the first time since Kay had approached his table. "I know I can."

"Well, you certainly have confidence. I'll give you that."

The owl spun his head. "And I suppose there's no talking you out of this?"

"No, sir." Arthur shook his head, walking over to Excalibur and giving it a thoughtful look. The sword was heavy enough when he wore it on his belt. He was pretty sure he wouldn't be able to swing it more than a time or two – and even then without much control and accuracy.

But if all went according to plan, he wouldn't need that.

Oh, Merlin, he thought, *I really hope you're right.*

After trying without much luck to swallow a quick breakfast, Arthur got dressed and made his way down to the castle courtyard, where the makeshift tournament was to be held. When he arrived, a crowd of spectators had already gathered, pushing and shoving one another as they fought their way up onto the wooden stands, trying to get the best spot to watch the fight. In fact, there were so many of them there, Arthur half wondered if they outnumbered the crowd at his coronation.

But then, it was not every day the king of England took on his own knight.

The Saxon king, Baldomar, met him at the gate. He looked down at Arthur, studying him carefully. "Are you certain about this?" he asked, his voice tense with concern.

Arthur squared his shoulders. Or he tried to, at least.

The chain mail armour he was wearing was supposed to be lighter than plate, but it was still unbearably heavy. "Don't worry," he said. "I have a plan. And I plan to win."

The king nodded, though he didn't look quite convinced. "I hope so," he said. "For I do not like the way your challenger looks at us. I get the feeling he will not be so eager to sign a treaty if he emerges victorious."

"No, he probably won't be," Arthur agreed, wanting to be honest. He shuffled from foot to foot. "In fact, it may be a good idea for you to head out of town now, while you still have the freedom to do so. Just in case. If the worst happens, I do not want you to have to pay for my failure as king."

King Baldomar looked at him thoughtfully. "You are wise beyond your years, boy king," he said. "And I can see you truly care for others, even above your own self. That's a rare quality in a leader." He smiled. "But like you, we are not cowards. We do not retreat in the face of adversity. We will stay and cheer for your victory. And *when* you emerge the winner," he added, emphasising the *when*, "we will sign your treaty."

Arthur's face flushed. It was all he could do not to break out into a happy dance. But he forced his feet to remain firmly on the ground. "Thank you," he said. "Then we talk this afternoon."

"I look forward to it." King Baldomar gave him a deep bow, then turned and headed back to where his men were gathered. Arthur watched him go, drawing in a slow breath. He appreciated the faith shown in him, and he just hoped he could prove worthy of it.

A moment later, Sir Pellinore approached. "Are you set, lad?" he asked, looking at Arthur a bit doubtfully. "Kay has indicated he's ready to fight."

A chill tripped down Arthur's spine, all of his earlier confidence in front of King Baldomar instantly deflating. He glanced out into the courtyard to see Kay warming up by swinging his sword against a wooden post. He was dressed in a full suit of plate armour and looked ten feet tall. Arthur cringed, looking down at his own paltry suit of chain mail that didn't even fit well. What was he doing? Archimedes was right – this was pure foolishness!

No! He scolded himself. It did him no good to panic before the fight even began. Keeping his head was the one chance he had to win this. And he had to win this. Everything depended on it.

"I'm ready," he told Pellinore, trying to make his voice sound calm and confident. He drew in a breath and walked past the older knight, heading out onto the makeshift field, keeping his head held high. The crowd broke out into loud cheers as they caught sight of their king, and shouts of "Long Live King Arthur!" resounded through the space. Arthur caught a quick glimpse of Kay's scowl before his foster brother put his helmet over his head.

"All right!" Sir Pellinore announced, stepping into the courtyard and addressing the crowd in a voice loud enough for everyone to hear. "The fight shall begin when I raise and lower this flag. The rules are simple. Fight with honour. Fight with bravery. And fight to the death."

Wait, what? Arthur stopped short at the last part. Clearly no one had thought to mention that pesky little 'to the death' detail earlier! While, yes, tournaments often ended with knights being maimed or killed, it was never the intended result. He gnawed on his lower lip. This was not good at all. Not only did he not want to die himself, obviously – he also didn't want to have to kill his foster brother if the fates turned in his favour. While he was truly angry at Kay for putting him in this position, that didn't mean he wanted him dead!

Worry about it later, he scolded himself. *Right now, you have to fight. And stay alive.*

Arthur watched as Kay unsheathed his sword and followed the move with his own, trying not to notice how heavy Excalibur felt in his hands, his muscles already wobbling from the effort. His heart pounded as he took a moment to gaze over the crowd before facing his opponent.

Suddenly, his eyes fell on Guinevere, who was sitting in the very back row of the stands, dressed in a simple homespun dress of undyed wool, her hair plaited into two matching braids. Arthur threw her a small friendly smile and waved in her direction, happy to see a familiar face. She smiled back at him – just for a moment – then bashfully dropped her gaze to her lap. But it was enough. Arthur felt his confidence rising again. She had come. Which meant she cared. And if he won this, perhaps they could dine together again.

It was almost reason enough to win, in and of itself.

It was then that he noticed something at her side – make that some*one.* An old woman dressed in common peasant clothes. Which wouldn't have normally struck him as unusual. Except…

The clothes were purple. And so was her hair.

He swallowed hard. Oh, no! Had Mim come back? Now of all times? And somehow she had found Guinevere! She must have heard that Guin had been his guest at dinner last night; from what Archimedes had told him, the whole town had been talking about it. Had Arthur put his new friend in danger? He tried to get Guin's attention again, but she had turned to look at Mim, who was whispering something in her ear. Guin looked uncomfortable as she glanced back out onto the field. What had the wizard said to her? It took all Arthur had inside of him not to rush the stands and make sure Guinevere was safe.

But at that moment, the trumpets sounded through the air, indicating the start of the fight. Arthur turned to see Sir Pellinore raising his flag, then dropping it.

This was it. The battle had begun. Before Arthur could even think of saving Guinevere, he'd have to find a way to save himself.

CHAPTER SIXTEEN
GUINEVERE

A fight to the death.

The words reverberated in Guinevere's ears as she watched Arthur take the field against Sir Kay. She could hear Mim's excited cackles beside her but couldn't bring herself to look in her direction.

"Why does it have to be to the death?" she asked, worrying her lower lip. "Why can't they just, I don't know, fight and declare a winner – like they do at the regular jousts?"

"Oh, my pet. You worry far too much about one downed little sparrow," Mim clucked. "Besides, it'll be much easier this way. If he dies, Merlin loses. We win."

Guinevere shot her a look. She shrugged. "And, you

know, the kingdom will be safe from destruction, blah, blah, blah – all that good stuff, too, of course," she added gleefully.

"It's just so… barbaric. I mean, he's only a boy," Guinevere found herself arguing.

"A boy under the thumb of an evil wizard," Mim reminded her. "Trust me, my sweet girl." She rubbed her hands together. "This will be so much fun!"

Guinevere felt her stomach squirm with nausea. Why couldn't her mother take anything seriously? Didn't she understand this wasn't a game? Arthur could die out there on the field. And whether he was meant to be king or not, he didn't deserve such a fate.

She watched as Sir Kay lumbered towards Arthur, swinging his sword with practised grace. Arthur stumbled backwards, trying to put distance between them, but only managed to fall on his backside. The crowd erupted into worried murmurs as their king scrambled to his feet just in time to dodge the heavy blow from his knight. The sword swung only a finger or two above his head in a near miss. Once he was clear, Arthur dashed to the other side of the field, trying to catch his breath.

It was not an auspicious start, to say the least.

"This might be quick!" Mim crowed. "If we're lucky, maybe I'll even have time to grab a few slugs at the market on the way home." She grinned widely. "I'm still craving that slug soup."

Guinevere ignored her, still watching Arthur closely. He was standing in the corner, panting heavily. He gave another look at Kay, then, to Guinevere's surprise, dropped his sword and began to unclip his chain mail armour. He let it fall to the ground in a pool of metal, leaving him wearing only a tunic and tights.

"What is he doing?" Guin gasped. "Why is he taking off his armour? He'll be completely unprotected!"

"Well, clearly he's not very bright," Mim said with a snort. "Not that we didn't know this already. I mean, with Merlin as his teacher..."

Guinevere frowned. But Arthur *was* bright – she'd witnessed it first-hand. And he definitely wasn't stupid enough to just take off his armour on a whim; he must have a reason for doing it.

But what could it be?

She held her breath as Kay stalked towards Arthur again, his sword raised and ready. Arthur had picked his own sword back up and was holding it in a defensive stance. But Kay was so much larger, towering over the boy king like a mighty beast, Guin realised it would be nearly impossible for Arthur to even get close enough to land a blow. How did he ever expect to win?

Kay swung his blade. But Arthur darted out of the way at the last second. Guin watched as he danced from side to side, nimbler without his armour. Kay, dressed in full plate, tried to catch him, but each blow landed a hair too late. Arthur would feint right, then dodge left when Kay took the bait. And then feint left, only to dodge right. Arthur wasn't landing any actual blows, but he was succeeding in tiring his opponent out. Kay's thrusts were getting weaker. His shield began to wobble in his hand. On his next swing, Arthur slid forwards instead of going to the side, ducking under the sword's arc and slamming his feet into Kay's ankles. The knight bellowed as he lost his balance and came crashing to the ground. Arthur rolled to the side to avoid being flattened. Then he scrambled to his feet, grinning at the crowd.

Guinevere let out an accidental cheer. Mim shot her an annoyed look.

"Sorry," she muttered. "But you have to admit, that was pretty good."

Mim grunted, turning back to the fight. The crowd was on its feet now, cheering loudly for their king – and jeering at his opponent. Kay cursed under his breath as he managed to get back on his feet. He charged after Arthur again, swinging his sword recklessly. He was angry now, Guinevere realised. Humiliated. Which meant he would start making mistakes.

Meaning Arthur might actually have a chance.

But just when Arthur moved in for a real blow, his feet suddenly seemed to come out from under him. He yelped in surprise as he fell sprawling to the ground, a cloud of dust kicking up in his wake. Guinevere gasped. Had he tripped over something? But there was nothing there!

It was then that she heard the giggle. Her head jerked in Mim's direction. Her mother was slapping her hand on her knee in excitement.

"Did you do that?" Guinevere demanded in a whisper. "Did you just use magic to trip him?"

Mim shrugged impishly. "The fight was getting boring," she declared. "I just wanted to mix things up a bit."

"But that's not fair!" Guin cried before she could stop herself.

"Fair, schmair." Mim grinned at her toothily. "If I'm going to have to sit here, I want to have some fun!"

Guinevere sighed, turning back to the fight. Arthur was trying to stand up, but it was like his legs weren't working right any more. Then Guinevere noticed something strange under his boots. Something that looked almost like mud.

Purple mud.

Kay barrelled towards Arthur. But this time Arthur couldn't leap out of the way. It was as if he was glued to the ground by the mud. His eyes widened in fear as the knight swung—

Kick off your boots, Guinevere begged silently. *It's the only way!*

Arthur threw himself forwards, slipping out of his boots at the last moment. He slammed chest-first into the ground, but somehow managed to scramble back up again, dashing shoeless to the other side of the courtyard, leaving Kay staring down at a pair of empty boots.

Yes! Guinevere cheered, remembering to do it inwardly now. She stole another glance at Mim. Her mother was leaning forwards in her seat, her eyes glued to the fight. Guinevere realised she wasn't going to stop until Arthur went down.

Which wasn't fair. It wasn't fair at all. She was fine with helping Arthur lose the throne, seeing as he wasn't the rightful heir. But she wasn't all right with killing him in order to do so. There had to be another way. A more civilised way.

Why couldn't her mother see that? Why was she being so cruel?

"Mother! Stop!" she tried, raising her voice. "You need to stop now!" Several people turned to look at her. Mim's smile dipped to a frown.

"*You* need to mind your business. Whose side are

you on, anyway?" Not waiting for an answer, Mim turned back to the fight just in time to see Arthur trip again. She giggled and shot a look at Guin, almost as if daring her to say something.

Guin couldn't take it any more.

"Excuse me," she said, rising to her feet abruptly. "I've got to go to the privy."

"Good. Because you're being a complete poop!" Mim muttered. "No slugs for you, later. You don't deserve them!"

Guinevere ignored her, making her way through the throng. After climbing down the risers, she circled around the back of them, where no one was standing. Her mind raced as she walked. She had to do something to make this right. Her mother wasn't going to stop. But what could she do to help Arthur, save going on the field and fighting Kay herself?

"You let go of the boy, you lousy old lout!"

Speaking of… Guinevere looked up to the sky just in time to see a small owl swooping down at Kay. Merlin's bewitched owl, she realised in shock. She'd just assumed he'd been stuck in the future along with the wizard himself. But evidently he'd escaped that fate. Maybe he'd be able to help.

Kay let out a scream as the owl pecked him hard on his bulbous nose. He waved his arms, trying to swat him away. But the owl kept at it, digging his claws into the knight's shoulder. Unfortunately, Kay's armour was too thick and the owl couldn't get a good grip.

"Archimedes!" Arthur cried, struggling to stand. "Look out!"

But it was too late. Kay swung out a fist. His metal glove smacked the owl straight on. Archimedes flailed for a moment, then dropped to the ground like a stone.

"No!" Arthur cried, sounding horrified. He dived towards the bird, throwing himself on top of him to protect him from Kay. Even from here, Guin could see the tears streaming down his bruised cheeks and realised his face was cut and bleeding. But he didn't seem to even notice, he was so concerned about the bird. "Oh, Archimedes!" he cried, his voice cracking on the name.

Guinevere's heart panged hard. He clearly cared for this animal. Like he cared for his people. Even his enemies. He wasn't Merlin. He wasn't anything like Merlin. And he didn't deserve to die.

Drawing in a breath, she realised what she needed to do. It was the last thing she wanted, and her hands started to shake just thinking about it. But she had no choice. She had to act – now. Or Arthur would die. And his blood would be on her hands.

"*Zim, zabberim, zouse!*" she whispered. "Make me a mouse!"

A moment later she felt her body collapsing in on itself, shrinking down, reshaping, just as her mother had taught her to do. She hated shapeshifting – it felt so disconcerting to fold into another shape. It made her sick to her stomach, too. And gave her a terrible headache.

But that was nothing compared to what Arthur was going through. And she was almost positive, if the tables had been turned, he would have done the same for her.

She drew in a breath, steadying her nerves. Then, using her tiny feet, she dashed under the risers and weaved through the standing spectators' legs at the front. She prayed no one would suddenly move their feet and squash her before she had the chance to get out onto the field. By the time she made it to the front, Arthur had fallen to his knees before Kay. He clearly had no fight left in him.

"You should have just walked away, Wart," Kay sneered. He removed his helmet and looked down on the young king, his mouth curling into a lazy smirk. "Did you really think you had a chance to beat me?"

Arthur stared up at him defiantly. Blood dripped down his face, but he ignored it, his mouth set in a thin line. The crowd was so silent you could have heard a pin drop.

"I had to try," he said simply. "For my people. For our kingdom."

Kay's face twisted into an ugly scowl. He raised his sword, ready to make the fatal blow.

Guinevere realised it was now or never. She raced across the field as fast as she could. Darting up Kay's boot, she found the small kink in his armour where it met with his knee. It wasn't a large spot, but it was the perfect size for tiny mouse teeth.

She bit down. Hard.

"Argh!" Kay screamed, falling backwards and dropping his sword. Guinevere scampered up his side until she found his armpit, biting down yet again into his soft flesh. The reek of sweat assaulted her nose, and it was everything she could do not to vomit. Instead, she forced herself to bite again. And again.

The crowd gasped as Kay began to roll on the ground, screaming in pain. Arthur took his moment, leaping up and kicking the knight's abandoned sword to the side, far enough away that he couldn't easily retrieve it. Then he stalked over to Kay – and placed his own sword at the knight's throat.

"You were saying?" he asked.

"Make it stop!" Kay begged. "Please!"

"Kill him! Kill him!" cried the crowd. "Show no mercy!"

But to Guinevere's surprise, Arthur lowered his sword. "No," he said simply. "I won't kill you. That's not how we do things here any more. You will be charged with treason against your king and you will be tried in court, by a jury of your peers. It will be up to them to decide your fate."

Kay began to blubber like a baby. He yanked off his gloves and threw them angrily at the crowd. Arthur motioned to his guards, who surrounded the disgraced knight and pulled him to his feet. Kay tried to fight them off, but he was too weakened from the battle. They dragged him out of the courtyard as the crowd jeered and threw pieces of food at his head.

Arthur watched him go, then turned to Archimedes, who was still lying motionless on the ground. He dropped to his knees, cradling the bird in his hands. Was he dead? But then Guinevere caught a slight movement at the wing. No, he was alive. She let out a sharp breath.

Arthur looked up at the crowd. "He needs a doctor," he said. "Is anyone here a doctor?"

A large muscular man pushed his way through the crowd. He took the bird from Arthur's arms and studied him with a careful eye. "He's stunned," he told the young king. "Maybe a broken wing. But he will be all right."

Guinevere watched as Arthur's shoulders drooped in relief. She felt relieved, too, a wave of emotion rushing through her telling her everything was going to be all right.

And while she'd never get credit for it, she had managed to save the day.

Using magic, of all things.

She felt a pang of guilt as she headed off the field, unseen by anyone in the crowd. They were all rushing Arthur to congratulate him on his win. She watched his lips curl in a bashful grin, and she wondered if she'd been right to do what she'd done. After all, it was exactly what she always chided Mim for – using an unfair advantage to manipulate a situation to your liking. But then, if she hadn't, an innocent boy would have died. That wouldn't have been right, either.

She sighed. Ever since she'd met Arthur, things had become very confusing.

She weaved her way through the throng until she was back to where she'd started, behind the risers. Where she could end her shift and transform back to her old self. She wondered how bad of a headache she'd have when she became human again. Magic took a huge toll on her each time she cast a spell. Mim claimed it was because she didn't do it enough – like exercise, magic got easier the more you did it. It didn't cost Mim anything to shift and shift again. But Guinevere would likely be weakened for a week.

It was worth it, though. She wouldn't have changed a thing.

But before she could utter the magic words to end the transformation, she suddenly felt a hand close over her mouse body. She squeaked in surprise and tried to squirm away, but the hand was too strong. A moment later, she felt herself being lifted up into the air.

The hand opened.

And she found herself face to face with Mim.

CHAPTER SEVENTEEN
MADAM MIM

"Well, well, well, what have we here?"

Mim squinted at the little mouse, at first unsure of what she was seeing. She knew it couldn't be a regular mouse – after all, regular mice did not tend to interfere with jousting tournaments. But what else could it be? Another one of Merlin's stooges, like that ridiculous owl who had tried and failed to save his minion? She wondered how many of the forest creatures this madman had manipulated.

But then, there was something oddly familiar about this particular creature. Something about its dark brown eyes… and long thick lashes.

Mim wrinkled her nose. No. It couldn't be. Could it?

"Guinevere?" she whispered.

Suddenly the spell broke and Mim found herself cradling a rather large and heavy thirteen-year-old girl in the palm of her hand. Shocked, she leapt backwards, her arms flinging out, and the girl dropped to the ground like a stone.

"Ow!" Guinevere grunted, landing hard on her bottom.

Mim stared down at her daughter, speechless for one of the first times in her entire life. "Why, it is you!" she cried out once she'd found her voice again, even though, in hindsight, the declaration was quite obvious. "What on earth were you doing as a mouse?"

Guinevere scrambled to her feet, a guilty look flashing across her face. "Hello, Mother," she muttered, wiping the mud off her backside. She looked a little dazed. Her hand lifted to her head and she rubbed it ruefully.

Mim shook her head in disbelief. "Why, I'll be a monkey's uncle!" she cried. "You used magic! But you hate magic!"

Guinevere scowled. "Maybe I hate cheating more."

Mim giggled. She couldn't help it. Guin was just so cute when she was mad. The way her little nose wrinkled and her eyebrows furrowed…

"Stop laughing! It's not funny," Guin protested, her scowl deepening.

"No, of course not!" Mim agreed readily, trying to

swallow down her mirth. "Not funny at all. Rather – amazing, really! Simply amazing. Such a good shift, too. You got all the mouse parts just right – and that's not easy to do! I have to admit, I'm impressed. So very impressed!"

Guinevere's frown faltered. "You're not mad?"

Mim laughed. "Mad? I'm delighted! Thrilled! Sure, I wanted the fight to go differently. And I'm not pleased about losing all the gold I wagered against the lad. But you, my dear, were magnificent! Marvellous! I'm just… tearing up with pride over the whole thing."

Guinevere pursed her lips together, looking very uncomfortable. "You were *cheating*, Mother! You were using magic to make him lose."

Mim nodded, not sure why her daughter insisted on stating the obvious. "And then you used magic to make him win," she added. She laughed again. "Did you see all the confused faces on the crowd when Kay dropped his sword? It was amazing. I couldn't have done it better myself."

"It's not a joke. Arthur could have been killed!" Guinevere retorted, her voice rich with indignation. Mim felt her amusement falter a bit.

"I wasn't going to kill him!" she protested. "I was just having a little fun is all. You really need to lighten up."

"Mother, this has gone too far," Guinevere shot back, not missing a beat. "We're supposed to be fighting for justice

– to save the kingdom, not tear it apart. If we start hurting people, we'll be no better than the evil Merlin himself!"

Mim's delight at the whole event was fading fast, replaced by a feeling she didn't like at all. Not one bit. Why was Guinevere being so mean?

"You know, you seem awfully concerned about the boy you've been working to take down getting taken down," she noted, a little crossly this time. She trailed off, noticing Guinevere's face reddening. Mim's eyes widened. Oh.

"Oh, my gracious! You're in love with him!" she cried, all the pieces coming together at once. "That's what it is, isn't it! He's charmed you with his riches and feasts and pretty clothes. And now you think if you can help him, he'll make you his queen." She tsked with her tongue. "I thought better of you, my girl. I really did."

Guinevere's face had turned the colour of a ripe apple. "That's not true!" she cried. "That's not even close to true. And I don't care about any of those things, either," she added. "It's just… I don't think Arthur is like Merlin. I think he's a good person, and he's been tricked, too. Maybe if we just tell him the truth, he'll do the right thing."

Mim was laughing so hard now she was practically rolling on the ground. "The truth! You want to… tell… him…" – she could hardly get the words out through her laughter – "the truth?" She stopped laughing abruptly. "Oh, my dear girl, you are more deluded than I thought. This little adventure in the outside world was clearly too much for you. You're not acting at all like your old, sweet self." She reached out, stroking Guin's hair. "We need to get you home, and fast."

For a moment, Guinevere looked as if she wanted to argue again. Then she sighed deeply, as if exhausted. "We should *both* go home," she said. "This has all got completely out of hand. We should go home and talk everything over – figure out what should be done like two rational people. There has to be a peaceful way to convince Arthur to abdicate the throne. I'm sure if we just thought it through..."

"That sounds lovely, my dear," Mim agreed. She patted Guin's head. "And I'm absolutely in favour of all of it and can't wait to do it. I just have one tiny little task to check off my list first. Then I'll head right home. You can even start dinner, if you like! And then we can have a dance party? Just like old times."

Guin frowned, looking suspicious. "What task?" she asked. "You're not going to hurt Arthur, are you?"

"Of course not! What do you take me for? Merlin?"

"Promise me." Guinevere's eyes were diamond hard.

"I promise! I promise!" Mim cried, rolling her eyes. "On the life of my new toad, Martha the Second. And you know how much I simply adore all her beautiful warts!"

Guinevere let out a breath. "All right," she said. "Thank you."

"Anything for you, my dear." Mim gave Guin a sloppy kiss on the cheek. "Anything for you."

Guinevere opened her mouth – probably to say something else annoying – but Mim had already wasted enough time talking. She had a plan, and she was eager to carry it out.

"*Zim, zabberim, zim!*" she incanted, waving her arms and poofing herself into a brand-new magical shape. Namely that of a certain young blonde girl with big brown eyes and thick lashes. A girl who had expertly captured the king's attention. Someone he trusted. Someone he'd never suspect.

Guinevere's jaw dropped. "No!" she cried. "What are you doing?"

"I'm just going to pay a quick visit to our dear king!" Mim replied, enjoying the way Guinevere's voice sounded on her lips. "Don't worry. I'll be home in three shakes of a slug's tail, ready for our dance party!"

"Mother! What are you—" Guinevere started, looking alarmed. But she didn't get to finish her sentence. For Mim took the opportunity to snap her fingers again, and Guinevere poofed out of her sight. Off on a one-way magical trip home to their cottage in the woods, where she would be safe and sound, and, if Mim were lucky, she would start on dinner. All this magic was making Mim very hungry.

Once Guin was gone, Mim looked down at her new and improved younger self. It had been a good shift – in fact, this time only her left foot and ankle were spotted with purple. Which was easily coverable by a boot or a dress hem. No one would ever notice.

She smiled, raising her eyes to the courtyard, where the celebration was now in full swing. Let them feast and drink and believe they'd won, she thought. They would soon learn the truth.

That no one messed with the Marvellous Madam Mim.

CHAPTER EIGHTEEN
ARTHUR

Arthur looked for Guinevere after the fight was over, but she seemed to have vanished from the crowd. So had Mim, for that matter, and Arthur started to worry that perhaps the mad wizard had done something awful to his new friend in order to get back at him. He was almost positive Mim had something to do with the strange happenings during their fight – she'd been using her sorcery to try to help Kay take him down. As if the fight hadn't been hard enough on its own.

Arthur winced as he thought back to the moment he was sure he was about to die. The point of the blade scraping at his skin. The fear pounding in his heart. Everything inside of him had wanted to beg for his life. But he also hadn't wanted to shame himself in his last moments, especially not in front of the Saxons.

Now he was thankful he hadn't. After the fight ended, the Saxons were so impressed by Arthur's performance – and show of mercy – they were more eager than ever to join forces and support the new king. And the crowd was thrilled – a boy taking on a giant and winning! A feat that would surely be sung about in the taverns for years to come.

But no one was as happy as Arthur himself. He had gambled it all and come out on top. He had shown everyone he was worthy of being their king. And it would be a while, he hoped, before anyone dared challenge his rule again.

Well, except for Mim, of course. She would never give up. And Arthur knew he'd have to keep a close eye out for anything suspiciously purple in the near future.

But for now? He'd take the win.

To say he was exhausted by the day's events would have been a drastic understatement. The fight had taken both a physical and mental toll on him, and all he wanted to do was crawl into bed and rest. So while Camelot celebrated with their new Saxon friends, he decided to retreat to his chambers early and ask that supper be brought to his sollar so he could eat alone.

Though not before checking on Archimedes. Fortunately, the owl seemed much better, if in a bit of a foul mood. Probably due to his broken wing – the doctor had told him he couldn't fly for a month. A grounded owl, it seemed, was a grumpy one.

Arthur was just settling in when there was a knock on the door. He assumed it was the steward, bringing him his dinner. But instead, he was surprised to find none other than Guinevere standing outside his door, carrying a tray with a bowl of piping hot soup and a small loaf of crusty bread.

Arthur smiled, delighted to see her. "Guin!" he cried, ushering her happily into his sollar and gesturing for her to put down the soup on the table. "I was looking for you after the fight! I was getting worried when I couldn't find you."

Guinevere set down the soup. "You were worried about me? Why?"

Arthur grimaced. Right. She didn't know. He led her over to the chair by the fire, then knelt down beside her, meeting her eyes with his own. "Look," he said, "I don't want to alarm you. But the old woman sitting next to you at the fight? The one in purple?"

"Purple?" Guinevere tapped her finger to her forehead. "Ah yes. I do seem to recall a woman in purple. She was quite lovely."

"Was she?" Arthur scratched his head. Lovely was not exactly the descriptor he would use when describing Mim. "Well, she can be quite clever in hiding her true self, I suppose. But in reality, she's a very powerful wizard. She's been snooping…"

Arthur scratched his head. Well, beauty was in the eye of the beholder, he supposed. "In any case, the woman in purple is a very powerful wizard named Madam Mim. She's been snooping around the castle ever since I became king, and I think she means to take me down." He gave her a helpless look. "I was worried she might try to hurt you to get at me."

To his shock, Guinevere giggled.

"What's so funny?" he asked.

"Sorry," she said, shaking her head. "Sometimes I laugh when I'm scared. It helps… relieve the tension." She smiled at Arthur. "Thank you for warning me. I will, of course, be on guard against this powerful purple wizard."

Arthur let out a breath of relief. He was glad Guin was taking him seriously. "I'm just happy you're all right," he said. Then he grinned. "And look! So am I! I told you I'd find a way to win."

Guinevere raised an eyebrow. Arthur felt his face heat.

"All right, fine. I didn't know for sure myself. Especially when Mim started tripping me up with her magic. But it all worked out in the end! And now the peace treaty is signed, and Kay is in prison. And all is well in the kingdom."

"I am very pleased to hear that, Your Majesty," Guinevere said, bowing her head.

He laughed. "Oh please! Don't start with that whole 'Your Majesty' thing. We know each other better than that now, don't we, evil knight?" He nudged her playfully with his shoulder.

"Oh, yes," she said. "We know each other *quite* well." She giggled again.

Arthur felt his cheeks heat, though he wasn't sure why. She was certainly acting a little strange. But then, it had been a very strange day.

"Are you all right?" he asked, just in case.

But Guin only waved him off with a laugh. "Of course I am! It's been a wonderful day! Simply marvellous! And I'm so glad you were victorious against that lousy knight. In fact, I made you a very special victory soup, just for the occasion. It's my secret recipe," she added with a smile.

Arthur smiled back at her. He'd almost forgotten Guin still worked in the kitchens. He was glad they were letting her cook now instead of just sticking her with the dirty dishes. She knew so much about various herbs and plants – she would be a great addition to their staff.

"Thank you," he said, rising to his feet and walking over to the table. He leant down and made a show of smelling the soup. It smelt odd, and a little unpleasant. But then, there were a lot of foods served in the castle he was still getting used to. Back at Sir Ector's, he had only ever been allowed to eat whatever scraps were left over from his foster father and brother's feasts – only one step up from the castle hounds, really – so his palate hadn't been prepared.

"What's in it?" he asked curiously.

"Slugs," she replied with a smile. "Super slimy slugs. With some rare, delicate mushrooms found high in the hills mixed in. Very special," she added. "Fit for a king." Then she looked at him expectantly, and he realised she wanted him to take a bite.

Arthur's stomach squirmed a little as he looked down at the soup. He wasn't sure he was going to like it – he'd never been fond of mushrooms, and while admittedly he'd never tried slugs, he was pretty sure he didn't like anything slimy. But Guinevere looked so hopeful, and he knew she'd worked hard on the meal, probably spent most of the evening preparing it; he couldn't insult her by turning it down.

And so he sat down at the table, picking up his spoon. He could feel Guinevere watching him as he dipped it in the bowl and brought it to his lips. The broth had a warm, spicy flavour that turned out to be actually pretty tasty, too. He smiled, relieved he could tell her the truth.

"It's good!" he pronounced. "Thank you!"

She nodded, looking pleased as she rose from her chair. "Now if you'll excuse me, Your Maj— er, I mean, Arthur," she corrected. "I must get back to the kitchens. Please let me know if you need anything else."

Arthur nodded. "I should be fine. I'm planning to go to bed the second I finish this delicious soup. But maybe we could find some time to spend together tomorrow? To celebrate some more, once I've had a full night's sleep?"

"Oh, I would absolutely *love* that!" she cooed. "It would be absolutely marvellous."

She rose to her feet and started out of the bedroom. Arthur watched her go, feeling happy and satisfied. It had turned out to be a really good day, despite its worrying beginning. And its ending was even better – with the promise of a wonderful tomorrow. He was so glad he'd run into Guin in the forest. She'd turned out to be a truly good friend, and he no longer felt so alone, being stuck in the castle, now that she was here.

In fact, it almost made it tolerable to be king.

Guinevere was just about through the door when her dress happened to catch on a lone nail sticking out from the wall. She grunted, annoyed, and yanked on the dress's hem to free it. Arthur frowned as he caught something flash at her exposed ankle, just for a moment, before she pulled the door closed behind her.

Something… purple.

"Wait!" he cried out, alarmed. He jumped from his chair and ran to the door, yanking it open, looking down each end of the hall outside. "Guinevere? Can you, uh, come back here for a moment?"

But there was no one there. No one at all.

Arthur's heart started to stutter in. He walked back into the room in a daze, going straight to the soup and staring down at it with sudden suspicion. Could it be? But no! It had to be just a coincidence, right? That was clearly Guin. They'd had a whole conversation!

A rather strange conversation, now that he thought back to it.

Suddenly he heard a rapping at the window. At first he assumed it was Archimedes, come to congratulate him on his victory. But no, he reminded himself, the owl couldn't fly with his broken wing. Instead, it was a small yellow bird, about a quarter of the owl's size, with long thick eyelashes curtaining its brown eyes. Did birds usually have eyelashes? Arthur's head was too foggy to remember.

"Go away," he muttered. "I need to think." He stared

down at the soup again. It did smell really strange. It tasted a little strange, too, now that he thought about it. Not bad, just… different. With this unfamiliar flavour…

Tap, tap, tap.

The bird continued to peck at the window with its beak. Arthur wondered if it was hurt or something. Finally, he decided to open the window to see for himself. Maybe he could bring it down to the castle's doctor and have him look at it.

The bird flew into the room at top speed. It was carrying something in its talons, but Arthur couldn't tell what it was. He watched as it dived straight to the soup and knocked the bowl off its tray. The contents splashed onto the floor.

"What are you—?"Arthur started. But he stopped short as he realised how thick his tongue suddenly felt. As if his mouth were filled with mud. A moment later, his stomach twisted and the room began to weave in and out of focus. He grasped at his chair as he lost his balance and started to fall.

"Oh, no!" he cried. "No, no, no!"

His eyes fell on the spilt soup. Poison? Had Mim really poisoned him?

The bird was frantically flapping above him. It looked as distressed as he felt. His eyes were so heavy he could barely keep them open, and soon they fluttered closed. *Just for a moment,* he thought. *Then I'll figure out what—*

"Arthur! Stay with me, Arthur!"

He opened his eyes with effort. To his shock, the bird had disappeared.

Instead, it was Guinevere who was leaning over him, a horrified look on her face.

CHAPTER NINETEEN
GUINEVERE

Guinevere looked down at Arthur, her insides feeling as if they were being torn out bit by bit. And it wasn't just the after-effects of shapeshifting for a second time without much rest in between – though those were admittedly brutal. It was more the realisation of what her mother had done.

Turned Arthur – sweet Arthur – into a giant slimy slug.

He looked up at her, his eyestalks waggling. She resisted the urge to vomit. She'd never seen something so vile – with its writhing greyish flesh undulating across the floor, leaving a slime trail in its wake. Arthur clearly hadn't fully realised what was happening to him yet. She didn't know if that was good or bad.

"Arthur, you're under a spell," she told him, hoping she didn't sound too scared. Or angry. *Why, Mother, why? This isn't funny!* "Don't try to move."

He squinted at her with tiny black slug eyes, looking quite scared himself. Then he seemed to nod, as if remembering. He opened his mouth to speak, but only managed a soft sluglike squeal.

"Don't try to talk, either," she added. She glanced over at the spilt soup on the floor – at the slimy little slugs squirming in the broth, mixed with her mother's favourite mushrooms. Her mind flashed back to the last time she'd seen this soup. Mim had been so proud of herself. *It turns people into slugs! Isn't that silly?* At the time Guin had wondered about the practicality of such magic. Who would ever want to be a slug? Now she was starting to understand. Her stomach twisted.

"Look, I'm going to give you something to help you. It'll make you very sick, but it will get the poison out of you. Are you all right with me doing that?"

He started to nod. Then he froze, staring in horror at something behind her. At first she worried it was her mother, come back to see the fruits of her labour. But then she realised he was staring into a silver mirror, seeing his reflection for the first time.

He began to scream – a horrible slug scream. His whole

body undulated with fear. Guinevere dived towards him, placing her hand on his slimy flesh, trying to calm him.

"I know, I know!" she whispered fiercely. "It's absolutely terrifying. But you have to stay with me. Be quiet. If you scream too loud, the guards will come, and they'll take me away, thinking I did this to you. And then I won't be able to help you." Her heart pounded. *Would* she be able to help him?

She felt him surrender, his blobby body sinking back to the floor. She let out a breath of relief and removed her hand, which she used to reach down and pick up the crystal vial she'd brought into the room as a bird. It was the largest one she could carry in bird shape, and she just hoped it'd be enough.

She removed the stopper and held the vial over Arthur's head. "Open," she instructed. "It's going to taste vile, but whatever you do, don't spit it out. You need all of it to make it effective."

Arthur obediently opened his mouth. Guin tipped the bottle, and a drop of green liquid splashed onto his slug tongue. He winced, looking as if he wanted to throw up from the taste, but forced himself to swallow the medicine down. Not wanting to waste a drop, Guinevere continued to drip the potion into his mouth until the bottle was completely empty.

"I know it's horrible, but unfortunately, what happens next is going to be even worse," Guinevere apologised. She ran over and locked the door. Then she grabbed the water bucket by the hearth. She brought it over to Arthur. Just in time for him to vomit into it.

Bright purple vomit.

Oh, Mother... you promised!

But then, her mother had kept her promise, hadn't she? At least technically. Guinevere had asked her not to hurt Arthur. And she'd stuck to her word, instead doing absolutely the next worst thing. Guinevere grimaced, imagining her mother's glee as she concocted her plan. Why, she probably thought it was perfectly hilarious. In fact, she was probably on her way back to the cottage at this very moment to brag about her cleverness over dinner.

What would she think when she learnt Guinevere had interfered again? Thwarted yet another of her plans?

Guinevere shook her head, turning her attention back to slug Arthur, who was writhing on the ground. As his body twisted and turned, it began to morph new parts. First an arm. Then a leg. Then another. Until – *poof!* He was fully human again.

"Did it work?" Arthur's eyes shot back to the mirror. He let out a shrill laugh. "Oh, my heavens, I've never been so happy to see my scrawny little body in all my life."

Guinevere smiled at him, relief coursing through her. She rose to her feet. "You'll probably feel a little rough for a while," she told him. "But you're going to be all right." She reached down and took the pail, then went to the window and dumped the contents out; she wanted to dispose of any evidence. Then she turned back to Arthur. "Get some rest. I'll talk to you later." She stepped towards the door.

"Wait!" Arthur called after her, his voice anxious. "You're leaving?"

She stopped in her tracks. "Well, y-yes," she stammered, turning to face him again. "I shouldn't be here at all. It's not proper for a servant girl to be in the king's chambers, unaccompanied."

"It is if she saved my life!" Arthur shot back, not missing a beat. He struggled to sit up. "Besides, you're more than a servant. You're my friend." His eyes, large and blue and earnest, locked on her face. "Please stay with me. I don't want to be alone right now."

Guinevere's heart panged at the desperation she heard in his voice. And suddenly she felt immensely guilty about all she'd done. She'd been angry at him for lying to her back in the forest, and yet now she was doing the same – though her deception was much, much worse. He trusted her. And she was betraying him with every breath.

Maybe he wasn't meant to sit on the throne of England. But he didn't deserve this.

No. She needed to stop this. Now. She needed to walk out that door and never come back. He would be sad, of course. She'd be sad, too. But it was for the best. Nothing good could come of this dangerous game. And if he ever learned the truth – that the girl he trusted was nothing more than a liar, a part of Mim's scheme from the start... She shook her head. She couldn't bear the thought.

Better she just walk away. Even if it hurt her heart to do so.

She started towards the door again. But before she got three steps in that direction, she felt arms wrap around her, Arthur pulling her into an embrace. For a moment, she stiffened, her heart in her throat – wondering if she should pull away. But his arms were so strong. So warm. Instead, she found herself turning and melting into them, laying her head on his shoulder. She wrapped her arms around his back, embracing him fully, and pushed all the doubts and guilt and worry deep down inside.

"Thank you," Arthur murmured against her shoulder. "I don't know what I would do without you."

The guilt raged again, almost suffocating her, and she forced herself to untangle from his arms and step back to put distance between them. "I'm just glad I could help," she said, hoping he couldn't hear the tremble in her voice.

He smiled at her, such a genuine smile it broke her heart. Then his eyebrows furrowed, as if something had just occurred to him.

"I think my head's still a little foggy." He closed his eyes and opened them again. "I was so out of it, I honestly thought you came in through my window as a bird."

"A… bird?" Guinevere had hoped perhaps he had been too sick to remember that part. She tried to make herself laugh, as if it were the silliest thing in the world.

"I know." Arthur blushed. "I told you I was out of it." He looked up at her. "You came just at the right time," he mused. "If you hadn't…" His voice trailed off, as if he didn't want to say what could have happened. "How did you know to come?" he added. "And how did you happen to have the antidote on you?" His voice held confusion, but not suspicion. Which made her feel even worse.

Guinevere thought fast. "I was coming to your room to deliver your dinner," she explained. "And as for the antidote, well, I told you I dabble in herbs." It was the closest to the truth she dared come. "Something my mother taught me. I usually carry around a whole slew of lotions and potions, just in case of emergencies."

She decided to leave out the part about being zapped back home by her mother, only to find a book of potions left out on the kitchen table, open to the slug soup spell. It hadn't been hard to put two and two together.

"Madam Mim did this," Arthur murmured, half to himself. "She came in here disguised as you. I should have known something was up, though. She was acting so strange. So unlike you."

Guinevere sucked in a breath through her teeth at the mention of her mother. So Arthur was aware of Mim's ill intentions towards him. She wondered who had tipped him off. Perhaps that owl of his?

Arthur raked a hand through his hair, groaning. "This has gone too far. Mim's determined to take me down," he moaned. "I just wish I understood why. Is she angry that I'm king, for some reason? But why would she care? I wish I could understand."

Guin held her breath, realisation hitting her like a lightning strike. This was her chance to tell him the truth. The truth about his destiny. She didn't want to hurt him, and she certainly didn't want him dead or to live life as a giant slug. But he deserved to know what was really going on. How he'd been used and manipulated by an evil wizard for his own gain. It wasn't fair, what Merlin had done to him. Or what Mim would continue to try to do because of it. Perhaps if he knew the truth, he could make the right choice for himself. He could step down from the throne willingly and allow the rightful heir to take his place.

Then Mim wouldn't have any reason to target him. And he would be safe.

Maybe they could even run away together.

Two birds, flying free.

She drew in a breath. "The thing is," she said, her voice a little hoarse as she tried to form the words. "The thing is…"

Arthur's eyes were on her now. He looked a little scared. "What is it, Guin?" he whispered.

"The thing is," she replied, "what if you were never meant to be king?"

CHAPTER TWENTY
ARTHUR

Arthur stared at Guinevere, for a moment too stunned to speak.

"What are you saying?" he asked, after finally finding a somewhat wobbly version of his voice. "Of course I'm meant to be king. I pulled the sword from the stone, didn't I?"

"Yes," she agreed cautiously. "But what if it was all some kind of trick?"

"A trick?"

"You know. Like a ruse – maybe by your teacher Merlin." Guinevere's voice took on a rush of words. "Maybe he wanted a puppet on the throne of England. So he could rule behind the scenes. And he picked you – because you worship him and would do anything he says, and no one would suspect a thing."

Arthur sank back into his chair, feeling his stomach swim with nausea once again. But this time, it wasn't from poison. It was from doubt.

"No..." he whispered. "That can't be true..."

But even as he said the words, he wondered. Because even though he didn't want to admit it aloud, part of her theory made perfect sense. After all, he'd never truly understood why pulling a blade from a rock entitled him to a crown. And wouldn't it make much more sense if it wasn't some magical destiny after all, but some kind of trick?

Merlin *had* picked him, after all, out of all the boys in all the world, to educate and train. Why would he do that – why would he bother wasting so much time with a nobody like him? When he'd pulled the sword from the stone, of course, he assumed Merlin had somehow known of his destiny – even if he never told him about it – and that was why he'd been chosen.

But what if the opposite was true – what if Merlin had used him from the start, knowing full well the power he could gain over the land if he managed to trick everyone into crowning some young boy as king? Merlin had never approved of their idea to hold a tournament to determine a ruler, believing a knight of the realm would only invite more wars and violence into the land, as others had done before him. Could Merlin have decided, instead, to take matters into his own hands to avoid that fate?

But if that was the plan, why hadn't he told Arthur? Maybe because he thought Arthur wouldn't go along with any of it had he known what Merlin was orchestrating?

Suddenly a thought occurred to him. "But Merlin didn't want me to come to London to be Kay's squire," he told Guinevere. "He wanted me to stay home and continue our lessons. And if I had done that, I'd never have even run into the sword, never mind pulled it out of the stone."

"Hm." Guinevere seemed to consider this. "Perhaps he only said he didn't want you to go, to make you want to go even more. An evil wizard trick, you understand. To get you to insist on doing something you never really wanted to do in the first place." She nodded to herself. "This way he could deny he had anything to do with it. Say it was all your idea from the start."

Arthur didn't like this. Not one bit. Especially since it was starting to make far too much sense. After all, what was more likely? That he, a mere orphan boy with no noble pedigree to speak of, should be destined by the heavens to become king of all England? Or that a powerful wizard, unhappy with how things were being run and worried someone like Kay would don the crown, would take matters into his own hands?

Merlin wasn't evil, Arthur was convinced of that. But he *was* tricky. And he did, admittedly, cheat sometimes. Maybe not for selfish purposes, like Guin presumed. But maybe it was his way of saving the realm.

"Fine," he said. "But if that's the case, where is he now? He dashed off to the future weeks ago, before I ever arrived in London. If he truly wanted to rule through me, wouldn't he be ruling now?"

"Not necessarily," Guinevere said. "If he were here from the start, people might suspect his involvement. Better he stay away and bide his time until everyone accepts you as king. Then, when he does come back, no one will think anything of it."

Arthur sank into his chair, scrubbing his face with his hands. When he looked up, Guin was giving him an apologetic look.

"Sorry," she said. "This is why I didn't want to tell you."

"Do you think other people believe this, too?" he asked, his stomach churning. "Are people saying this behind my back? That I'm nothing more than an imposter king?"

She nodded slowly. Arthur groaned.

He leant back in his chair, staring up at the ceiling, which had been painted in fancy gold swirls that twirled around one another in complicated patterns. He'd never seen a painted ceiling before coming here. He hadn't even known that people painted ceilings in the first place, or why they would want to. Just one more example of how much he didn't belong here. How he should have never come here at all.

Oh, Merlin, he thought. *How could you do this to me?*

He dropped his gaze back to Guinevere. She was sitting across from him, pity swirling in her deep brown eyes. His stomach wrenched again. He thought back to their first meeting by the well. It felt like a lifetime ago after all he'd been through in recent days.

"It's funny," he murmured, half to himself. "From the very start I didn't believe I should be king. I didn't even want to be. In fact, I would have given almost anything to get rid of the crown. But now..." He shrugged. "Now I feel like I've been making a difference. Helping people. Keeping the peace. Like maybe I might be a good king after all."

"You *are* a good king," Guinevere said softly. "But that doesn't make you the right one."

Arthur felt his face crumble. He didn't want to cry, especially not in front of Guinevere, but he was afraid he couldn't help it. The past twenty-four hours had been both the most joyous and most terrible he'd probably ever experienced in his life. He'd defended his throne. He'd brought peace to the realm. And now what?

"You can just walk away," Guinevere said softly, as if she could hear his thoughts. "Leave all this behind. Live your life. Stay safe." She paused, then added. "We could go together…"

Arthur's heart wrenched at the thread of hope he heard in her voice. She really cared about him – in a way he wasn't sure anyone had ever cared about him before. And for a moment, he almost agreed. It sounded like a dream to just run away with Guin. Go back to living a simple life. The life he was likely meant to lead.

But deep down, he knew it could never be that easy. Even if he wanted to give up the throne, he couldn't exactly do it without a good explanation. No one would allow it. But he also couldn't just go tell everyone the truth – they'd assume he'd been lying from the start. They might even try to execute him for treason.

But then, if he stayed on the throne, Mim would keep trying to get to him – and at some point he was sure she would succeed. And – his head was spinning now, faster than a top – what if Guinevere was wrong about Merlin's alleged trickery? What if Arthur actually was, by some wild miracle, the true destined king of England? It seemed impossible, but he couldn't just walk away from his destiny and let England fall back into the dark ages if that were the case. Then he'd be a traitor of a different sort.

He bit his lower lip. "Look," he said to Guinevere, "before I make a move, I need to know for sure. I need proof that Merlin was behind all of this. And if he is, I need to know why he did it."

Guinevere frowned. "Isn't it obvious? He wants power."

"We don't know that for sure," Arthur replied stubbornly. "You don't know Merlin like I do. He's a good man. He may be a bit set in his ways at times, but he always has good intentions – I know he does."

Guinevere squirmed in her seat. She still looked conflicted, but there was also something else in her eyes now. A look like she truly wanted to believe him. And he found himself suddenly determined to convince her.

"If Merlin was responsible for putting me on the throne, then he would have a very good reason to do so," he added. "I need to find out what the reason is. Only then can I make a decision on what to do."

Guinevere nodded slowly. "I understand," she said after a pause. "And I'll help you in any way I can."

Arthur's heart swelled at this. "Thank you," he said. "That means a lot." He rose to his feet, stalking the room, his heavy steps eating up the distance between the walls. "First, I need to get to Merlin's tower. Maybe he's left a clue there. That's how we found out about Mim." He rubbed his chin with his hand. "I'd send

Archimedes again, but he's got a broken wing..." He pressed his lips together. "No. I need to go myself. I can't trust anyone else. Of course I'll have to find a way to sneak out of the castle."

Guinevere looked up. Her eyes sparkled. "Well, *that* I can help with."

Arthur turned to her in surprise. "Really?"

She nodded eagerly. "We can disguise you as a dishwasher and sneak you out the servants' passages." She looked up at him. "Where are we going again?"

"Sir Ector's castle in the Forest Sauvage," Arthur replied. "So not exactly nearby."

She nodded. "I know of a supply wagon that makes the journey twice a week. They bring everything right to kitchens. If we can stow away in the wagon, they'll take us right to where we need to go."

Arthur felt his heart pound with excitement. "Guinevere! You're brilliant!"

Her cheeks turned bright red. "I don't know about that," she hedged. "I mean, it may not even work."

"It'll work," Arthur declared. "I'm sure of it." He paused, then added awkwardly, "Also, you just said 'we'. Does that mean you're coming with me?" He held his breath, waiting for her reply. He knew he should tell her she didn't need to get any more mixed up in this than she already was. That he didn't want to put her in danger. But at the same time, he really didn't want to go alone.

At first she said nothing, and Arthur feared she'd been just caught up in the moment and never meant to volunteer herself for the quest. But at last, she looked up at him, her eyes shiny. "Yes. I'm coming with you. Whatever happens? We're in this together."

CHAPTER TWENTY-ONE
GUINEVERE

This is for the best. It's really for the best.

Guinevere silently repeated the mantra in her head as she led Arthur down the back stairs towards the kitchens, praying they didn't run into anyone important along the way. She'd disguised Arthur as best she could, bringing him clothes 'borrowed' from one of the stable hands, then shearing his head to his scalp. He looked a lot older with the new hairstyle, and once she'd dirtied him up a bit with some mud she'd brought in from outside, he actually looked like a servant. Maybe not surprising, since that was the role he was actually born into.

The hardest part was getting him to leave his sword and crown behind. But in the end, she convinced him it was for the best. If they were seen on the road with such treasures by bandits, they could be robbed or kidnapped and held for ransom. Or they could be called out as thieves themselves – as Guin had thought Arthur was when they first met in the woods – for possessing items clearly above their rank. She didn't need them thrown in prison before they were able to reach their destination.

She still couldn't believe she'd agreed to go with him. It was one thing to sneak him out of the castle – to keep him safe from whatever mischief her mother planned next. Quite another to agree to accompany him on his journey to the belly of the beast. Still, she couldn't help being a bit curious about the opportunity to find out more about Merlin. Was he truly the evil murderer her mother had warned her about? Or the loving mentor that Arthur adored? Guin hoped that travelling to his tower might shed some light on the man. And his true intentions.

She stole a glance at Arthur. He was so sure his mentor meant only good. Merlin was like a father figure to him. How disappointed he would be if he learnt that the man he looked up to was actually an evil mastermind out for destruction. It was going to hurt, that was for sure. At least she would be there to soften the blow. And then, maybe, he'd finally be able to walk away from it all.

She would achieve her quest – remove the wrongful ruler from the throne – without any unnecessary violence or magic or tricks. Just the simple truth.

While her mother might not agree with her methods, she would have to accept the outcome.

"I can't believe we're doing this," Arthur whispered, shooting her an excited grin. "I never would have been able to manage it without your help."

She gave him a weak smile, trying to push down her rising guilt. What would he think if he knew the truth? Why she'd come to the castle in the first place. Why she'd befriended him. How she'd really known he was in trouble, and how she'd known how to cure him. Would he hate her for all the lies she'd told? Would he cast her out of his life forever?

She shook her head. She couldn't think like that. She just had to stay the course. She was helping him – that was the important thing. She was keeping him safe and aiding him in learning the truth. She couldn't be blamed for that.

They were halfway down the tower steps when they heard a door slam somewhere below them. Someone was coming up the stairs. They froze, looking at each other. On the narrow landing, there was no place to hide.

"Maybe it's just other servants," Arthur reasoned.

But even as the words left his mouth, voices rose from below them.

"The king needs to be informed of this," said the first – a deep male voice, echoing up the stairs.

"Let's go wake him, then," the second voice urged.

Guinevere glanced over at Arthur, seeing his face had gone pure white.

"Belvidere and Gawain," he whispered. "They're coming this way. There's no possibility they won't recognise me, even with these new clothes and this hair."

Guinevere's pulse quickened. She looked up the stairs, wondering if they should make a run for it. But even if they did manage to make it back to his chambers, there would be no time for Arthur to change before the knights arrived, and his clipped hair and dirty face would cause all sorts of unfortunate questions.

"What do we do?" she whispered. The voices were getting closer.

"I don't know. Maybe I could hide my face from them?" Arthur tried to turn to face the wall, an attempt to shield himself from view. But he looked so obvious and ridiculous, Guin knew it would only catch their attention. But what other option did they have? Could she shield him somehow? But that would be obvious, too.

Unless…

Suddenly an idea came to her. She met Arthur's eyes with her own. Her hands were trembling, but she shoved them behind her back.

"Just go with it, all right?" she asked. There was no time to explain anything.

Fortunately, he nodded. The voices were just around the corner. Guinevere stepped up to Arthur, drawing in a shaky breath, then pressed him against the wall, covering him with her body.

"What are you—?" he started to say.

But she silenced him with a kiss – just as Belvidere and Gawain rounded the corner.

"Well, well, what have we interrupted?" Gawain asked jovially.

Belvidere made a tsking noise with his tongue. "Servants! No wonder nothing gets done around here!" He rolled his eyes and kept climbing the stairs. Gawain flashed Guin and Arthur a knowing grin, then scurried off behind Belvidere. A moment later, their footsteps faded and Guin and Arthur found themselves alone again.

Guinevere stepped away from Arthur, turning her head to avoid his eyes. She couldn't believe she'd just done that! She'd never kissed anyone besides her mother before, and her stomach was doing flip-flops like a fish out of water.

"S-sorry," she stammered. "I just… I wasn't sure what else to do."

Arthur didn't reply at first, and finally she allowed herself a peek back at him. He was staring at her with awe in his eyes. She felt her cheeks burn. *Say something,* she begged him silently. *Anything!* She wondered if his lips were still buzzing from the feel of hers, like hers were from his.

"Wow," Arthur whispered at last. "That was…" He shook his head. "Wow."

"Come on!" she urged, beckoning him impatiently. Mostly to get rid of her embarrassment. "We've got to go or we'll miss the wagon."

Arthur seemed to wake from his trance. He followed her down the stairs, into the kitchens. Here, they didn't have to worry about anyone noticing them – everyone was too involved in their own tasks to pay them any heed. Just as well, Guinevere decided, for another kiss like the one on the stairs might have done her in completely.

They slipped out the back door just in time to see the supply wagon roll up. The driver jumped off his seat and began unloading his supplies.

"Once he's done, he'll go into the kitchens and get Mistress McCready to pay him for his deliveries," Guinevere explained. "That's when we'll have our chance to hide under that blanket."

"All right," Arthur agreed with a vigorous nod. "We'll just—"

But he never got a chance to finish his sentence, for at that moment, a small owl hooted loudly. She looked up to see none other than Archimedes, his wing still in a sling, staring down at them with beady eyes.

"Archimedes!" Arthur cried, his face paling. "What are you doing up there? You're not supposed to be flying, remember?"

"Pinfeathers! What are *you* doing outside the castle?" the owl demanded. "And your hair! What have you done to your hair?" He glanced from Guinevere to Arthur with suspicious eyes.

"Look, it's a very long story and I don't have time to fully explain. But I need to get back to Merlin's tower to figure some things out," Arthur explained. "Since they won't let me out of the castle, I had to come up with another way."

Archimedes seemed to consider this. "Well, then, I will come with you," he declared. "I'm sure I could help." He lifted his left wing and tried to fly towards them. But without his right wing, he lost his balance and went tumbling off the tree. Arthur had to dive to catch him before he collided with the ground.

"I'm sorry, old bird," Arthur said, looking down at Archimedes with pity in his eyes. "You need to stay here and get better. It's what Merlin would want, and you know it."

The owl ruffled his feathers. "Well, I suppose I could hang around and keep an eye on things. But don't be gone too long. The kingdom needs their king. If they find out you're missing..."

"I'll be back soon, I promise," Arthur replied. "They'll barely even know I'm missing." He leant over and gently set the owl on the ground. Archimedes waddled a few feet away, looking very disgruntled.

"Be careful," he told Arthur. "And whatever you do, don't go and get yourself killed."

"Of course," Arthur agreed, giving the owl a fond look. He turned back to the wagon, realising the driver had finished unloading his wares and had gone into the kitchen, as Guinevere had predicted. Now was their chance. He turned to Guin. "All right. Let's go."

They dived towards the wagon, throwing themselves inside of it. Arthur pulled back the tarp and crawled underneath, holding it up for Guin to follow. Once they were both hidden from view, he dropped it, covering them completely.

Guinevere could feel her heart beating madly. It was one thing to come up with this plan, quite another to carry it out. Would they get away with this? And what would Mother think when she realised Guin was gone – and Arthur along with her? A chill tripped down her spine. Maybe this was a bad idea…

But then she felt something warm on her palm. She glanced down. In the darkness under the tarp, she could barely see the outline of a hand slipping into hers. A moment later, she felt a small, comforting squeeze.

"This was a good plan," Arthur whispered.

And suddenly she didn't feel afraid any more.

CHAPTER TWENTY-TWO
ARTHUR

Travelling in the back of a wagon over bumpy roads wasn't exactly comfortable. After the first moments of adrenaline wore off, Arthur realised it was rather boring, too. To make matters worse, the driver had a penchant for singing, but not the voice for it. And his off-key, overly loud, sometimes bawdy tunes made for a very long day with very little chance to sleep.

At least Arthur had Guinevere next to him. Even if they didn't speak for fear of being discovered, it gave him some comfort to feel her warm breath on his face and know he wasn't alone. He couldn't imagine trying to do any of this without her. And he was so grateful she'd agreed to come along. This wasn't her fight, after all. But she was a good friend.

A good friend…

His hands reached involuntarily to his lips. No, he couldn't think of that any more. She'd only been trying to save him from being recognised by his knights. It went no further than that.

He reminded himself of Archimedes's words: *You don't have time for romance.* But even still, his fingers lingered a moment longer on his lips, remembering. Merlin had given him a lecture on love, and at the time he hadn't understood it one bit.

But now he thought maybe he did. If only a little…

Eventually, the wagon came to a stop. Arthur and Guin held their breaths as the driver stepped down from his seat. Arthur peeked out from under the tarp, watching him head into a small farmhouse at the edge of a great forest.

"We're here," he whispered. "That's the Forest Sauvage. I'd recognise it anywhere!"

"Quick!" Guinevere cried. "Let's slip out before he gets back!"

Arthur didn't need a second invitation. They climbed out from beneath the tarp and jumped off the wagon. Arthur almost fell as his feet hit the ground hard, his legs weakened from all that time cramped up without being used. He grabbed on to the side of the wagon for support, then shook out each leg, waking it up in turn. Beside him, Guinevere did the same.

"We made it," he said. "I can't believe we made it."

"Well, not quite yet," she hedged, looking out at the forest beyond them, worrying her lower lip with her teeth. "We still have to get through *that*."

Oh, right. In his excitement, Arthur had forgotten how dangerous the Forest Sauvage could be, filled with creatures and other nasty things that went bump in the night. He didn't have any weapons on him, either, since he'd had to leave Excalibur behind (something he was still a little bitter about).

But there was no other way to Sir Ector's castle. So through the forest it was.

"Come on," he said. "We want to get through before dark."

As they stepped under the trees, the world seemed to darken, the vast canopy of leaves above them all but blocking out the sun. It also felt colder here without the warm rays of sunshine kissing their skin. Arthur suppressed a shiver as they walked.

"I never liked this place," he remarked. "It always scared me."

"I don't know," Guinevere replied with a shrug. "I grew up here. So it's kind of like coming home."

"That's right!" Arthur exclaimed, turning to her. "I forgot you said you lived here once. What made you move, again?'

Guinevere gave an awkward shrug. "Ask my mother. It was her idea."

Arthur nodded. "It must be nice to have a mother," he remarked. "I never did. Even Sir Ector, my foster father, had already lost his wife before I came to live at his castle. But I've always imagined having a mother would be really nice."

"What happened to your parents?" Guinevere asked, suddenly sounding very curious. "Were they… killed?" She mouthed the word *killed* a little awkwardly, as if hesitant to use it.

"I don't actually know," Arthur admitted. "Sir Ector never told me – I don't know if he knows, to be honest. He found me on the castle steps, only a few days old, screaming blue murder. He took me in and allowed me to live in the castle with him and Kay. But never as a true son," he added, his voice revealing his bitterness. "More as a servant he didn't have to pay."

His mind flashed back to his foster father's face in the castle hall as Kay had come up to challenge him the day before. The man who had raised him, now plotting his demise. Arthur had always wanted to impress Sir Ector – gain his approval. And it hurt more than he wanted to admit to know the feeling was not mutual.

"I'm sorry," Guin replied. "That must have been rough."

Arthur shrugged, not wanting to be pitied. "We can't choose our birth story. But we can choose how to live the rest of our lives."

Guinevere nodded, not replying. Arthur turned to look at her. "Your mother won't be worried about you, will she?" he asked. "When she realises you've gone?" He hated the idea of worrying this poor, unknown woman.

Guinevere shrugged. "I don't know if *worried* would be the word I'd use."

Arthur could tell he was making her uncomfortable and decided to drop the subject. Still, he couldn't help a small stirring of pity for Guin, who obviously had a complicated relationship with her mother. Arthur had always assumed mothers were good and kind and loving. But maybe, as with foster fathers, this was not always the case for everyone.

He was about to try to change the subject when they heard a rustling noise in the bushes. Arthur froze in his tracks, grabbing Guinevere by the arm. She turned to look, her eyes widening as they fell upon what Arthur was already staring at across the path.

A pair of unblinking yellow eyes, shining out from the darkness.

"Don't make any sudden moves," Arthur whispered. "Maybe it'll go away."

The eyes blinked twice. Then, to Arthur's horror, they began to emerge from the bushes. As they came into the light, he realised they belonged to a long, lanky grey wolf.

A very hungry-looking long, lanky grey wolf.

The wolf lifted its head and howled, a mournful, lonely sound that made Arthur's skin crawl. This was not good. This was not good at all.

And the wolf looked right at them.

"Guin, run!" he cried. "Now!"

They burst into action, dashing down the trail as fast as their legs could carry them. For a moment, Arthur dared hope that maybe the wolf would be caught off guard and they could get far enough away before it began pursuit. But unfortunately, that didn't happen, and soon they could hear the creature behind them, gaining ground. The wolf was fast – so fast. And it became very clear to Arthur that outrunning it was not an option.

"What do we do?" Guinevere cried. She wasn't as fast as Arthur because of her long dress and slippers, and she was already falling behind.

"I don't know," Arthur replied, his heart beating fast. He looked around the forest, trying to find a big stick or rock, but saw nothing large enough to scare away a grown wolf.

"Maybe we should try to climb a—" Guinevere started,

then screamed as her foot caught under a root. Arthur watched in dismay as she careered forwards, slamming face-first into the dirt.

"Guin!" he shouted, retracing his steps to get back to her. She looked up at him with tears glistening in her brown eyes.

"I'm stuck," she confessed, tugging on her foot. It was firmly lodged in the root. Arthur got on his hands and knees, trying to pull it out. But he couldn't.

There was another howl. The wolf was getting closer. They were running out of time.

"Leave me," Guinevere told him. "Get to Merlin's tower."

"Not a chance," he said, shaking his head. "I won't leave you."

"Then he'll kill us both!"

"Maybe." He drew in a breath. "Maybe not." Scrambling to his feet, he looked down at Guin. "Lie still. I'm going to lead him away from you."

Guinevere's eyes bulged. "No!" she cried. "You can't! He'll kill you!"

"Everyone wants to kill me these days," Arthur reminded her wryly. "I'm getting kind of used to it."

"Arthur—"

"Trust me, all right? I know what I'm doing."

In truth, he had no idea what he was doing. But that didn't sound as comforting. Instead, he grabbed the largest stick he could find and waved it in the air.

"Over here, you big bad wolf!" he called out. Then he dropped the stick and started running in the opposite direction.

For a moment he worried the wolf wouldn't take the bait. But soon his ears caught more crashing sounds behind him as the wolf dived through the bushes in pursuit. He let out a breath of relief and pushed onwards, his mind racing for a plan. He couldn't outrun the wolf, that was for sure – his legs were already tiring, and he was almost completely out of breath. And he couldn't dodge the wolf like he had with Kay – it was much nimbler a creature than his foster brother in armour. He looked for trees to climb, but saw nothing with branches low enough to reach. He couldn't hide in a cave, either – the wolf would just scent him easily and follow.

So what to do? The forest was getting thicker and darker the further he ran, and he started to worry that even if he managed to lose the wolf, he'd get lost himself... forever.

Don't panic, he scolded himself. *Just think.*

What would Merlin say in a case like this? Probably something grand like *Use your wisdom, not your might.*

Which was all well and good until you tried to actually do that and still run at the same time.

Knowledge.

Wisdom.

What do I know about wolves? he asked himself. After all, he'd grown up in the Forest Sauvage and had been schooled constantly on their danger. What had Sir Ector taught him back when he was little in case he ever came face to face with such a creature?

They're as afraid of you as you are of them.

And suddenly he realised exactly what he had to do. He had to face down the wolf. Man to beast.

He had to stop running.

This was, as you can imagine, easier said than done. Because he had no idea, in reality, if Sir Ector had been right. It was one thing to boast about facing down a wolf and quite another to actually do so, all alone in the woods.

But he didn't have a choice, did he?

It took all his willpower to slam his heels into the ground. To turn around, to draw in a breath. Make his shoulders square. Lift his chin. Raise his hands menacingly in the air. Try to look two times his size.

And then he let out a roar. As loud as he could.

The wolf skidded to a stop. It stared up at him for a moment, its eyes bulging from its head. Arthur roared again, taking a menacing step towards the creature. He knew the wolf could kill him at any moment – end this ruse. But first the wolf had to realise that, too.

And it didn't seem to get it.

Arthur roared a third time, this time charging at the wolf. The creature let out a scared whimper and started running in the other direction. Arthur chased it for a moment, feeling a thrill of excitement roll through him as he went, arms still raised, voice still roaring.

Until the wolf had disappeared completely. And he was alone once again.

He dropped his arms and sucked in huge mouthfuls of air. He'd done it! He'd actually done it.

"Arthur!"

He looked up to see Guinevere limping towards him. She had a huge smile on her face. "You did it!" she cried. "You defeated the wolf!"

Arthur felt his cheeks heat. His first instinct was to brush off her words, to protest and insist it wasn't that big of a thing. But it *was*, he suddenly realised. He, Arthur, had faced down an actual wolf and won. He *should* be proud.

And he was.

"Are you all right?" he asked Guinevere, looking down at her ankle.

"I'm fine," she said. "It's just a little bruised." Her eyes levelled on him. They looked soft somehow in the dim forest light. "Thank you," she said simply. "You saved my life."

"You saved mine first," he reminded her with a sheepish grin. "I guess now we're even."

"Perhaps so," she agreed with a smile. "Now let's get to Merlin's tower."

CHAPTER TWENTY-THREE
GUINEVERE

The rest of the trip proved much less eventful. Arthur, fortunately, still remembered the way to his foster father's keep. Soon he was leading Guinevere out of the dark forest into a golden afternoon with the magnificent castle in full view. Even better was the fact that, since Sir Ector and his son were back in London, Guin and Arthur were able to walk right into the place and head straight to the tall, crumbling tower where Merlin had stayed once upon a time.

As they climbed the old, decrepit stairs to the very top, Guinevere began to feel a growing nervousness in the pit of her stomach. They'd escaped a castle, a wolf and a dark wood. But now they were entering the inner lair of the evil wizard who'd murdered her parents. What vile monstrosities would they find inside?

Turned out, a lot of junk.

"Did… someone rob the place?" she couldn't help blurting as they walked into the room. Toppled piles of books and random papers made the place look as though it had been ransacked or torn apart by a storm. She noted a huge hole in the roof and a bucket placed underneath, now filled with rainwater. The tower had clearly seen better days.

Arthur looked around the dishevelled room. To her surprise, his lip curled in amusement. "Let's just say housekeeping isn't one of Merlin's specialties," he joked. "And he left rather in a hurry." He pointed to the hole in the ceiling, as if indicating this was how the wizard had made his exit.

"Did Merlin make you clean for him, too, like Sir Ector did?" Guinevere asked curiously, remembering what Arthur had said about his foster father.

"Merlin usually leaves the cleaning to magic," Arthur replied. "Which is… interesting… if not always effective. You should have seen the one time he tried to use magic to help me with the castle dishes!" He laughed, as if remembering the moment fondly.

Guinevere watched, curious despite herself, as Arthur

walked over to a round blue ball painted with strange brown markings and set on a stand. He spun it with his hand and it twirled around and around, the markings blurring as it went. It was still disconcerting to Guin to hear Arthur talk about Merlin. His voice took on an affectionate tone when he spoke of his teacher – as if he loved him a lot. It was clear he was some kind of father figure to him, as Mim had been a mother to her. Did he have any inkling of the darkness lurking inside this madman who had taken him under his wing?

She tried to imagine how she'd feel if the tables were turned. If Mim were the evil one, and Guin had been tricked by her treachery. The idea made her feel quite uncomfortable.

"How did you meet Merlin, anyway?" she asked, mostly to change the subject.

"Oh! It was kind of an accident," Arthur said, looking bashful all of a sudden. "I was trying to get Kay's arrow, which had gone into the woods. I accidentally fell through his ceiling just as he was having tea. And he invited me to stay." He grinned at the memory. "He told me he had been expecting someone, but he didn't know who until I dropped in – literally."

"So he didn't seek you out?" Guinevere asked, surprised. "*You* found *him*?"

"I guess so." Arthur shrugged. "He told me he wanted to be my teacher. And I was thrilled to have him. No one ever really paid me any attention before then. As I said before, I was not much more than a bother to my foster father and brother. And I was always breaking dishes in the kitchen, so the cook wasn't fond of me, either. But Merlin – he treated me like a real person. Like someone with value." He stared down at the floor. "Everything I am now, the person I've become – it's all because of him."

Guinevere nodded, not sure what to say. The Merlin described by Arthur sounded nothing like the man she'd been told to fear all her life. He sounded almost… kind. Decent. Like Arthur himself. How could a man like that murder her parents in cold blood? It didn't make any sense. She thought back to how she'd asked Mim why he'd murdered her parents. All she'd said was that he was evil. But that wasn't a real reason, was it? There had to be something else. Something Mim didn't want her to know.

But what could it be?

"So now what?" she asked, looking around the room. "Are you going to look for some writings of Merlin's? Something to prove his plan?"

"No," Arthur replied with a grin. "I'm going to try to bring him back."

"What?" Guinevere cried before she could stop herself. This was not part of the plan.

But Arthur was already shuffling through papers on a nearby table. "There's got to be a spell," he murmured. "He used a spell to send himself to Bermuda. There has to be another spell to return him home." He turned to a towering bookcase full of books. "We just have to find it."

Guinevere's heart pounded, seemingly louder and faster than when confronted by the wolf in the forest. It was one thing to search an evil wizard's lair. It was quite another to conjure up the actual evil wizard.

But she couldn't exactly say that to Arthur.

"That might be easier said than done," she reminded him instead, pulling out a book at random. It was titled *The Tome of Terrible Turnips*, which didn't seem particularly applicable to their current situation. "There are so many books in here. How will you ever be able to find the right one?"

"I'm not sure," Arthur confessed. "Especially since I can't exactly read."

"You can't?" Guinevere stared at him, astounded. She couldn't imagine life without books. It would be like life without… well, life.

"I mean, I know my ABCs, thanks to Archimedes," Arthur amended, looking a little embarrassed. "But we didn't have a chance to get much further than that. Let's just say reading wasn't a big priority in the kitchens of Sir Ector's castle. In fact, I'm not sure even Kay can read – and he's a noble knight."

Guinevere considered that this was probably true, judging from what she'd seen of the oafish lad in question. And if Arthur was never meant to be more than a squire, there would have been no practical reason to educate him. If it hadn't been for Merlin...

She shook her head. "Well, then, I don't know how this is going to work," she said. "I can read, but I'm only one person. It would take ages for me to get through all these books to find the correct spell. Even if I did know what I was looking for, which of course I don't."

She knew she was talking too fast, making too many excuses. And it hurt to see Arthur's face crumble at each one. But what other choice did she have? Undo her mother's spell, free an evil wizard from captivity, and set him loose on the world? Because that was essentially what they were talking about here.

Arthur sighed deeply, walking across the room to the window and picking up a book on its sill. "I suppose it's too much to ask for them to read themselves..."

Suddenly, to Guinevere's shock, the book seemed to leap from his hands. She watched, amazed, as it hovered in the air, then popped itself open to its first page. A moment later, a low-pitched voice rose to her ears.

"It's doing it!" Arthur cried excitedly, pointing to the book. "It's actually reading itself!"

Sure enough, the book was, indeed, reciting the words on its page. When it had finished, it turned itself to the next page and kept going.

"That's it!" Arthur exclaimed. "I completely forgot. All of Merlin's possessions are magical. He used to have this teapot that filled cups of tea on its own. And these books all packed themselves when we left his cottage for the tower! Of course they'd be able to read themselves, too! That just makes sense if you think about it!"

Guinevere watched the book, her heart pounding. Magic. This whole place was bursting with magic. And they had no idea what they were dealing with. What was she thinking, agreeing to come here? She should leave now. Before—

"I have an idea!" Arthur blurted out. "What if we commanded the books to find the spell we're looking for?"

Guinevere paled. "Do you think they'd listen?" she asked.

"They listened when I mentioned reading themselves," he reminded her. "It's worth a try, right?"

Guinevere found she couldn't argue with that. The look on his face held too much hope, mixed with desperation.

"I suppose it can't hurt," she agreed reluctantly.

Arthur nodded, looking excited. He turned to the shelf of books. "Look, um, well, I don't know if you've noticed, books, but Merlin is missing. We need to find him. Do you happen to have a spell… or something… to help us do that?"

He paused, looking at the shelf expectantly. But nothing happened. The books remained still and unread. Only the first book, which had settled onto a small table by the window, was still reciting its text.

"So much for that," Arthur muttered, sounding discouraged. He sank down in a chair by the cold, ashy hearth and put his head in his hands. "I should have known it couldn't be that easy." He sighed deeply and rubbed his face. "What am I supposed to do? Why did I even come here?"

Guinevere squeezed her eyes shut. She let out a long breath, then opened them again. "I… think you need some magic words," she said slowly. "I mean, at least to get them started…"

Arthur's head jerked up. "Of course," he said, his voice filled with excitement again. "Merlin always had magic words for each spell! Good idea, Guin!"

Guin gave him a wan smile, her insides churning. *What are you doing?* she scolded herself. *You're going to ruin everything!* After all, Mim had trapped Merlin in the future to help keep the kingdom safe. And now Guinevere was helping to bring him back?

"We just need to figure out what they are." Arthur looked down at the book that was still reading itself. A moment later, his eyes lit up and he beckoned to Guin. She stepped towards him, her knees wobbly and her hands shaking. Arthur pointed to the page, where, sure enough, a string of strange words had been illuminated in glowing golden letters.

"What do they say?" he asked, looking up at her, his blue eyes shining with hope.

She swallowed hard. *Lie!* she told herself. *Just make something up.*

But instead, the real words rose to her lips. *"Higgidis… piggidis?"* she whispered.

The room burst into life. Books started flying from the shelves so quickly, Guin was forced to duck so as not to be struck on the head. As she and Arthur watched, each book began flipping madly through its pages, faster and faster, the words blurring into one another as they read.

"It's working!" Arthur cried excitedly. "It's actually working!" Instinctively, he leapt up and threw his arms around Guinevere, locking her into an exuberant embrace. "Guin, you're like a real wizard!" he gushed happily.

"I'm not a wizard!" Guin protested before she could stop herself. She struggled out of the hug, putting her hands out in front of her as if to ward off the words. Her cheeks began to burn.

Arthur looked at her, completely confused. "I— I was just joking..." he stammered. "Sorry."

Guinevere closed her eyes, drawing in a long breath. Then she opened them again. "No, I'm sorry," she said. "It's just... well, magic scares me, if you must know."

"I understand," Arthur said, his voice softening. "I felt that way once, too. But Merlin showed me that magic can be used for good. It can help people. It can make things better."

Guinevere nodded stiffly, not trusting herself to speak. Her head felt as if it was swimming with confusion. She wanted to run from the room and never look back. But at the same time, she couldn't bear to leave Arthur's side.

The books began to move faster, words on each page lighting up one after another after another as they told their stories to the tower room. Their voices rose in a cacophony of sound until Guinevere just wanted to put her hands over her ears to block them all out.

At last, she watched as a heavy golden tome, bigger than

the rest, slipped down from the very top of the bookshelf, where it had been hidden behind a small book with a crimson cover. It flew across the room, landing on the table with a loud thump and then opening itself to a gold-leafed page. Guinevere and Arthur ran over to it and scanned the text.

"What does it say?" Arthur asked.

"It's written in Latin," Guinevere told him. "So I can't be quite sure. But I believe it says, 'How to find someone through time.' "

"That must be it!" Arthur exclaimed. "Should we—"

He was interrupted by the sound of a slamming door down below.

"What was that?" Guinevere whispered, worried.

Arthur ran to the tower door and put his ear to the wood. "Oh, no!" he exclaimed. "I think Sir Ector has returned. He must have fled the castle after they arrested Kay." He swallowed hard. "If he sees me, he could try to kill me. Like Kay wanted to. I'm sure he was the one behind the challenge in the first place. No chance Kay had enough smarts or ambition to come up with it on his own."

Guinevere gnawed on her lower lip. "What do we do?" she asked. "Should we try to get out of here?" She looked out the window. It was a long fall to the ground. Maybe she could try to find another shapeshifting spell? One that would work for both of them?

More magic. It had become a true slippery slope.

But Arthur shook his head, walking back over to the table and the spell book. "We can't leave. Not without Merlin. This is our only chance to reach him. We need to try to cast this spell, whatever it is. It's the only way."

Guinevere picked up the book and looked down at its golden words. Her heart was beating very fast. The last thing she wanted to do was try to cast a random spell without having any idea of what she was doing. Especially a spell to conjure up an evil wizard.

But then, if Arthur was right – and Sir Ector meant to kill him – Merlin might be their only hope.

"All right. Let's give it a try," she ventured. "But no promises it's going to work."

"I believe in you," Arthur said simply. And she felt a tug in her heart again.

Sorry, Mother. But I have no choice...

Drawing in a breath, she looked down at the golden words on the page. Here went nothing. *"Iter per tempus..."* she began chanting, and the golden letters started to glow on the page as she spoke them. *"Iter per tempus... tempus viator..."*

And suddenly everything went black.

CHAPTER TWENTY-FOUR
ARTHUR

Arthur opened his eyes and looked around, blinking a few times to get used to the sudden bright light that shone down on him with an intensity that was almost blinding. A moment ago, the tower had been dim, not to mention damp and chilly. Now everything was sunny and warm. He was practically sweating under his tunic and tights.

"What's happening?" he asked, trying to force his bleary eyes to focus. Something in the air smelt strangely of salt. "Did the spell work?"

"Um..." Guinevere stepped up beside him, looking quite dazed herself. She was still holding the book in her hands, but the golden letters had dimmed to black.

She blinked a few times, too, then her mouth dropped open like a fish's. "Oh..." she whispered. "Oh, no."

"What is it?" Arthur asked just as his vision began to clear. When he finally got a good look at his surroundings, he gasped out loud.

"Where are we?" he whispered.

One thing was for sure: they were definitely not in Merlin's leaky old tower any more. In fact, they were not in a tower at all, but rather outside, on the ground, standing on some kind of sandy patch of land on the shores of a vast sea.

Where were they? And how had they ended up here?

"Wait," Arthur said, a slow realisation beginning to wash over him. "Did something in that spell...?"

He trailed off, feeling embarrassed to voice his wild theory. But still, what other explanation could there be? One moment they were in one place, the next somewhere else entirely.

"Don't be alarmed," Guinevere said slowly, reaching down to scoop up a handful of sand. Arthur watched as the tiny crystals slipped through her fingers and rejoined the beach below. "But I think the spell didn't work exactly how I thought it would." She looked up, meeting Arthur's eyes with her own worried brown ones. "Instead of returning Merlin to us," she said, "I think it took us to Merlin."

Arthur stared at her, for a moment unable to speak.

The spell had taken them to Merlin? Merlin… who had been trapped in the future?

Were *they* in the future?

In Bermuda?

An unexpected thrill prickled his skin. He knew he shouldn't be happy about this accidental time travelling; it was bound to bring about even more complications than they were already facing, which admittedly were quite a few. But still! How could he not be just a little bit excited about the prospect of seeing the future with his own eyes?

Merlin had always talked lovingly about the future. All the amazing inventions humanity would develop and use in everyday life: machines that travelled faster than horses, medicine that healed like magic, and hot running water inside people's own homes to bathe in anytime they wanted, without having to jump into a freezing lake to do it. In fact, Merlin had claimed these people of the future were even able to fly from place to place using big winged inventions called planes – no shapeshifting necessary. And, even wilder, the world had actually become round!

No. The world had *always* been round, he corrected himself, remembering Merlin's words. It was just now, everyone knew it.

"This is amazing!" he cried, twirling in a circle, taking it all in. "I can't believe we're here!"

"Me neither," Guinevere agreed, though she sounded a lot less enthused. Arthur glanced at her, surprised. She looked almost frightened, wringing her hands together in front of her. On instinct, he placed a hand over hers.

"It's going to be all right," he assured her. "We're going to find Merlin. And he'll know what to do."

It was then that he spotted some kind of castle behind them. But it was unlike any castle he'd ever seen before. Three strange-looking manor houses were set in a U shape around a courtyard, each three stories high and featuring impossibly large glass windows, lined up in triple rows, all along their sides. Arthur gave a low whistle. He'd never seen so much glass in his life. And it was so smooth, too, not bubbled and rough like the glass back home.

He looked down at the courtyard, which was taken up almost entirely by a very large pond filled with the clearest crystal-blue water Arthur had ever seen. Around the pond was some kind of smooth stone perimeter – filled with strange-looking beds covered in brightly striped cloth. Each bed had a large cloth banner hanging above it, held up by a shiny metal stand, providing shade from the sun's harsh rays.

But that wasn't even the strangest part – not by far. For lying on some of these beds were people – in a horrifying state of half undress. Arthur stifled a gasp as he watched a woman wearing only two small strips of fabric saunter by them, casually carrying a wine goblet in her hand, as if it was nothing out of the ordinary to do so.

"Why, they're all practically naked!" Guinevere gasped, joining him in taking in the scene. "Have they no modesty in the future?"

"Perhaps they have different ideas about that," Arthur rationalised. "Merlin often talked about different styles, different customs," he mused. He hadn't really grasped the wizard's full meaning at the time, but now he could clearly see it for himself, on full display everywhere he looked. The world had truly changed over the years, and its people along with it. And suddenly Arthur felt the almost overwhelming desire to know everything – see everything – that this magical future had to offer.

Guinevere, on the other hand, still looked rather doubtful about the whole thing. Arthur watched as her eyes drifted from the people on the beds to something behind them. "At least the food looks nice," she observed.

Arthur turned to watch a young man dressed in a crisp white shirt and short brown trousers walk by them carrying a heaped tray full of strange-looking but heavenly-smelling food. There was some kind of flattened brown meat, Arthur noted, placed between two slices of puffy brown bread. Accompanying the meat was a tall pile of golden-coloured sticks with a splotch of thick red liquid beside them. It was all Arthur could do, as the man walked by, not to reach out and pluck one of the golden treasures from the plate to try for himself.

"Do you see Merlin anywhere?" Guinevere asked, drawing his attention away from the food.

Arthur scanned the courtyard again, taking in each person lying on a bed around the pond. For a moment, he worried he'd find Merlin in a state of similar undress as the others. But a further look told him the wizard was not among the pond dwellers.

He pressed his lips together. "No. I don't. Maybe we should ask someone?" he suggested. "Someone has to have seen him, right? I mean, let's be honest, Merlin doesn't exactly fit in here."

Neither did they, he realised suddenly, looking down at his tunic and tights and Guinevere's heavy wool dress. He wondered if they should attempt to find more appropriate attire before beginning their quest so they could blend in with the local population.

"Excuse me, did you just say *Merlin*?"

Arthur whirled around at the sound of the new voice. The man who had walked by them earlier with the tray of golden sticks was now standing behind them, his tray regrettably empty. Perched on his nose were spectacles – similar to what Merlin wore – but with dark glass obscuring his eyes. How did he see out of them?

The man looked at them curiously, his brows furrowing above his glasses. "Okay, seriously, is there some kind of Renaissance Faire going on around here that I don't know about?" he asked.

"A fair?" Guinevere asked, cocking her head in confusion, clearly not quite understanding. "What kind of fair?"

"We're just… not from around here," Arthur tried to explain, realising the man was put off by their clothing, as he had suspected. "We're from London," he added, hoping that London was still a real place in the future. And, if it was, it had a different sort of wardrobe than here.

"Yeah, I figured from your accents," the man said. "Don't worry – this place is full of Brits. You must be sweltering, though," he added, gesturing to Guinevere's dress. "We do have a gift shop on-site with lots of summery clothing and bathing suits, if you want to find something more suitable for the beach."

Gift shop. Arthur stored the words away in his mind. That must be where people received their clothing in the future. And how nice of them to give the clothing away as gifts instead of charging money like they did in the shops back home. No wonder Merlin liked the future so much! Good food, free clothes, warm weather. Why – it was almost paradise. In fact, if the entire fate of England hadn't been at stake at the moment, he might have actually thought about staying here for a while himself.

"Um, thank you?" Guinevere said. "I'll, uh, keep that in mind."

Arthur stepped forwards, trying to steer the conversation back to the missing wizard. "You asked if we mentioned Merlin. Have you seen him here? We're actually looking for him. He's been… gone for quite some time, and we're a little worried."

The man nodded, seeming relieved. "I figured someone would come for him eventually. He didn't have an ID on him, so we couldn't call anyone. He kept babbling these nonsensical words by the pool and was starting to freak out some of the guests. Probably just too much sun for the poor guy. It happens to the best of us." He stopped as if something had just occurred to him. "Wait, you're not Wart, are you?"

"I am!" Arthur exclaimed, shocked to hear his old name spoken by a stranger in the future. "I mean, that's my nickname, anyway. Merlin always called me Wart."

"I thought you might be," the man said. He gave Arthur a stern glare. "Look, I don't know what kind of fight the two of you got into, but your grandfather seems really shaken up by it. It might be nice if you forgave him for whatever it was he did. I mean, trust me, I have a grandfather, too. I know how they can be. But still. The poor old—"

"Where is he?" Arthur interrupted, starting to get impatient. "Where can we find him?"

"I have no idea," he said with a shrug. "Security took him away a few hours ago. Like I said, he was acting really strange. Mumbling to himself. Telling people he's a famous wizard – like the Merlin of the King Arthur legend or whatever."

"Wait," Arthur said, his turn to interrupt. "Did you just say *King Arthur legend*?" He glanced at Guin. She looked back at him, raising her eyebrows.

"Yeah, you know. The whole Knights Of The Round Table, Guinevere, Lancelot?" The man looked at them strangely. "I would have thought you'd be all over that kind of thing, judging from the way you're dressed." He shook his head, looking disappointed. "Kids these days. No sense of history."

"Uh, yes, sorry, yes!" Arthur barked a shaky laugh. "Of course we know all about King Arthur and his… round table," he added. Wow. Had the circular table he'd just installed back home in his meeting room somehow become legendary in the future? It seemed an odd detail for people to remember throughout the annals of time, but he was flattered nonetheless.

Also, who was Lancelot?

He realised the man was looking at him strangely. He

swallowed hard. "And, uh, yes, my… grandfather… gets, uh, confused sometimes," he added, still fake laughing. "He likes to imagine he's a time traveller from the past."

"Yes!" The man's eyes lit up. "That's right! He did say something about time travel." He snorted, giving them a rueful grin. "Between you and me, I kind of liked the old guy. He was funny. Weird, but funny." He looked out over the courtyard. "You see that man over there? His name's Joe. He should know where you can find Merlin."

"Thank you," Arthur said, feeling relief wash over him. "We'll ask him."

"Good luck," the man said. "And take care of your grandfather, won't you?"

"We will, I promise."

The man nodded and headed off in another direction. Arthur turned to Guin. "First let's go to the gift shop," he said. "We'll get clothing to fit in better. Then we won't have to deal with questions every time we talk to someone."

They headed in the direction of the 'gift shop', which turned out to be not much different from the shops back home in London – though the 'gifts' were quite different in style. Still, after a few moments of studying the others who were shopping in the store, they were able to pick out a few items of clothing that seemed more in line with what people in the future wore but weren't made of the barely-there fabric that some seemed to prefer.

Arthur grabbed a pair of brightly coloured trousers that stopped at his knees and a large shirt that Guinevere translated to read, "I survived the Bermuda Triangle." Arthur had no idea what that was, or if they had indeed survived it, but they had survived time travelling, and since there were no shirts bragging about that particular achievement, this would have to do.

Guinevere emerged from the small booth used to change clothes, looking beautiful in a long, frothy blue gown of the lightest, silkiest material Arthur had ever seen. It wrapped around her body in swaths of fabric, but left her arms uncovered. She walked up to the mirror at the end of the shop and stared at her reflection.

"I don't know," she murmured, looking doubtful. She turned to Arthur. "Do you think this is suitable?"

"I think you look lovely," he said honestly. And when Guinevere smiled, he knew he'd said the right thing. "Now come on. Let's find Merlin."

They started to head out of the shop. But before they got to the doors, a woman wearing a colourful flowered shirt suddenly stepped into their path. "Are you planning to pay for those?" she asked, looking at them angrily.

Arthur frowned, confused. "Aren't they meant to be gifts?" he asked. "This is a gift shop, yes?"

"Very funny." The woman rolled her eyes, dragging them both back to a small table in the centre of the shop, on which there sat a strange machine Arthur didn't recognise. She reached over and plucked a paper tag off each of their outfits. "The dress is thirty-nine ninety-nine," she said. "I'll throw in the shirt and shorts for an even sixty."

It took Arthur a moment to realise she was talking about money. He should have known the gifting idea was too good to be true. No future could be that perfect.

Guinevere glanced at him. "Do you have any coins?" she whispered.

Did he? Arthur reached into his satchel, feeling around. Being king, he normally had no reason to carry around gold on his person. But he had distributed coins to the poor a few days before and managed to find one leftover coin at the bottom of his bag. He pulled it out, holding it up to the woman.

"I only have this," he said apologetically. "Will it do?"

The woman stared at the coin, her eyes widening to saucers. She reached out and plucked it from Arthur's hand. "Is this gold?" she asked, looking quite astounded. Arthur watched as she bit down on it with her teeth, then stared at it again.

"Is it enough?" Arthur asked worriedly.

But the woman was ignoring him now. She had set down the coin on the table and was tapping on a small black object with a glass face in her hand. A moment later, she looked up. "Is this real?" she asked suspiciously. "It says on the Internet it's from the Middle Ages."

"Um, yes. It's very old," Guinevere agreed. "And very valuable." She glanced at Arthur. He held his breath. "It's also all we have to pay for the clothes. Is that all right?"

"Yes!" the woman replied excitedly, hastily slipping the coin in her pocket. Then she seemed to remember herself. "I mean, I suppose it'll do." She reached behind the table and handed them two hats and two pairs of the dark glass spectacles that the man had been wearing. "Take these sunglasses, too," she said hurriedly. "It's really bright out there."

Guinevere and Arthur dutifully took the hats and placed them on their heads. Arthur felt a little ridiculous in his, which fit fine, but had a strange little brim that shielded his eyes. Guin, on the other hand, looked rather lovely in her wide straw-brimmed bonnet that wasn't much different from what the serfs wore in the fields back home.

Then he tried the 'sunglasses', resting them on his nose as he'd seen the others do. Suddenly, his vision dimmed. Startled, he ripped them off his head.

"They make you go blind!" he exclaimed.

"Oh, yeah, they're a little on the dark side. But trust me, you'll thank me once you get outside. That sun is brutal today. I can't believe you've been out there without them."

"Thank you," Guinevere piped in. "We appreciate it." She grabbed her own sunglasses and began to drag Arthur out of the shop.

"Have a nice day!" the woman called out after them before turning to her next guest.

"I'm glad she took that coin," Guinevere remarked once they were outside again. "I'm not sure what else we could have offered her."

Arthur nodded, setting the sunglasses on his nose again. This time, they didn't blind him entirely, but it was as if someone had turned off a very large lamp.

"What a brilliant invention," he marvelled, taking them off for a moment to stare down at them before returning them to his face. "Those working in the fields back home could greatly benefit from something like this."

"Maybe you should invent it for them," Guinevere said with a smile. "Once you're not king, you're bound to have a lot of time on your hands. Why, you'll be able to do all sorts of interesting things with your life."

Arthur nodded, his enthusiasm deflating a bit as he was reminded of their mission. As fascinating as the future was, they weren't here as guests on a holiday. They were here to learn whether Merlin had really decided to make him king and how he could successfully abdicate the throne without managing to get his head chopped off in the process.

Guinevere caught his eye. "Come on," she said. "Let's go speak to this Joe."

They headed over to the man who had been identified as Joe. When they approached, he was tapping on one of the same rectangular glass objects the woman in the gift shop had been using.

"Excuse me," Arthur ventured. "I'm sorry to bother you. We're looking for a man named Merlin. He's old? Maybe dressed in a blue hat and robes? Do you happen to know where he is?"

The man looked up from his object, frowning for a moment. Then a flicker of recognition crossed his face. "Oh, you must mean the old dude from this morning," he said. "We brought him down to the infirmary. I think he got too much sun." He shrugged. "Not sure if he's still there."

"Where's the infirmary?" Guinevere asked.

The man pointed down a path, then turned back to tapping on his glass rectangle – conversation clearly over. Arthur really wanted to ask him what the rectangle did and why everyone seemed to be so fascinated by it, but he knew it would just make him stand out again. Instead, he turned to Guinevere.

"Come on," he said. "Let's go find him."

They dashed down the path, as directed, following the little white signs with red crosses that read 'infirmary', according to Guin. At the end of the path, they came across a small white one-storey building with the same red cross painted on its door. They glanced at each other excitedly. This must have been it.

"Come on," Arthur said, and headed through the doors.

Inside, it was also white. And really clean. In fact, it might have been the cleanest place Arthur had ever seen, and he wondered how they kept it so pristine. In the centre of the room was a woman with black hair in neat braids, sitting behind a table, wearing an outfit that was also white and clean – to match the room, Arthur assumed.

"Excuse me?" he said, walking up to the woman. "Do you have a man named Merlin here, by any chance?"

The woman looked up from yet another small black rectangle. These people of the future *really* seemed to love whatever these things were. "Merlin?" she repeated, looking a little drained. "Oh, he's here all right." She rolled her eyes. "Just follow his loud bellyaching down the hall. You can't miss him." She groaned. "And please take him with you when you leave. My migraine will thank you."

"We will," Arthur promised, though he had no idea who the migraine was or why they would thank him for retrieving his teacher. "Now where—"

"Higgidis piggidis! No, no, NO!"

Arthur's eyes lit up. "Merlin!" he cried. There was no mistaking his teacher's voice.

He started running down the corridor, fast as his feet could take him. He could feel his heart pound in excitement as they reached the door at the end. The chanting was louder here, definitely coming from the other side of the wall. Arthur grinned widely.

Merlin. We've found you at last.

CHAPTER TWENTY-FIVE
ARTHUR

"Merlin!"

Arthur yanked open the door, bursting into the room. His heart swelled as his eyes fell on his teacher, who was sitting up in a small bed and waving his hands in front of his face. Merlin was dressed oddly, in a strange, thin cotton robe printed with drawings of cute baby ducks. And his beard looked in desperate need of a brushing.

But it was him. There was no mistaking it.

"Merlin!" Arthur cried again, his heart feeling as if it would burst with joy. "Oh, Merlin. It's so good to see you!"

The old wizard looked up, his watery blue eyes lighting in recognition. "Wart?" he exclaimed, his voice filled with astonishment. "Am I dreaming? Is that really you?"

"It's really me," Arthur assured him, crossing the room and throwing his arms around his teacher, giving him a huge hug. Merlin grunted a little, clearly surprised at the unexpected gesture of affection, but he managed to pat Arthur awkwardly on the back before they parted again. Arthur smiled down at him. "It's so good to see you," he gushed. "Are you all right?"

"Oh. I'm fine." Merlin huffed, looking down at his strange attire. It was then Arthur noted he had a tube of some sort sticking out of his arm. The tube led to a small bag hanging from a pole and containing clear liquid. Merlin caught Arthur's worried look. "Don't mind that," he said quickly. "They're just trying to rehydrate me. For some reason they're convinced I've got heatstroke." He snorted. "As if I would ever allow myself to get heatstroke. Why, if I could survive a dragon blast in the middle of the Sahara, surely I can deal with the paltry sun of twenty-first century Bermuda."

Arthur bit back a laugh. It was Merlin all right. And he hadn't changed a bit. "I'm just happy you're here," he said, pulling up a chair and sitting beside the wizard. "I have so much to tell you. So much has happened since you've been gone."

"Of course it has," Merlin grumped. "I'm sure she's taken full advantage of my absence to cause as much havoc as possible." He made a disgusted face. "I should have picked a longer lasting disease," he muttered. "That would have shown her not to trifle with me!"

Arthur frowned. "Who are you talking about again?" he asked, though he had a sneaking suspicion he knew.

"Madam Mim, of course," Merlin blurted. "Try to keep up!" He squeezed his hands into fists. "I'm positive she's the one who tangled with my spell-casting skills, making it impossible for me to get back home. I can still time travel, you see. But I'm unable to pinpoint where – or when – I want to go. You can't imagine all the places I've been to since I first left you in the tower. The twentieth century, the twenty-second century – I don't recommend that one bit, by the way!" he added as an aside. He tapped his finger to his chin. "Then there was the twelfth century – that one was actually quite pleasant, if you must know; almost felt like home. But now I'm here, in the twenty-first century, where no one seems to believe a thing I say." He sighed dejectedly. "And maybe they're right. All of this has surely scrambled my noggin. And no type of hydration is going to help with that!" He stared bitterly down at the clear tube in his arm, as if blaming it for everything.

Arthur nodded dutifully, though, in truth, he had only understood about half of what the wizard was saying. But he was used to that, he supposed. And nothing could dampen his joy of being back with his teacher.

"So... you can't get back home," he tried to interpret.

"Of course I can't get back home! Haven't you been listening to a thing I've been saying?" Merlin burst out. He shook his head, his long white beard swinging from side to side. "It couldn't have been easy for Mim to do this, so I assume she had some kind of nefarious reason for doing it. Or maybe she's just still bitter that I beat her in that duel. Even though she's the one who cheated in the first place!" He waved his fist in the air. "Why, if I get my hands on her again—"

He was interrupted by a small, anxious squeak. Arthur whirled around, remembering, for the first time since he'd seen Merlin, that he hadn't come alone. Guinevere was hovering by the doorway, wringing her hands together nervously.

Merlin also seemed to notice her for the first time. "Excuse me, young lady. Do you mind? We're trying to have a private conver—" He stopped short. His eyes widened. So wide that for a moment Arthur thought they would pop out of his head.

"What's wrong, Merlin?" he asked.

"No," his teacher murmured. "It can't be..."

Guinevere flinched, almost as if she'd been struck.

She started to back away. Arthur's heart beat uncomfortably. What was going on here? Why did they look like they knew each other?

"Camile?" Merlin questioned. Then he shook his head. "No. That can't be right. Camile would be older now. You're just a child. But you look so much like her… A daughter? But then, she never had any more children after…" His face turned bright white. "You're not… You can't be…"

"This is Guinevere," Arthur blurted out, unable to stand the suspense any more. "She's my new friend. She saved my life and helped cast the spell for us to get here to find you."

"Guinevere," Merlin whispered in disbelief. Then his eyes lit up and his face broke out into a huge grin. "*Guinevere!* You're alive! And practically grown up, too!"

"Wh-what?" Guinevere stammered, still looking as if she was about to bolt from the room.

"Oh, your parents are going to be so happy when they find out," Merlin gushed, clapping his hands together with glee. "This is the best news ever!"

"You must be mistaken," Guinevere protested. "My parents are… dead." Her mouth dipped to a frown. Then something seemed to flicker across her face. Something very dark that Arthur had never seen before from his friend.

"You *know* they're dead," she added, with more force. "You..." She sucked in a breath. "*You*... killed them!"

"Wait, what?" Arthur cried. He couldn't have been more shocked if Guinevere had just accused Merlin of masquerading as a purple polka-dotted dragon. "What are you talking about, Guin?"

Guinevere turned to him. Her brown eyes flashed fire. "I'm sorry, Arthur. But you need to know the truth. Your precious Merlin killed my parents in cold blood when I was just a baby. And he tried to kill me, too!"

"No!" Arthur cried, horrified. "That's impossible! Merlin wouldn't do that!" He turned to his mentor. "Would you?" he asked, suddenly feeling a flicker of doubt.

"Of course not!" Merlin sputtered, sounding angry. "Why would I kill her parents? They're dear friends of mine." He stroked his beard. "Also, they're not dead – well, at least not back in our rightful time. So there is that, too."

Now it was Guinevere's turn to look confused. "What are you talking about? Of course they're dead," she said. But Arthur could hear a thread of doubt in her voice. Mixed with a thread of painful hope.

"Actually, King Leodegrance of the Summer Country and his wife, Camile, are very much alive," Merlin replied. "*You're* the one who is supposed to be dead."

"You're lying!" Guinevere spit out. "You have to be lying!" Her voice caught on the words. "You're trying to trick me."

Merlin shrugged. "I'm happy to prove it to you, if we can ever get out of this place. Queen Camile is just going to be beside herself with joy when she finds out. She never did have another child after you disappeared from your cradle that night. She was too distraught by losing you."

Guinevere just stared at him, not replying. Her knees trembled, and Arthur ran to grab her before they buckled out from under her.

"Guin, it's all right!" he whispered. "This is good news, right?"

Guinevere turned to him, her eyes filled with tears. "Yes… but… how can it be true? How can it possibly be true?"

"Who told you they were dead?" Arthur asked. "Was it your foster mother? Maybe she… didn't know?"

Guin's face twisted, and Arthur's heart squeezed at the pain and betrayal he saw cross her face. Whoever had told her this lie had clearly been someone she trusted. And now she was doubting everything she'd ever been told – maybe for her entire life.

Guinevere squeezed her eyes shut, then opened them again. Her shoulders drooped as if all the fight had gone out of her. Arthur watched as she bit her lower lip, then shuffled from foot to foot.

"Guin…" He placed a hand over hers, but she jerked it away. She gave Merlin one last look, then mumbled an apology and fled the room. Worried, Arthur started after her, but Merlin stopped him at the door.

"No, lad," he said gently. "It will do no good to chase her down. Let her have the time she needs to sort her thoughts. She'll come back when she's ready."

Arthur reluctantly turned back to his mentor. He knew Merlin was right, even if he didn't want him to be. He sighed deeply. "This has all turned out to be such a mess," he moaned. "Ever since the day you left. Nothing has been normal since."

Merlin frowned. "Maybe you should start at the beginning. Tell me everything that's happened since I've been away." He stroked his beard. "For example, did you ever go to that blasted tournament? What clod-headed oaf managed to win the thing? Who's our new king?"

"Well—" Arthur began.

Merlin scowled. "Oh, no. Don't tell me it was that lunkhead Kay. He's the last person on earth who should be wearing the crown. Though I'm sure Mim would love it. All the chaos he would end up causing. It would be a disaster – just as she likes it…" His voice trailed off as he caught Arthur's expression. "Well, what is it, boy? For goodness' sakes, you look like you swallowed a bee." He shook his head. "Don't leave me in suspense. Who is the king of England?"

Arthur felt his cheeks turn bright red. "It's… well, sort of, um… *me*?"

Merlin's eyebrows furrowed. He stared at Arthur for a moment, and Arthur could almost see the smoke coming from his brain.

"I, uh, pulled the sword from the stone," he added weakly.

"Well, I'll be!" Merlin suddenly let out a huge whooping cheer, startling Arthur and forcing him to take a quick step back. "*You* pulled the sword from the stone? The legendary sword Excalibur?"

"That's the one," Arthur agreed. "Evidently whoever pulls it out is meant to be king."

"Yes, of course. I know the legend. I just had no idea it was about you! Though I suppose it makes perfect sense. I always knew you were meant for greatness, of course."

"It does?" Arthur stared at Merlin, perplexed. "You did?"

"Ever since that day you crashed through my roof." The wizard grinned. "After all, why do you think I took such an interest in your education?"

"I don't know. I guess I just thought you were being nice," Arthur said. His mind was whirring with confusion and a little bit of worry. Merlin didn't seem *too* surprised about his student's very unlikely destiny. Was that because the wizard had planned it all along?

Arthur shuffled from foot to foot. "Merlin..." he began, not knowing how to bring it up.

"What is it, lad?"

"You didn't... I mean, you hadn't... just... by some means..."

"Well, spit it out, boy! What are you talking about?"

"You didn't plan this? You didn't cast a spell on the sword so only I could pull it out and it would look like a miracle?"

Merlin's eyes widened. "Why on earth would I do a thing like that?"

Arthur shrugged, squiriming a little. "I— I mean, I don't know," he stammered. "So maybe you could rule through me?"

For a moment, Merlin was speechless. He stared at Arthur, his expression unreadable. Then he leapt out of bed, ripping out the tube attached to his arm. Arthur winced, not sure that was the best way to go about it.

Merlin stalked towards Arthur. "Have you just met

me, lad?" he demanded. "You think I wanted to be king of England?"

Arthur took a small step backwards, looking a little frightened. The last time he'd seen his teacher so agitated was just before he'd blown himself to Bermuda. And Arthur *really* didn't want to have to track him down in yet another time period just to finish their conversation.

"Merlin, sit down," he begged. "It was just a theory..."

"Well, it was a very bad theory," he sputtered. "With no factual evidence to back it up." He huffed and plopped back down on the bed, looking extremely miffed. "Besides, even if I had wanted to do something like that, it wouldn't work. The magic of the sword in the stone goes deep. No mere wizard could just disenchant it on a whim to allow a person of their choosing to pull it out. Otherwise someone would have done it a long time ago."

Arthur drew in a breath, his thoughts whirling in his head. "So then... you're saying..."

"That you're the foretold king of all England?" Merlin shrugged. "It certainly appears so."

Arthur felt his heart skip a beat. Could it be? Could he really be the true king after all?

It seemed impossible. Yet what other explanation could there be? Certainly no one else would want him to be king – or have the ability to make it happen. He felt an unexpected thrill spin up his spine. He hadn't realised how much he'd been hoping for this until it actually happened.

"Of course, there's only way to find out for sure," Merlin added. "We need to consult the Internet."

CHAPTER TWENTY-SIX
ARTHUR

"The inter-net?" Arthur repeated doubtfully. "What is that? Some kind of oracle?"

"Not exactly," Merlin replied. "The Internet can't predict the future like an oracle. It can only reveal words and pictures of the past. And sometimes videos, too." He snorted. "So many videos! Though the good majority of them seem to be of cats doing silly things. For some reason people here really like their cats."

"Cats?" Arthur was so lost it wasn't funny. Merlin sighed.

"Here's the deal. Since you are from the past, the Internet can reveal your future – which is also in the past, at least at this present time," he explained. "Does that make sense?"

"Not really," Arthur replied. "And anyway, don't you already know the future?" he asked, puzzled. "You've bounced all around it! Surely you would have heard about me being king!"

"No offence, but as important as that little detail might be to you personally, it certainly is but a mere ripple in our vast universe," Merlin replied, sounding a little irritated by the question. "And besides, even I have my limitations. Remember when you first crashed through my roof? I knew you were going to be of some importance. And that I was meant to be your teacher. I just didn't know what I was teaching you for." He shrugged. "Now it's starting to all make sense. And I'm sure the Internet will be able to fill in the gaps."

Arthur nodded doubtfully. "So where is the Internet?" he asked.

Merlin swung his legs off the bed and onto the floor. Standing up, he looked around the room. "I know the nurse at the door has a computer at her desk. We'll have to borrow that." He started heading towards the room's exit with purposeful steps.

"Um, Merlin?" Arthur ventured nervously. When the wizard turned to look at him, he gestured to the duck-covered dressing gown he wore, which was, for some unfortunate and completely inexplicable reason, wide open in the back.

The wizard's cheeks turned bright pink. "Oh, right! Clothes!" He grabbed his wand off the table and waved it with a flourish. *"Bibbidi bobbidi—!"* he chanted. Then he winked at Arthur. "I learned this one from a lovely fairy godmother while stuck in 1800s France. Sweet lady, really. Though quite hung up on punctuality." He waved his wand. *"BOO!"*

There was a sudden poof, and the wizard went up in a plume of smoke. He emerged a moment later dressed in a pair of short trousers decorated with funny-looking trees and a very brightly coloured striped shirt. Which didn't exactly help him fit in. But it was better than his previous attire, so Arthur decided to let it go.

"Now," Merlin said, turning to address Arthur. "I need you to distract the nurse. Once she's gone, we'll jump on her computer and see what we can find out."

"Jump on it?" Arthur raised an eyebrow. "Won't that break it?"

"Not literally, my boy," Merlin said with a groan. "Just a figure of speech. They have a lot of those in this time period. You'll need to try to keep up."

Arthur nodded dutifully. "How am I supposed to distract her?" he asked. Then he had an idea. "What if you turn me into a mouse? Are people in the future still afraid of mice?"

"Oddly, yes," Merlin replied. "Though I've never understood why." He nodded absently. "Yes, that might actually work. Good thinking, boy." He patted Arthur on the back, and Arthur couldn't help beaming from the approval.

A moment later, Merlin was waving his wand in his direction. *"Misculus, moosculus, Mickey Mouse!"* he chanted, and suddenly there was another poof of smoke. Arthur squirmed as he felt his body collapse in on itself, just as it had so many times during their lessons. And soon he was standing on his hind legs, twitching his tiny pink nose.

Merlin clapped his hands in delight. "Huzzah! I still have it!" he declared. "Now go on, boy. Do your thing. And, uh, don't get stepped on," he added with a sheepish grin.

Arthur gave him a little mouse salute. Then he skittered out of the room and down the hall. When he reached the room with the woman at the desk, he paused only a moment, then leapt up onto her lap. She looked down, her eyes bulging from her head.

"Boo!" Arthur tried to say. It came out more like '*squeak*', but turned out to still be extremely effective. The woman leapt from her chair, screaming.

"Mouse! There's a mouse!"

Arthur felt himself go flying. He hit the ground hard

and saw stars. By the time he could see normally again, the woman was running from the building, slamming the door shut behind her.

"Not bad," Merlin remarked, walking into the room. "Not bad at all." He grinned at Arthur. "Just like old times, am I right?"

Arthur nodded, smiling through his whiskers. He had to admit, it was good to have his teacher back. Even if it did always end up leaving him animal-shaped.

He watched as the wizard walked around the table, then huddled in front of a strange little box with a glass window on the front. "Now, let's get to work," he said. "She'll be back in a few minutes with someone to deal with the rodent problem. We need to do this fast." He leant over and started tapping on a tray of buttons.

Arthur squeaked loudly, trying to get Merlin's attention again. After all, working in a kitchen most of his life, he'd seen first-hand how mice were 'dealt with', and it would likely put a damper on any possible future of him as king – or anything else, for that matter.

Merlin looked down, surprised. "Oh. Right. Sorry. You probably want to be human again, don't you?" He absently waved a hand in Arthur's direction. A moment later Arthur poofed back to his old self. He let out a breath of relief, then turned his attention to Merlin's tapping on the tray of letters.

"So is that the Internet?" he asked curiously, pressing his finger against the machine.

"It's a computer," Merlin corrected. "You access the Internet through a computer."

Arthur cocked his head. "The Internet is inside the computer?"

"No. The Internet is everywhere."

"Everywhere?" Arthur looked around, feeling bewildered. "Is it invisible?"

Merlin groaned. "Look, I'll be happy to give you an in-depth lesson on twenty-first-century technology the moment we get back home. But right now, we need to concentrate on your past— er, future."

"Sorry." Arthur leant over and placed his hands on the table, watching Merlin tap on the tray again. As he tapped, words appeared on the glass window in front of him.

"The Internet is quite miraculous," Merlin explained. "You simply type in a question, and it will spit out answers. It's as if every book in the world is inside of it, and you don't have to turn any pages to read them."

"Wow," Arthur said. "That truly is magical."

"Actually, it's scientific," Merlin corrected. He tapped on the buttons again, and something appeared on the glass. *"King Arthur destiny..."* he murmured as he tapped.

The wizard hit another button, and Arthur held his

breath as the words on the glass shifted. A moment later, a new page revealed itself.

"What does it say?" he asked anxiously. This was it. The moment of truth. The Internet was about to tell him who he really was. And once he knew, there was no going back. Suddenly he found himself wishing Guin were here. Whatever the answer, he knew she would find a way to make him feel better about it all.

Merlin cleared his throat, then started reading. "'Arthur was destined to become the once and future king and unite the land...'"

Arthur's heart leapt to his throat. Merlin kept reading, but he could no longer focus on the words.

Arthur was destined...

"So it's true?" he breathed. "I am the destined king of England?" He couldn't believe it. But there it was, spelt out clear as day on the Internet.

"The Internet never lies," Merlin assured him. "If it says you are the destined king, then you are the destined king." He scanned the window, his lips pursed. "And it seems you were a pretty legendary one, at that. In fact, it appears you even have books and major motion pictures all about you!"

"What's a motion picture?" Arthur asked.

"Oh. It's like television that's not broken up into

parts," Merlin explained absently, still reading the window. "Though it appears you have a few streaming series about you, too. Too bad we don't have more time to binge them." As if that cleared anything up.

But it didn't matter, really. The point was, Arthur was king. He was the rightful king.

Merlin straightened, giving Arthur a rueful grin. "Well, my boy! It seems there's no getting out of it. It's your destiny, and you're stuck with it." He slapped him on the back. "You know, I knew from the start, with your spirit and the way you put your heart and soul into everything you did, that you'd be worth something someday." He humphed. "Archimedes didn't believe me, but I was right! It says so right there." He tapped on the glass. "King Arthur and his Knights Of The Round Table."

Arthur felt his cheeks heat, but this time with pleasure. "I need to tell Guin!" he exclaimed. "She's not going to believe it." He grinned widely, then declared, "And then I need to get back to England, before someone else tries to take over in my absence. Or Mim tries something else."

"Something else?" Merlin repeated, turning to look at him questioningly. Arthur realised he hadn't told his teacher all that had happened with the evil witch. He quickly related the main points – including the disgusting slug thing, which still gave him the shivers. When he had finished, Merlin huffed angrily.

"Ridiculous! Just ridiculous! I'm going to have a word with her when I get back! More than one, if you must know! Why, I'll make sure she never dares mess with you again."

"That would be great," Arthur said, feeling so relieved. This was exactly what he needed. Everything was going to be all right. He could feel it in his bones.

Merlin crossed the room, then crossed back, tapping his forehead with his finger. "The question is – how do we get back home? My spell book is completely scrambled. If we try to time travel, we might end up in the Jurassic era – and eaten by dinosaurs. That would really put a damper on your destiny."

Arthur didn't know what a dinosaur was, but he was pretty sure he didn't want to be eaten by one. Luckily, he did have another idea. He stepped into Merlin's path. "Guin has your book," he told him. "From your tower. It got us here. Surely it can also bring us home."

"Yes! YES!" Merlin did a little jig. "This is wonderful news! Wonderful! With my book in hand, I'll be able to reverse Mim's spell and get us all back home safe and sound!"

Arthur let out a small cheer. "And then I can get back to being king."

"Indeed, my boy, indeed. And together we can stop Madam Mim from causing any more mischief." Merlin wrinkled his nose. "Now, come! There's no time to waste! Let's get that book – and get you back to your future!"

CHAPTER TWENTY-SEVEN
GUINEVERE

Guinevere stared out at the vast sea as the sun dipped below the horizon, bruising the sky with vivid blues and purples and reds. The same sun she'd seen set a thousand times before back home. But somehow it felt different here. Now.

Everything felt different. Like she was out there, in that wild sea, unmoored, adrift. Every truth she'd ever been told in her life had become a violent wave crashing over her, threatening to drown her with doubt.

Lost in thought, she didn't hear Arthur approach. When he reached out to touch her arm, she jumped.

"Sorry," he said. "I didn't mean to startle you."

"It's all right," she said quietly, not taking her gaze off

the horizon. In truth, she was afraid if she looked at him, she'd break out into tears all over again. She felt as if she'd been crying for hours, and still her eyes were wet.

"Are you all right?" he asked softly.

She swallowed hard, pausing before answering. "I don't know," she said at last. "I mean, I feel like my whole world has been turned upside down. I don't know what to think, what to believe." She shook her head. "My parents, alive? Could it really be true?" Her voice cracked on the last bit. She couldn't help it.

But there was a bigger question in her mind. One she couldn't share with Arthur. The one that felt like a sharp knife stabbing her in the gut. Had Mim known all this time that her parents were alive? Had she lied to her face over and over again as Guinevere grew? Her foster mother's words seemed to echo in her ears. *I saved you. You would have died without me.*

All this time she had felt so grateful to her mother. But now that gratitude tasted like sawdust in her mouth. How many times had Mim called Merlin a monster?

What if it was actually Mim, not Merlin, who was the true monster?

She thought about all the time they'd spent together over the years. The singing and dance parties in their cottage. The games of cards where Mim would badly cheat and Guin would laughingly catch her at it. All the lessons Mim had patiently taught her about magic and herbs. Yes, Mim had certainly enjoyed causing mischief from time to time – but could she really have gone so far as to steal away a child from her parents?

It was almost too much to think about.

Arthur reached out, pressing his fingers against her cheek, turning her head gently – so gently – until she was looking into his deep blue eyes. She swallowed hard, powerless to turn away.

"We will find out the truth. Whatever it might be," he said firmly. "Together."

Her heart squeezed. A tear slipped down her cheek, but she didn't bother to swipe it away.

"I would like that," she murmured. It was all she could say. But at the moment, it was enough.

Arthur smiled at her. Then he turned to look out at the sea. For a moment, he said nothing. Then, "It's so pretty here," he murmured. "And so warm." It was almost as if he could sense she was at her breaking point and needed a change of subject.

"Yes," she agreed, kicking off her shoes and digging her toes into the crunchy wet sand. She wondered how Merlin was doing on his spell. He'd found her earlier and taken the book from her, promising to find a spell that would get them safely back home. He said it could take a little while and that she should enjoy the beach while he worked. And so she had, even procuring a tray of those little golden sticks, which had turned out to be delicious. "It's almost magical."

"If only I didn't have my entire destiny and the future of England waiting for me back home," Arthur joked. "I'd stay much longer. Maybe even learn how to stand on water, like them," he added, gesturing to the people out on the water riding the waves on strange long boards.

She turned to him, surprised. "So it's true?" she asked. "You're really England's king? It wasn't a trick after all?"

"I'm afraid there's no getting out of it," Arthur said, a little sheepishly.

"You're going to make a great king," she blurted out before she could stop herself. But even after she said the words, she realised she meant them. Arthur was everything a good king should be. England was lucky to have him. And Mim would just have to accept that.

A sob escaped her throat as she thought of her foster mother again. Maybe Mim had also been deceived? Maybe she truly believed what she'd told Guin all along. Because the alternative – that she'd been the one to steal Guin away from her own parents and had lied to her for her entire life – was too cruel to even consider.

But then, what about Arthur? Merlin? Mim had been so insistent that Merlin crowned Arthur because he wanted the power for himself. But was this merely another lie – another game? How could Guin know for sure?

It was too much to think about. Far too much. She forced herself to push it down deep inside to deal with later once their immediate problems were solved. When she arrived back home, she would go straight to her mother and demand to know everything – the whole truth this time. No more lies. No more deception. And if her mother wouldn't agree to this, then Guin would leave. She would find her true parents – if they were indeed alive. She would start a new life.

She realised Arthur was still watching her. "I don't like seeing you so sad, Guin," he said. "I wish there was something I could do. Or say. Or—"

On impulse, she reached down and slipped her hands into his. His skin was warm and slightly rough at the fingertips. But his hands were strong as they clasped her own. "You're here," she told him. "That's all that matters."

"I don't think I've thanked you yet," he said softly. "I mean, definitely not enough. You saved my life. You helped me rescue Merlin. I don't know what I would have done without you." He paused. "I'm lucky to have met you, Guin."

Guinevere couldn't help a small flinch at his words.

At the grateful look radiating from his eyes – a look she didn't deserve. If only he knew the truth: that their meeting was not the accident he thought it to be. That she'd purposely befriended him with the intent to bring him down. To destroy his life and his rule.

The thought tore at her heart. She hadn't known Arthur long, but in the short time they'd been together, he'd become a true friend in every sense of the word. A friend like she'd never had before. A friend like she'd probably never have again.

Which meant she could never tell him the truth. He could never know what she'd once intended to do. And from now on, she'd be the best friend a person could be. She would support him, stay loyal and true. And if anyone ever tried to hurt him again, she would be the first to stop them.

She felt his eyes on her, and she lifted her head again. He was staring at her, his hands still clasped in hers. Her breath caught in her throat as he reached up, brushing a lock of hair from her eyes.

"Guinevere," he whispered. And that was enough.

Their lips came together. Soft. Sweet. A little clumsy, too. But that was to be expected – neither one of them had much experience in the act. Guinevere felt her knees weaken. She started to sway, but Arthur held her up, his strong hands clasping her at the waist.

"Arthur," she murmured. "Oh, Arthur…"

"ARTHUR! WHERE ARE YOU, BOY?"

They broke apart, stumbling backwards to put distance between them as Merlin stomped down the beach, carrying his bag. He was dressed once more in the blue robes Arthur had described, though he seemed to have forgotten to remove his sunglasses, even though the sun now dipped below the horizon. He stumbled on a small rock and fell face-first into the sand.

"Argh!" he grumped as he tried to climb back to his feet. "Who turned out the lights?"

Arthur laughed and ran over to his teacher to take the sunglasses from his face and pocket them. Merlin looked around and huffed loudly.

"That's better," he remarked. Then he turned to the two of them, glaring with suspicion in his eyes. "Am I interrupting something?" he asked.

"No!" they both blurted out at once, then looked at one another awkwardly. Merlin rolled his eyes.

"You two are as bad as those silly squirrels," he muttered. Then he shook his head. "Now let's get going. The past won't save itself, you know."

CHAPTER TWENTY-EIGHT
ARTHUR

It was raining when Arthur, Guinevere and Merlin time travelled back to Merlin's tower. They realised this immediately, since the ceiling had so many leaks in it and all the buckets Merlin had placed to catch the water had long overflowed and flooded the floor. It took but a moment for them to be thoroughly drenched.

"Oh, dear!" Merlin exclaimed, looking over all his sopping wet books. "Thank goodness these are magically protected. Or else we'd have a disaster on our hands."

"I miss Bermuda already," Arthur moaned, looking down at his twenty-first-century garments. They were so comfortable – even when wet. He dreaded having to change back into his royal robes.

"Still, I'm glad the spell worked," Guinevere remarked, looking around the room. "I was half-afraid we'd be stuck in the future forever." She grimaced. "Not that it wasn't a nice place and all. But we have… things to do." She stared out the window, wringing her hands. Arthur wondered if she was thinking about her parents and how to find them.

"Well, I need to get back to the castle immediately," Arthur said. "Before anyone notices I'm gone." He frowned. "I wonder how long we *have* been gone, actually. Has any time passed here since we left?"

"It's tough to tell," Merlin said, "since watches have yet to be invented." He walked over to the window and peered outside. "But from the buds on the trees and the birds chirping, I'd say it's nearly spring."

"Nearly spring!" Arthur exclaimed. "But we left in the winter. It wasn't even a month after Christmas."

"Oh, dear," Merlin said. "Perhaps my spell casting is still a bit off."

"We need to get back to the castle!" Arthur cried, his heart pounding. "They must be frantic, wondering where I've been." He swallowed hard, a horrible thought occurring to him. "What if they think I'm dead? What if they've already selected a new king?"

Merlin looked at him solemnly. "That would be very bad," he said. "The number one thing to avoid when time travelling is accidentally changing history. If you're no longer king like you're meant to be, the future as we know it could spiral off into an alternate reality. Meaning everything that is meant to be, may no longer be." He paced the room, his steps eating up the distance between walls. "Oh, dear. This is all my fault. You should have just left me to rot in the future. It would have been better for everyone."

"I'd never do that," Arthur said vehemently. "You're too important to me. I'm glad we rescued you. And I'm sure we can sort everything out. We just need to get back to the castle – quickly."

"And we shall," Merlin agreed. "Just let me get packed first. Won't take a second!"

Arthur opened his mouth to tell the wizard they didn't have time for packing. But before he could get a word out, Merlin waved his wand, and the books around them came to life once again, shaking themselves off and marching towards Merlin's suitcase. Arthur had to leap aside in order not to be trampled by the parade.

"Merlin!" he cried, trying to be heard over the commotion of stomping books. "We really don't have time to—"

He was interrupted by the sound of a slamming door somewhere down below. Rushing to the window, he peered out only to see Sir Ector himself, charging up the stairs, looking sopping wet and angry. Arthur cringed. He'd almost forgotten his foster father had returned home just before they'd travelled to the future. Which was months ago, by this point.

"Quick! Hide!" Guinevere cried. "Before he sees you!"

Arthur looked around the room in a panic. "Where?" he asked.

"Behind those books!" she suggested, pointing to a towering pile in the corner that hadn't marched itself away yet. Arthur nodded and dived behind the pile, hoping it would stay put – at least for a little longer. A moment later, Guinevere joined him in the tight space.

"I say, what's going on in here? I thought I heard a ruckus!" Ector cried, barging into the room. Merlin whispered a word and the books all dropped to the floor, as if they'd never been animated at all. Ector scowled, his eyes shooting straight to Merlin.

"Marvin!" he bellowed, as usual not getting the wizard's name right. "I should have known!"

"Why, hello, Sir Ector," Merlin said gallantly. As if nothing at all was amiss. "I see you're back from London."

Ector grunted. "Of course I'm back. I've been back for two months. Ever since my fool of a son got himself arrested for treason. I tried to tell the Wart it was an honest mistake – it could have happened to anyone! – and what did he do? The lad threw me out of the castle!" He spat on the floor angrily. "Why, I raised that boy from a baby, and this is the thanks I get?"

"It's more than you deserve," Arthur muttered from behind his pile of books, soft enough so his foster father couldn't hear. Then something struck him. "But wait, I didn't throw him out of the castle," he whispered to Guin. "I mean, I definitely planned to. But I never had time to do it – before I was poisoned and you took me away."

She frowned. "That's odd. Do you think he's making it up?"

"Maybe," Arthur mused. "But to what benefit? I mean, why would Merlin care?"

Guinevere shrugged, and they turned back to the conversation. Merlin was patting Ector on the back with a comforting hand. "I'm so sorry you've had such rotten luck," he was telling the lord. "And I have no interest in adding to it now. So I'll just pick up my things and take my leave. I'll be out of your hair in no time at all."

Ector looked around the messy room, clearly dubious about the estimated time of departure.

"Using magic, of course," Merlin amended quickly.

"Oh." Ector scowled. "Well, I suppose that's all right then. Though perhaps before you take your leave, might you have a look at Kay? The boy hasn't been right in the head since the Wart freed him from prison. Not that he was a scholar to begin with, mind you. But now he seems downright dazed and confused. He keeps babbling about Wart not actually being Wart. Which of course doesn't make any sense. I'm thinking perhaps he got hit on the head a bit too hard during the fight." Ector frowned. "Though I don't remember him actually getting hit at all, now that I think about it. In fact, I still don't understand how he lost to begin with. He was doing so well…"

Arthur frowned. "Did he just say I let Kay out of prison?" he asked. "Because I definitely didn't do that!"

"No, of course not," Guin agreed, looking worried. "Maybe someone else did?"

Arthur looked up again, thankful to see Merlin ushering Ector out the door. "Let's go take a look at the boy," the wizard told the father. "It's probably nothing. He's likely just a little tired, that's all. I'm sure he's going to be just fine. Just fine indeed." He followed Ector down the stairs, closing the tower door behind him. Once they were alone, Arthur and Guinevere scrambled from their hiding spots.

Arthur ran to the window to watch Ector and Merlin approach Kay in the courtyard. "I don't understand," he murmured. "How could I have freed Kay from prison and thrown Ector out of the castle? I haven't been there in months. Maybe someone in the castle has been covering for me?"

"Covering for you," Guin replied in an uneasy voice. "Or… pretending to *be* you."

"What?" Arthur turned to her, eyebrows raised.

"You heard Sir Ector," Guin reminded him. "He said Kay keeps babbling about you not really being you." She bit her lower lip. "What if someone's pretending to be you? Someone with the power to shapeshift."

Arthur's eyes bulged from his head. "You don't think…" he began, then his voice trailed off. He was too horrified by what Guin was implying to even speak it.

"Yes," Guinevere said flatly. "You wanted to know what Madam Mim's been up to since you've been gone? Well, I think you have your answer."

CHAPTER TWENTY-NINE
GUINEVERE

Guinevere didn't consider herself a violent person. In fact, in most instances, she was very kind and gentle and good. But at the moment, it was all she could do not to punch a wall with her fist. She should have known Mim wouldn't be content to just sit around in Arthur's absence and let things play out as they were supposed to. No, she had to meddle once again.

And put herself on the throne of England.

Guin thought back to all Mim's complaints about Merlin and how he wanted the power all to himself. And yet all this time, it was *she* who had wanted the throne of England. Or maybe she hadn't planned it – maybe she suddenly decided it would be perfectly hilarious to take over, to trick everyone into thinking she was Arthur. Then she'd acted exactly the opposite of the way he would if he'd actually been there. Who knew what mischief she'd already caused in the two months she'd been in power? And who knew what was still up her sleeve?

They had to stop her. Now.

Guin sighed, frustrated. All she wanted to do was go to the Summer Country and see if what Merlin had said about her parents was true. But that would have to wait until she sorted this out. After all, it was her fault they were in this predicament to begin with – if she hadn't sneaked Arthur away from the castle, Mim would have never had the opportunity to take his place.

Her fists tightened. *Why, Mother. Why?*

"Are you all right, Guin?"

She felt Arthur come up behind her, placing a gentle hand on her back. She knew the gesture was meant to be comforting, but it only brought tears to her eyes. Arthur had been so good and kind to her from the start. If only he knew how little she deserved it. What if he learnt her true role in this thing? He'd never speak to her again.

Guin couldn't bear the thought.

"I'm just worried," she said. "What if we're too late? What if you can't get your throne back and the future spirals out of control like Merlin said? What if people are hurt? What if people die?"

"I won't let that happen," Arthur declared, sounding much braver than she'd ever heard him sound before. "We know now that I am the rightful king. And I plan to take back my throne, no matter what it takes."

He sounded so sure of himself. And for a moment, all she could think of was the boy she'd first met in the woods, who only wanted to fly away. Arthur had grown up so much since then. He'd faced his enemies and made them his friends. He'd fought a fierce battle and won – through brains instead of brawn. And he'd been willing to give it all up to travel across time and space to rescue his teacher and friend. When she looked at him now, she no longer saw a boy playing at being king, but a boy who had accepted his destiny – despite the danger it foretold.

A boy who deserved to sit on the throne.

She just hoped they weren't too late.

Merlin walked back into the tower, muttering under his breath. Guinevere looked up at him, searching his face. "What is it?" she asked.

"I'm afraid it's not good," Merlin said gravely. "According to Kay, Arthur – or someone who appears to be Arthur – is still on the throne. But he's completely changed his tune. He's refused to sign the Saxon treaty and declared them to be England's enemies, locking up their king and his men. He's raised taxes, cut food to the poor. There's massive unrest in the streets. Violence. Chaos. And it's all being done in Arthur's name."

Arthur's face paled. "This is terrible! We need to get back there. Now! Make things right. No matter what it takes."

"I agree," Merlin said. "And there's no time to waste. My poor books will have to wait a little longer, I'm afraid. This calls for faster travel – and there's no room for luggage." He waved his hands, gathering them to his side. Then he lifted his arms.

"*Higgidis… piggidis… diggidis, dundon.* Magic, carry us to London!"

And poof! They were gone.

A moment later Guinevere opened her eyes. Her lids felt heavy – as if she'd been asleep a very long time. When she blinked, clearing her vision, she looked around. "Are we here?" she asked. "Are we in London?"

Suddenly her eyes fell upon a small stone in the centre of what appeared to be a churchyard. On top of the stone sat an anvil. She scrambled to her feet, approaching it curiously.

"That was it." Arthur's voice came from behind her. "Where I pulled the sword from the stone."

She turned to watch him walk over to her and stare

down at the anvil. "It seems so long ago," he said softly. "And yet, at the same time, like yesterday."

"I still can't believe you managed to do it," Merlin remarked, coming up behind him, shaking the dust from his beard. "I only wish I had been there to see it."

"Believe me, I wish you'd been here, too," Arthur replied wryly. "Then maybe everything wouldn't have turned into such a disaster."

Merlin's face grew serious. "I know," he said softly. "And I am truly sorry for that. I let my temper get the best of me. And you didn't deserve it. You were just excited about going to a tournament. And I acted like a complete selfish buffoon." He hung his head.

Guin watched as Arthur approached his teacher, laying a hand on his arm. "It's all right," he said. "I know you were only trying to help me reach my potential. And without your teaching, I never would have lasted a day as king. So I think, maybe, we're even?" he asked, looking up at Merlin hopefully.

Merlin's face broke into a toothy smile. He reached over and pulled Arthur into a huge hug. Arthur squirmed and protested at first, but at last laughed and hugged the wizard back.

Guinevere smiled from a distance, feeling the love between the two of them, almost as if they were father and son. It made her think of Mim and their relationship. And how it could never be the same again now that she knew the truth. It hurt more than she wanted to admit.

She shook her head. There was no time for thoughts like that now. Right now they had a much more important quest: to stop Mim's mischief once and for all and get Arthur back on the throne where he belonged.

CHAPTER THIRTY
ARTHUR

Arthur stared up at the castle gates, gnawing his lower lip nervously. It was funny; for so long he'd wanted to escape these walls. Now he just wanted to get back inside. But that was easier said than done, Merlin reminded him. For if Mim really was in charge now, she wasn't going to be thrilled to see Arthur walk back through that door.

"Can't you just zap her back to her old shape?" he asked the wizard. "Make everyone see she's an imposter?"

But Merlin only shook his head. "For all her faults, Mim is a powerful wizard, and her magic is as strong as mine. I can't undo her spells. We must find another way to expose her lies to the people of Camelot."

Arthur frowned, feeling discouraged. "Well, she's not just going to admit it if we ask nicely," he countered. "And no one's going to take me at my word if she looks just like me. I'm going to have to prove I'm the real Arthur somehow." He paced back and forth, thinking hard. "But how will I do that?"

"What about the sword in the stone?" Guinevere asked suddenly.

Arthur looked up. "What about it?"

"That's how everyone knew you were king to begin with, right?" Guin reminded him. "Maybe if you pulled it again…? And Mim, well, couldn't?"

"Guin, you're a genius!" Merlin exclaimed. "That's exactly what we should do!"

"But…" Arthur scratched his head. "Couldn't Mim just magically make the sword come out of the stone on her own?"

Merlin shook his head. "The sword in the stone's magic is much older and stronger than Mim's or even mine. And just as I cannot undo Mim's spells, she cannot undo the stone's enchantment or make it work in her favour."

"Then that's what we'll do," Arthur declared, confidence rising inside of him. This could actually work. "We'll make her prove she's who says she is. And if she can't, well, then people will have to believe us."

"It's a good plan," Merlin agreed. "If you can get her to agree to go along with—"

He was interrupted by a sudden rush of people heading through the castle gates. Arthur found himself being shoved in one direction, then the next, for a moment getting separated from his friends.

"Where's everyone going?" he asked.

"It's petitioner day!" exclaimed a man rushing along with the rest. "Today's the day we get to ask the king for help."

Arthur's eyes widened. Of course! Petitioner day! The day he had once dreaded most as king. But now it could very well be the thing he needed to force Mim's hand. She'd be there in the throne room, along with half the kingdom. And if he challenged her there, in front of everyone, she couldn't very well ignore him.

"Come on," he said once he was back with his friends. "Let's go see this king!"

Guinevere took a step forwards. But to Arthur's surprise, Merlin took a step back.

"You two go ahead," the wizard said, gesturing with his hand. "I will hang behind. It might be wise not to let Mim know I'm back yet. After all, when she can't pull the sword from the stone, she's going to get angry. Very angry.

And I want to be there, in the shadows, to protect you and the people from whatever she might try to do."

"Good idea," Arthur replied, relieved at the idea of Merlin's being there to protect him. He turned to Guin. "All right. Let's do this."

•

CHAPTER THIRTY-ONE
GUINEVERE

Guinevere felt her knees trembling as if they were about to buckle under her as she and Arthur walked up to the castle's great hall. Arthur seemed so confident this plan would work. But he didn't know Mim like she did. And she was worried. Very worried.

They pushed their way inside the large room and looked around to gain their bearings. The place was packed with people, and everyone seemed to be yelling at once.

"What is happening?" Arthur asked, looking worried. "They all seem really angry."

Guinevere nodded, looking around at the agitated crowd. It felt as if a brawl could break out at any moment. "Maybe they sense something's wrong with their king?" she suggested, standing on her tiptoes to try to see over people's heads. She sank back to her heels, discouraged.

"We need to get to the front," Arthur said, "so we can see what's going on."

Guinevere nodded in agreement and began elbowing her away through the crowd. She got shoved back at least three times before she found people sympathetic enough to let her pass without much complaint. When she made it to the front of the room, she stopped short as her eyes fell upon the boy on the throne.

It was Arthur. Except, of course, not really. But it looked just like him. Same crown, same robes, same shock of blond hair from before he'd cut it. In fact, if she hadn't known any better, she would have been completely fooled. Like everyone in the room evidently was.

But then she caught something slightly off. A blush of violet at the king's ears.

Mim.

Mother.

Guinevere felt her knees wobble as her worst fears came true. She hadn't realised until that very moment how much she'd been hoping that she had been wrong – that it was someone else who had risen to take Arthur's place. But, of course, that was preposterous.

Who else had the power to shift into the body of another? It was always going to be Mim, and deep down, she had known it.

But still. Anger rose inside of her. She thought back to all those conversations she'd had with her mother. How offended Mim had acted when she talked about Arthur stealing the throne from its rightful ruler. Yet now she'd done the very same thing herself. And she didn't look the least bit sorry for it.

Merlin was right. Mim had been the one out for the throne all along. And Guinevere had all but helped her take it. Suddenly she felt so ashamed.

"Oh, my!" Arthur suddenly gasped beside her. "Is that…?"

He trailed off, but Guin followed his gaze and was horrified to see a small golden cage hanging next to the throne. Inside was a small owl with ruffled feathers.

"Poor Archimedes," Arthur whispered, his face pale. "I should have never left him here alone. With a broken wing and everything! If anything happens to him…"

"It won't," Guinevere promised, though in truth she had no idea what they could do about it. It was clear from all of this that Mim had fooled everyone with her ruse. She had the people; she had guards. She had knights. She had no reason at all to prove herself to anyone, least of all them.

"I'm going up there," Arthur declared. "The people deserve to know they're being deceived."

"Wait." On instinct, she grabbed his arm. He turned to her, puzzled. "Just... be careful. You don't want to make her angry." She swallowed hard, thinking. "Maybe... make it like a game instead," she added, an idea suddenly coming to her. "She's much more likely to go along with your challenge if she thinks it'll be amusing."

Arthur gave her an odd look, and she realised, too late, that she'd probably said too much. She wasn't supposed to know Mim. So how would she know about her love of games?

"Merlin told me that!" she added quickly.

"Right." Arthur scratched his head. "She does seem to like to play games, that's for sure. That's why she was so eager to duel Merlin. She thought it would be fun."

"Exactly!" Guinevere agreed, letting out a nervous breath. "Now go! I'll wait back here." The last thing she needed was for her mother to see her at Arthur's side.

Arthur smiled nervously at her, then pushed his way through the crowd towards the throne.

She watched as he approached Mim, squaring his shoulders and lifting his chin.

He looked so brave. And also, incredibly stupid. Did he have any notion how powerful Mim was? Sure, she acted like a giggling fool on the outside. But her true power ran deep. If she wanted to, she could cut Arthur down right then and there. And that would be the end of it.

Guinevere shuddered, unable to bear the thought of it.

Arthur's voice suddenly rang through the hall. "What is the meaning of this? Who is this imposter who sits on my throne?"

The rowdy court went silent immediately. Mim looked down at Arthur, a look of pure shock on her face. She hadn't expected to see him, that was for sure, and Guin allowed herself a moment of satisfaction to see her mother so unsettled. But then the shock cleared from Mim's face and her upper lip curled to a sneer.

"Well, well, what have we here?" she purred, looking Arthur up and down. "A little court jester come to play?" She grinned widely. "Oh, but you are so cute!" She turned to her court. "Look at how funny he's dressed!"

Guinevere winced, remembering they were still wearing their twenty-first-century clothes – why hadn't they changed? And why, oh, why, had she shorn his hair? In truth, he'd never looked less like a king.

But Arthur didn't falter. Instead, he leapt up onto the dais, turning to face the crowd. All eyes were now glued to him.

He cleared his throat. "My good people," he called out

to the crowd, "you have been deceived. This king who sits before you is an imposter. A wizard who practises sorcery. She has used this to shapeshift herself into looking like me, but I am your rightful king."

Mim started to laugh. Guin cringed as the squeaky sound echoed through the hall. It was Arthur's laugh, but at the same time, not. It sounded harsh, mocking, mean.

"Now, now," Mim protested. "Who's to say it's not the other way round?" She held up her hands in innocence. "Perhaps it is *you* who dabbles in sorcery. Perhaps it is *you*" – she pointed a finger at Arthur – "who has stolen *my* identity and is trying to trick these good people."

"Hmm," Arthur replied. "It seems we are at an impasse. Perhaps we should play a game to settle it all."

Mim raised an eyebrow, clearly intrigued despite herself. "A game?" she asked. "What sort of game?"

Arthur puffed out his chest, facing down his fake self. Guinevere held her breath.

"Isn't it obvious?" he asked. "We're going to play who can pull the sword from the stone."

CHAPTER THIRTY-TWO
ARTHUR

Arthur could hear the collective gasp from the crowd in the great hall. But he refused to turn around, keeping his eyes locked on the imposter before him, trying to read the expression on her face. For a moment he wondered if she was just planning to arrest him and throw away the key – or maybe even kill him outright – without giving him a chance to clear his name.

But instead, an amused smile slipped across her face. "That sounds fun!" she agreed with a giggle. She turned to the crowd, clapping her hands in delight. "What do you think? Shall we play this game?"

The crowd burst into nervous conversation – clearly conflicted about who was telling the truth. Once again,

Arthur would have to prove himself in front of his subjects. Fortunately, this time it wasn't a fight to the death. Just a simple task that had been no problem for him before.

"All right, then," Mim declared. "Off to the churchyard we go!"

The crowd poured out of the great hall and through the courtyard towards the old church down the road, eager to secure a good spot to watch the fun. Mim sauntered past Arthur, escorted by Arthur's own guards, throwing him a smug look as she passed.

Once she was gone, Guinevere appeared back at his side. "That was great!" she exclaimed. "Good work!"

"Thanks," he said, feeling his face flush with pride. "But that was the easy part. Now I have to go pull the sword from the stone again."

Guinevere placed a hand on his arm. "You can do this," she said. "And remember, you're not alone. You've got Merlin out there. And you have me, too."

His heart warmed at her words. He met her eyes with his own. "That means a lot," he said softly. "Thank you."

She reached out and slipped her hand into his. It was so warm, contrasting with his own, which felt half-frozen with fear. And when she squeezed it tight—

"Ahem! Are you lovebirds going to get on with saving

the realm anytime soon? I mean, don't let me interrupt or anything!"

They whirled around, startled. Archimedes hooted from his cage. Arthur's face broke out into a big grin. He turned to Guin.

"Can you free Archimedes?" he asked. "Mim's waiting for me."

She nodded. "I'll meet you in the churchyard." She smiled. "Go teach her a lesson!"

When Arthur arrived in the courtyard, he found Mim already holding court in front of the stone and anvil, along with what felt like half the kingdom standing around, watching eagerly. He felt an involuntary shiver spin down his spine.

When Mim saw Arthur, she clapped her hands excitedly. "There you are!" she exclaimed. "I was hoping you weren't going to chicken out!" She giggled. "Then the game would be over before it even began."

"Of course not," Arthur replied, trying to sound sure of himself. She certainly seemed confident. Did she know something he didn't? But no. Merlin assured him she couldn't manipulate the stone's magic. This was going to work.

"Sir Pellinore!" Mim cried. "Bring me Excalibur."

The old knight stepped through the crowd, carrying Arthur's sheathed sword. He made a great show of presenting it to both Arthurs as well as the crowd, and even Arthur saw there could be no doubt that this was his sword. It even had the little ding on it that it'd received during his fight with Kay. He watched as Sir Pellinore slid the sword into the anvil just as it had been on that fateful day. It slipped in easily, as if it were loose. But when Pellinore tugged on it once it was in place, it was stuck fast, just as before.

Arthur felt his confidence rise. This was going to work, he was sure of it.

"All right, then," Mim declared, circling the stone like a vulture to its prey. She looked much too comfortable for Arthur's comfort. "You say you can pull it out. Well, let's see you do it."

"You don't want to go first?" Arthur asked, rather surprised.

Mim giggled. "I'm feeling generous this evening. I'll let you have the first try."

Arthur pursed his lips. He wasn't sure why, but suddenly this was feeling a little like a trap. But how could it be? It was the same sword, he scolded himself, the same stone, the same anvil. Which meant it had the same magic. Magic Mim couldn't manipulate.

He stepped up to the stone. He could feel the eyes of half the kingdom on him, watching breathlessly. Even more breathlessly, he realised, than on the first day he'd done it, when the sky had opened up and a ray of beautiful light had shone down on him with the sound of angels singing in the air.

Of course, there was a lot more at stake this time.

Arthur looked out into the excited crowd, catching sight of Guinevere, who had now appeared at the back row. He gave her a questioning look, and she nodded, ever so slightly, causing him to let out a breath of relief. Archimedes was safe. And Merlin was somewhere nearby. He wasn't alone.

He turned back to the sword. This was it; the moment of the truth. He wrapped his hands around the hilt, then gave the blade a tug. Gently at first – the last time he'd done it, the sword had slid out like a knife from hot butter, and he didn't want to fall backwards from using too much force. But this time it didn't give as easily, and so he put more strength into the attempt, yanking on it with all his might.

The heavens did not open with holy light.

There was no sound of angelic music.

The sword did not budge.

The crowd gasped. Arthur felt his face turn red. He pulled a third time, but it was no different. The sword was stuck fast. He glanced over at Guinevere, who gave him a helpless gesture. What was going on here?

He tried again.

Still nothing.

A fifth time!

Nothing.

Nothing.

Nothing.

The sword – his precious sword – was stuck in the stone. Just as it had been all those years before he'd acquired it.

The crowd seemed to deflate. They'd been rooting for him, he realised. On some level they seemed to believe his claim. Which was good, but not enough, if he couldn't prove it to them.

"M-maybe something's wrong," he stammered. "Maybe it's been too long. Or the magic has gone, since it already worked once."

"Maybe," Mim said, stepping forwards. "But do you mind if I give it a try?"

"Go ahead," Arthur said, feeling deflated. He tried to remind himself of what Merlin had said about the stone's magic – Mim wouldn't be able to manipulate it with her own. But he was starting to feel less confident about that. What if Merlin was wrong? Or Mim's power was actually greater than they knew?

Mim grandly stepped up to the stone and anvil, making a great show of the whole thing by waving her arms in the air. She turned to her audience and bowed low, giggled a little as she straightened, and then turned, reached down, and dramatically wrapped her hands around the hilt. She drew in a breath, then pulled on the sword.

The heavens opened.

Light shone down.

Heavenly music started to play.

And the sword easily slipped from the stone.

Arthur watched, horrified, hardly able to believe his eyes. She'd done it. Somehow she'd done it. She'd pulled the sword from the stone as if she had been born to do it.

As if she were truly England's destined king.

Mim raised the sword above her head in triumph. A few people in the crowd began clapping hesitantly, still not quite sure what they'd just witnessed. Arthur began to back away, but he was quickly stopped by two guards.

Mim's eyes settled on him. Her lips curled to a smile.

"Seize this traitor," she told the guards. "And send him to the dungeon."

The guards made a move towards Arthur. He scrambled away, trying to put distance between them, but was stopped by the thick crowd behind him, who inadvertently prevented his escape. His eyes darted around the churchyard with desperation. Where was Merlin? Now would be a good time for the wizard to show himself. To save the day! To poof Arthur to safety.

But the wizard was nowhere to be seen. Instead, it was

Guin who suddenly burst from the crowd, her hair flying behind her and her eyes wild. "No!" she cried. "No, please!"

"Guin—" Arthur protested in panic. He didn't want her to be arrested, too.

But Guin ignored him, stopping just in front of Arthur-Mim and crossing her arms in front of her chest. She glowered at the wizard. If looks could kill, Arthur thought wildly, Mim would be nothing more than a puddle on the ground.

"This needs to stop, Mother!" Guin cried. "Now!"

Wait, what? Arthur did a double take.

Mother? Had she just said… *mother*?

Suddenly everything froze, just as it had that day in the great hall when Mim had first come to Arthur as Morgan le Fay. Everyone in the audience – every commoner, noble and guard – completely stuck in place. The only other person still moving, Arthur realised, was Guinevere.

Mim laughed heartily. As Arthur watched in horror, her disguise seemed to melt away, revealing her old wild-purple-haired self. She strode over to Guinevere. When she reached her, she patted her lovingly on the arm. "Oh, my sweet girl," she clucked. "There's no need to pretend any more. It's all over now. You can rest. You did your job, and you did it marvellously. Better than I could have ever dreamt!" She grinned, showing off crooked grey teeth. "I'm so proud of you, my dear. I can't even begin to explain."

"W-wait, what?" Arthur stammered. "What is she talking about, Guin?"

Guin stumbled backwards, almost tripping over a gravestone in the process. Mim cackled loudly, sheathing Excalibur and setting it on the ground. Then she turned to Arthur.

"Oh, my poor little sparrow. Did you think she was on your side this whole time? How adorable is that? She really is a good actress, isn't she? Those pretty, wide brown eyes. Those long lashes. That sweet smile. You'd never know in a million years she was working for me."

"No." Arthur shook his head vehemently. "I don't believe it. You turned me into a slug. She saved me."

"All part of the plan. You would have never left the castle with her otherwise. Which was quite considerate of you, by the way – just walking away like that and handing me the keys to the kingdom?" She grinned toothily. "Though you probably shouldn't have come back. Then I wouldn't have had to kill you."

Arthur looked from her to Guinevere, his heart feeling as if it were about to shatter in his chest. "Is this true?" he demanded, his voice cracking on the words. "Is Mim really your foster mother? Did you befriend me only to try to take me down?"

He waited with bated breath, his eyes locked on her,

begging her to deny it all. To call Mim a liar of the worst sort. To assure him she would never betray his trust. She cared about him. She'd kissed him on the beach. That had to mean something, right?

But instead of denying it, her face only crumpled. The light seemed to die in her deep brown eyes.

"Guinevere?" Arthur tried again, his voice hitching on her name. "Please… tell me the truth."

"I'm sorry," she blurted out. "Mim lied to me. She told me you weren't meant to be on the throne. That it was Merlin's evil plan to destroy England." She trailed off, staring at the ground. "I thought I was doing a good thing."

Arthur staggered backwards, as if he'd been struck by a blade. And maybe that would have been better. Maybe that wouldn't have hurt half as much as Guinevere's words. The girl he'd trusted. The girl he'd shared everything with. The girl he'd fallen in love with.

And she had betrayed him utterly.

"Oh, don't look so glum!" Mim scolded, wagging a finger at Arthur. "She really is quite fond of you. She told me so herself. But that makes no difference now. For I'm afraid you're not going to live long enough to ever see her again."

"What are you going to do with me?" he asked, trying not to despair. At the moment, he wasn't sure if he even cared. He'd lost his kingdom, and he'd lost Guinevere. What did he have left?

"Throw you in the dungeon, of course," Mim replied breezily. "Weren't you listening earlier? And then we're going to throw a marvellous party and execute you in front of the entire kingdom in the morning. Won't that be lovely?" She nodded to herself. "Why, we can even have that Saxon king of yours done at the same time! Two for one! That's bound to sell a lot of tickets. Especially if we serve slug soup. This kingdom is woefully short of slug soup, don't you think, darling?" she asked, slinging her arm around Guinevere. The girl shrugged her off, storming to the other side of the churchyard. Mim watched her go for a moment, then giggled again.

"Anyway, this has been fun! But I really must go. I have a kingdom to run into the ground. Toodles!"

She snapped her fingers, shifting herself back into Arthur's twin. Then, turning to the crowd, she waved her arms, unfreezing them. Her guards burst to life and charged towards Arthur.

"Take this imposter away," Mim crowed as the two men grabbed Arthur's arms, pinning them behind him. "Throw him in the dungeon where he belongs!"

CHAPTER THIRTY-THREE
GUINEVERE

"Did I mention how proud of you I am, my pet?" Mim asked after the sword and the stone performance, dragging Guin back to Arthur's chambers, where they could be alone. Once she'd shut and locked the door, she poofed back into her old purple self, walked over to a nearby chair, kicked off her boots, and placed them on the table. The sweaty shoe smell made Guinevere's stomach turn. Which was quite a feat, considering how nauseated Guin already was from what had just transpired in the churchyard.

Her mind flashed back to Arthur's face. The look of betrayal deep in his blue eyes. The way he had gazed at her – as if she were some kind of monster. But then, was he really wrong? Because of her, he was about to lose everything – including his life. What monster could do worse than that?

"This is what you were planning from the start, wasn't it, Mother?" she accused, her voice still shaky as she planted her hands on her hips. "Merlin never wanted the throne to begin with. It was you all along. You wanted the power for yourself."

"Power? Don't be silly, my pet. Since when have I ever cared about power?" Mim spit out dismissively. "I *much* prefer chaos! Sweet, beautiful chaos! And thanks to you, I have it in spades! Arthur was so stuck on his law and order, and peace, and rules, and juries of his peers – such nonsense! So boring! But now! Now everything is so pleasantly unpleasant! And who knows what fun will happen next? Something truly gruesome and grim, if we're lucky! And I'll have a front-row seat to it all." She beamed at Guin. "And I couldn't have done it without you! Why, my dear, whatever can I do to repay you? Do you want a pony? I remember when you were little, all you wanted was a cute little polka-dotted pony."

"I don't want a pony," Guinevere snapped. "I want the truth. You've been lying to me my entire life, haven't you? Not just about this, but about everything. Even my parents!"

"Your parents?" Mim's smile faltered. "What about your parents?"

Guinevere clamped her mouth shut, realising perhaps she'd said too much. The only way she could have known about her parents was through Merlin, and Mim didn't know Merlin was back. If Guin had any hope for Arthur to be saved, she had to keep it that way. The truth about her parents would have to wait – Arthur's life depended on it.

"Nothing! It doesn't matter! Just stop these games! Let Arthur be king like he's meant to be!"

Mim laughed – actually laughed. "Oh! You're so cute when you're angry!" She reached out and tweaked Guin's cheek, as if she were a baby. "But I promise you, I'm not as terrible as you seem to think. Maybe I *did* make up the whole Merlin-putting-Arthur-on-the-throne thing. But that doesn't mean he's the destined king of legends, either. Why, in fact, he's nothing more than a random boy who happened to be in the wrong place at the right time."

"What?" Guinevere frowned, suddenly uneasy. "What are you talking about? Only the rightful king could pull the sword from the stone." But even as she said the words, she wondered. Arthur *hadn't* been able to pull the sword from the stone a second time. Which meant something wasn't right.

"The *real* sword in the stone, perhaps," Mim agreed cheerfully. "But I swapped that out ages ago. After all, we couldn't just have *anyone* become king of England. It's far too important of a job." Her eyes rested on Guin, bright and shiny. She looked far too pleased with herself. "I needed someone completely unqualified. Someone I could easily control. Someone like your dear sweet Arthur." She cackled.

So that's how she'd done it. Mim couldn't overpower the magic in the stone, so she'd replaced it entirely with a stone of her own. One with her own magic at its heart.

Guin remembered how angry she'd been when Mim had first told her about Merlin's alleged trickery. So indignant that anyone would try to twist the strands of fate to their favour. But it hadn't been Merlin. It had been Mim from the start.

"I don't understand," she said, her voice quavering. "If you somehow made Arthur king in the first place, why did you want to take him down?"

"Oh." Mim's mouth dipped to a frown. "Well, that was a bit of a miscalculation, you see. I had no idea at the time Arthur was Merlin's protégé and that he would have all sorts of ridiculous ideas in his head because of it. Of course, by then, it was far too late to pick someone else, so I had to get creative."

Guinevere squeezed her hands into fists. "Creative? You tried to kill him!"

"I did nothing of the sort!" Mim blustered, looking offended. "He could have happily lived out his life as a giant slug. Slugs can live about six years, you know.

And they can have up to twenty-seven thousand teeth! Imagine all the lovely dinners you could chew up with those. Why, it would have been a quite pleasant existence for the lad, if you ask me! He should have been thanking me for the privilege!"

"Mother—"

"But evidently *you* couldn't accept that. So *you* took him away from the castle. Not me! Which left a glaring vacancy on the throne of England. I mean, what was I supposed to do if not waltz into the place and stand in for him to keep things going in his absence? In fact, no one batted an eye. Even when I ripped up that ridiculous treaty with the Saxons." She giggled, then sighed. "Of course I was worried at first that you wouldn't come back, either. I would have missed you dreadfully, you know. No one to play cards with or dance with. It would have been so sad. But now you're back! And everything is as it should be. Or will be, anyway, once we rid ourselves of that pesky little sparrow for good."

Guinevere drew in a shaky breath, her heart aching in her chest. This was all her fault. And Arthur would never forgive her for it. Why, oh, why hadn't she told him the truth about who she was from the start? Or at least once she realised her mother might be up to no good. It would have been hard for him to take, but at least the words coming from her own mouth could be seen as a confession, rather than a betrayal. Instead, she'd kept silent, too afraid of what he might think, hoping her dark secret would stay buried forever.

But secrets always came out in the end. She should have known that.

"So about that pony!" Mim added cheerfully. "Purple spots or pink?"

"I told you – I don't want a pony!" Guin shot back, her voice cracking on the words. "I don't want anything from you ever again!"

"Oh, fine!" Mim rolled her eyes. "Be glum and gloomy if you must! But I won't let you rain on my parade! I'm still your mother! And I'm grounding you until your attitude improves!"

"What?" Guinevere startled. "What do you mean, grounding me?"

Mim raised her hand in Guin's direction and muttered something under her breath. Guin felt a tug inside of her, like something was being yanked out. She clutched her stomach, confused.

"What are you doing?" she demanded.

"It's for your own good," Mim declared, standing on her tiptoes to kiss Guinevere's cheek. "Goodbye, my darling. I love you, and I'll see you soon."

And with that, she flounced towards the door, stepped out, and slammed it shut behind her.

A moment later Guin heard a loud click.

Mim had locked her in.

CHAPTER THIRTY-FOUR
GUINEVERE

Guinevere looked around the room, her heart pounding. For a moment, she felt paralysed in place. Then she sprang into action, running to the window – the same window she'd come through as a bird to rescue Arthur from life as a slug. Now her only possible escape.

Did Mim really think she could keep her here? That Guin wouldn't just shapeshift and fly away? The wizard might have won the battle, but as long as Guinevere had breath in her body, she would not concede the war. She would not let Arthur suffer or die on her account. She'd saved him twice.

Third time would have to be the charm.

She drew in a breath, reaching inside of herself to draw

up the magic she needed for a shapeshifting spell. But to her surprise, she couldn't find it. It was as if there was a well inside of her, and it had been thoroughly depleted.

Panic flooded her. No. That wasn't possible. She tried again.

Nothing.

It was then that she remembered the tug she'd felt just before Mim left. The feeling of something leaving her body. Had it been her reserves of magic? Had Mim stolen them out from under her?

And without magic, what could she do?

She looked out the window again, trying to fight the sinking sensation in her stomach. She couldn't fly, but maybe she could climb down somehow. The roof was steep, but if she took some of the blankets from the bed, she could tie them together and make a rope…

It didn't seem like a good idea. But it was the only one she had.

She ran to the bed and grabbed the blankets; she twisted each one and tied them at their ends, then snaked them out the window. The makeshift rope grew longer as she worked, but soon she was out of blankets – and the ground was still too far from the end of the rope for comfort. If she tried to jump, she'd likely break her bones.

But what choice did she have? She couldn't stay up here and simply wait around for Arthur to be killed by Mim.

Oh, Arthur, she thought. *I'm so sorry.*

She closed her eyes, trying to gather her courage. She thought of Arthur facing that wolf, deep in the woods of the Forest Sauvage. He'd been afraid, too. But he'd faced his fears. To save her.

Now it was her turn to do the same.

She opened her eyes, tied up her dress to her thighs, and started to climb out the window. But just as she was about to swing her leg over the sill, she felt a giant shove in the opposite direction, sending her barrelling back into the room.

"Argh!" she cried as she hit the floor hard, seeing stars. "What are you doing?"

A new voice rose into the room. "I should probably be asking you the same thing."

Guinevere looked up, heart stuttering. A towering shape stood silhouetted in the light streaming in from the window. For a split second, she thought it was Mim again, foiling her escape plan. But then she realised the shape was too tall, too narrow, too pointy-hatted to be her.

"Merlin!" she cried, her voice croaking with relief.

All her life, Guin had been deathly afraid of the wizard. Yet now he was the most welcome sight in the world.

She collapsed on the floor, breathing heavily and telling herself everything would be all right: Merlin was here.

Merlin stepped further into the room, looking down at her with a grumpy look in his eyes. "What in heaven's name did you think you were doing?" he demanded gruffly. "You could have fallen to your death, for goodness' sake. Not very wise, I must say."

She hung her head. "I know," she said. "But I didn't know what else to do. Mim locked me in, and I had to get out to help Arthur."

She watched as Archimedes flew through the window, hooting at her angrily. "Help Arthur?" he repeated scornfully. "Why, from what I understand, you're the reason he's in this mess to begin with! The poor lad! Why, Merlin should have left you in the twenty-first century! Or the twenty-second – which, by all accounts, is far worse!"

"Now, Archimedes," Merlin scolded. "Give the poor girl a break. We all make mistakes." He reached down and held out a hand. Guinevere took it, and he pulled her to her feet, then walked her over to a nearby chair and helped her settle into it. Waving his hand, he conjured up a steaming pot of tea, complete with a little sugar dish, on the table beside her.

Guinevere looked at the wizard gratefully. She couldn't believe she'd once thought him evil. Instead, he was kind and good. Perhaps better than she deserved.

"He's right," she said, giving Archimedes a rueful look. "I've made mistakes. I won't deny that. But you have to understand why." She sighed. "I grew up with Mim. And my whole life, she told me that *you* were the evil one. That you killed my parents and tried to kill me."

Merlin huffed. "That's the most ridiculous thing I ever heard! Whyever would I want something like that? Your parents are lovely people. Why, your mother once knitted me the nicest jumper you ever did see. And you certainly don't kill people who knit you nice jumpers."

"I suppose not," Guin agreed. "But I didn't know that at the time. And so when she told me I was England's only hope to save the realm, I thought I was doing something good and just." She hung her head. "It wasn't until I met Arthur and saw what a good person he is that I realised I might be fighting for the wrong side."

"Brilliant conclusion," Archimedes hooted. "Too bad you didn't think of it sooner."

"Now, now, Archimedes," Merlin scolded the owl again. "Let's not be rude. This girl clearly has seen the light." He peered at her with watery but sharp blue eyes. "Why, I think she cares for the boy. And I can only assume she wants to help us set things right."

"I *do* care about Arthur," Guin admitted. "And I don't want anything bad to happen to him. I also don't want anything to happen to England. I'm prepared to do whatever I can to help – even if it costs me my own life," she added bravely.

"Well, hopefully it won't come to that," Merlin replied. "But I do admire your courage. And your affection for our boy. Love is a powerful thing, you know. Perhaps the most powerful force in the universe."

Love. Guinevere startled on the word. Did she love Arthur? She wasn't even sure she understood the feeling. The only person she thought she'd ever loved before was Mim. And look how that had turned out.

But Arthur – that feeling was different. So different. Maybe it was love. Just a different sort.

"So what do we do?" she asked. "How do we rescue Arthur?"

To her surprise, Merlin shook his head. "We don't."

"What?" Guinevere cried before she could stop herself. "He's in prison. Mim's sentenced him to death for treason. He's to be killed in the morning!"

"Yes, I am well aware," Merlin said, pacing the room. "But if we simply go rescue him, we'll be right back exactly where we started. Otherwise I would have saved him in the churchyard. But it wouldn't have done any good."

"Except, of course, Arthur wouldn't be in prison," she ventured. "So, that'd be good, right?"

"Yes, yes, of course. But don't worry. It's only temporary. And I promise you, that sorceress won't be able to harm a hair on his head," Merlin assured her impatiently. "But in the meantime, we must find a way to expose Mim's treachery to the people. That's the only way to be rid of her for good."

"How do we do that?"

Archimedes hooted. "He was hoping you'd know. That's why we're here."

"Me?" She blinked, surprised.

Merlin nodded vigorously. "After all, you grew up with the woman. You know her better than anyone else. If anyone knows a weakness, it would be you."

She frowned. That made sense, of course. But what was Mim's weakness? She'd never thought about that before. Mim had always seemed so strong. So powerful.

"Is there something she cares about?" Merlin pressed. "Something that would upset her to lose. Or startle her. Or scare her, even."

"I'm… not sure," Guinevere mumbled, hating the look of disappointment that followed her words. Archimedes huffed and fluffed his feathers.

"I told you this was a mistake," he muttered.

"No!" Guin cried. "I can help. I'm sure I can. Just…" She thought hard, fast. "Why don't I go back to Mim's cottage?" she suggested, her words coming in a rush. "She might have left something there. Something we can use. She has diaries, too. She's always kept them in her room. Maybe there's some clue there."

Merlin stroked his beard. "Yes," he agreed. "That sounds very practical. Except for the fact that the cottage is quite far away. Sure, I can zap you to the Forest Sauvage, but it will take you a very long time to get back again. Time we don't have."

"Actually, it won't," Guinevere corrected. "Mim poofed our cottage to the outskirts of town just before Arthur became king. Now it's not far at all." She thought for a moment. "Do you know where the well is just outside of town? If you can get me there, I can make it the rest of the way on my own."

"I can certainly do that," Merlin agreed, looking relieved. "And while you're gone, I will go see the boy. He's got to be terrified at this point, and I don't want him to think we've abandoned him."

"And what about me?" Archimedes asked.

Merlin smiled. "Don't worry. I have an important errand for you," he told the bird. "But first, let's get our girl on her way." He waved his hand, reciting the magic words. Guinevere drew in a breath, preparing herself for another teleportation. She hoped this one wouldn't leave her with a huge headache. Still, she supposed, even that would be better than climbing down a tower holding on to nothing but blankets.

"Good luck!" Archimedes chirped just as Merlin was about to finish his spell. "Don't fail us!"

I won't, she thought as she poofed into thin air. And she meant it, too. Maybe more than anything else in her life. This was her one chance to make things right.

She wasn't about to waste it.

CHAPTER THIRTY-FIVE
ARTHUR

Arthur paced his small dungeon cell, his stomach churning with unease. He'd lost track of how long he'd been stuck here – there were no windows to give him any clues. The place smelt like overripe fruit, and there was nowhere to sit down except the cold hard floor. There wasn't even a bed, just a thin pile of straw in the corner, probably covered in fleas.

This was not good. Not good at all.

Oh, Merlin, he thought. *Where are you? Why didn't you save me like you promised?*

He'd been so sure the wizard would appear as the guards dragged him away, to make a dramatic rescue and take him somewhere safe. But the wizard never appeared. Arthur hoped nothing had happened to him.

His heart squeezed as his mind flashed back to the scene in the churchyard. The moment he hadn't been able to get out of his head. When he'd learnt the truth about Guin and her mother. What she'd been sent to do, under the guise of friendship.

She hadn't even tried to deny it.

His stomach heaved. He was close to throwing up, his mind torturing him with the memory of that Bermuda beach in the future, of Guin's lips brushing against his and him feeling as if he would live forever.

But no. It had all been a lie. Every sweet look, every embrace. A vile lie to help take him down so an evil wizard could ascend the throne in his place.

So Mim could pull the sword from the stone.

How had she done it? There was only one way he could think of: she had to have replaced the real stone with her own. One that her magic could control. But how had she known to do it in time for the challenge? And why did it appear exactly as it had the day he'd pulled out the sword the first time?

Not that it mattered how she'd done it. Just that she had.

Leaving Arthur looking like a liar in front of the kingdom.

He sank to the ground, no longer caring about the cold floor. He scrubbed his face with his hands. "What am I to do?" he wailed.

"Who's there?" asked a gruff voice from the next cell. Arthur lifted his head blearily. It sounded vaguely familiar.

"It's me, Arthur," he said. "Who are you?"

"Arthur?" Suddenly there was a man on the other side of the bars. Arthur gasped to realise it was none other than Baldomar, the Saxon king. "Why are you down here with the rest of us?" he scoffed, his voice filled with scorn. "Aren't you busy breaking your word and treaties?"

"That wasn't me," Arthur cried. "I'd never do that." He sighed. "It's kind of a long story. Let's just say I might have won the battle with Kay, but I have lost the war for my crown."

"As have I, lad," King Baldomar replied, pacing his small cell. "I'm told they're to execute me tomorrow. Which is fine, I suppose. I don't want to go home anyway. They'd never accept me after how I've failed them."

"You didn't fail them," Arthur protested. "I did." He closed his eyes. "And I'm sorry."

"So that's it?" King Baldomar asked. "You're sorry? You're done? You're content to die like me tomorrow?"

"No, of course not," Arthur said, feeling suddenly ashamed. He scrambled to his feet. "I don't plan to die," he assured him. "Merlin will save me." He paused, then added, "He will save *us*."

"Merlin? Is he one of your knights?"

"He's a wizard, actually. And very powerful," came a new voice from behind Arthur. Arthur whirled around to find a man dressed in ragged beggar's robes, stooped over a cane. Arthur frowned, confused. Then he caught a flash of sparkling blue under the robe's hood: eyes he'd recognise anywhere.

He ran to the front of his cell, grasping the bars with his hands. "Merlin!" he cried. "Where have you been?"

"Shh!" the wizard scolded. "Do you want to wake the whole prison? I'm in disguise, in case you didn't notice."

"Sorry," Arthur whispered. But his heart soared. Finally, he was here! Arthur had never been so happy to see someone in his entire life. "You've come to rescue us, right?" he asked, gesturing to the Saxon king. His heart beat fast.

But to his surprise, the wizard only shook his head.

Arthur's heart stuttered. "You mean you can only rescue *me*?" he asked, tossing an apologetic look at the Saxon king.

"Actually, I can't rescue anyone. At least not at the moment."

"What?" Arthur let go of the bars. "What do you mean

you can't rescue anyone? Turn me into a mouse, like you did in Bermuda! Or a squirrel or a bird, even! Just something small enough to let me slip through these bars and escape. It'll be easy!" he added, hating the desperation he heard in his voice. "Just use your magic."

"Sorry. I suppose I misspoke," Merlin said, clearing his throat. "Yes, I *could* stage a magical rescue – I certainly have the powers to do so. But I'm choosing not to."

"*This* is your big hero?" The Saxon king raised an eyebrow.

"I don't understand," Arthur said, ignoring him. "Don't you care that I'm about to die?"

"Of course I do!" Merlin huffed, looking a bit offended. "And I'd never let anything happen to you – you must know that. You just need to have a little patience. After all, a magical rescue now will solve nothing. You'll just be arrested again, and we'll be back where we started. Even if you did manage to escape somehow, you'd never be able to take back the throne. Which means Mim would remain in power – and that would be a disaster of epic proportions. No." Merlin shook his head, his beard waving from side to side. "We must be smart about this. We can't act rashly. The magic will help when the time is right – and no sooner."

Arthur took a step backwards, feeling defeated. He didn't

want to admit Merlin was right, but his words made an unfortunate amount of sense.

"So what's the plan?" he asked.

"Well," Merlin said, "first we need Guinevere to return. And then—"

"Guinevere?" Arthur interrupted. "You can't trust her! She betrayed me! She was on Mim's side from the start."

"From the start, yes," Merlin agreed amicably. "But I have reason to believe she's changed."

"Bah," Arthur spit out, pacing his cell. He didn't want to admit to Merlin how much Guinevere had hurt him. He was sure the wizard could never understand. "I don't want her help!"

"If you want to live, you do," Merlin scolded. "Didn't you learn anything from our lesson?"

Arthur sighed, leaning against the side of his cell, the fight going out of him. "Which one?" he asked, feeling exhausted.

Merlin rolled his eyes. "The one about love, of course! How love is the most powerful force on earth."

"Love?" Arthur glanced over at the wizard, his heart thudding. "What about love?"

Even as he asked, his mind flashed back to the lesson in question: the time Merlin had turned them into squirrels, and he'd met a red-headed girl squirrel who'd started chasing him around the tree. At first, he'd found her incredibly irritating. But in the end, she'd saved his life.

Because she loved him.

That love business is a powerful thing, Merlin had said.

Arthur's head shot up. "Does… Guinevere love me?" he asked, his voice hoarse.

Merlin burst out laughing. "Of course she does, silly boy! You'd have to be blind not to see it."

"Wow," he said, feeling his head spin. "I had no idea."

"Guinevere made some mistakes, yes. But she's always had good intentions. And she truly does want to help. Which is lucky for us, since she's the only one in the right position to do so." He shook his head.

Arthur sighed. "This is all such a mess. Sometimes I wish I never pulled the sword from the stone to begin with. Then none of this would have happened."

"And then some clod like Kay would have been our king after the tournament," Merlin reminded him. "That wouldn't have been ideal, either, if you think about it." He brushed a spider off his beard. "If only we had democracy. But I suppose that won't be introduced here for hundreds of years."

"De-mah-cracy?" Arthur repeated doubtfully. "What's that?"

"Oh." Merlin waved a hand. "It's a government they have in the future. People get to choose their leaders by voting for them. It's more civilised than a tournament. And much smarter than just letting someone pull a blade from a stone."

Arthur considered this for a moment. "That does sound—"

But his words were interrupted by the banging of a door. The guards were on their way back. Merlin waved a hand.

"I have to go! I'll see you tomorrow. And be ready for anything!"

And with that, he poofed out of the room, leaving only a cloud of smoke behind. A moment later, the guards stepped into the room, looking around suspiciously.

"I thought I heard talking," one of them said.

"Yes, I was speaking to my friend King Baldomar," Arthur assured them.

"We were having a lovely conversation on the joys of love," the king added cheerfully. He beamed at the guards. "Has either of you two ever been in love?"

The guards looked at one another and grunted, then stormed out of the room again. Arthur glanced over at King Baldomar and smiled. He smiled back.

"You think this plan of Merlin's will work?" Baldomar asked.

"I hope so," Arthur replied. "Because it's the only chance we've got."

CHAPTER THIRTY-SIX
GUINEVERE

Guinevere looked around. Her head was spinning, and she felt a little sick to her stomach. But she was no longer trapped in a tower, so there was that. Merlin's magic had worked. She was at the well, not too far from her mother's cottage.

Her eyes fell upon the stone well in question, and she felt her heart ache a little. She thought back to the last time she'd drawn water from this well, when she'd been talking to a very nice boy she'd just met about becoming a bird. If only she'd known at that moment all that was in store for the two of them. She wondered if she wouldn't have just turned them both into birds right then and there and convinced Arthur to fly away forever.

Oh, Arthur, she thought. *I hope someday you can forgive me.*

She shook her head. There was no time for these thoughts. Arthur was depending on her, and she couldn't let him down. She took off down the path, fast as her legs would carry her, until she arrived at the cottage and burst through the door as she had so often done in the past, when she'd greet her mother with a cheery smile. Not a care in the world.

Of course, today, Mim was not at her favourite table, playing her favourite game of cards. The cards were still there, but they were covered in a thick layer of dust. So was everything else in the place. It was clear Mim hadn't been here in months. But then, why would she come back to these humble surroundings? She had a castle now. She'd stolen a kingdom.

Guin looked around the cottage, feeling an unexpected ache in her throat. Memories came flooding back, uninvited, of all the nights she'd spent playing games at the same table, laughing as Mim would try to use magic to cheat. Or the times they'd clear the table away to create a dance floor. Or curl up by the fire and tell stories. The two of them against the world.

But it had been nothing more than a lie.

Guin shook her head. She couldn't think of that now. It hurt too much and would only prove a distraction.

And she couldn't afford to be distracted – not while Arthur was in danger.

She forced herself to turn away from their game table and all the memories it contained. Instead, she headed back to Mim's bedroom, where she kept her diaries hidden away. Mim had never liked Guin coming back to her room, saying she needed her private space. But there was no one to stop Guin now.

The bedroom was messy and also covered in dust. There were bookcases rising high, not unlike Merlin's in his tower, filled with books and vials and beakers, potions and herbs. Guin supposed whether you were a bad wizard or a good one, you used the same supplies.

She located the shelf with the diaries easily enough, grabbing one at random and paging through it. The book was filled with rants and raves and prophecies and recipes for disturbing-sounding diseases, all scrawled in messy handwriting across the pages without regard for margins. There were drawings, too: sick and twisted figures and animals with too many heads or legs.

Guin set the book down, feeling sick to her stomach. How had she not seen the signs? How had she not known her mother's mind? Mim had always been a bit odd, almost childlike in her naughty behaviour. But in a harmless, fun way. Guinevere had no idea how deep her foster mother's madness truly ran.

She didn't want to read any more, but she knew she had no choice. Arthur needed her to find something – anything – to help him. And so she forced herself to pick up another book, then another. The diaries were not filed by date, and even inside, they were not always in any obvious order. There were scraps of spells, purple doodles, bad poetry. But here and there she found actual entries – some of them distinctly about her.

One caused her breath to catch in her throat.

> *Those fools! They have no idea what they've lost. She is a treasure. A true princess of the Summer Country, born of fae blood with all the gifts it entails. And now she is mine! All mine – to mould as I wish. Why, she will become the most powerful wizard in the world under my tutelage.*

Guinevere drew in a breath. And there it was. The proof she'd been dreading all along. Mim had stolen her away, just as Merlin said. She had purposely taken Guin from a loving family, making them think she was dead. All for her own selfish purposes.

Anger rose inside of her, her blood feeling as if it were boiling under her skin. She thought of all the stories she'd been told. Mim always played the role of hero, defeating Merlin and saving Guin's life.

It was too much. Far too much. All she wanted to do was collapse into tears. To surrender to the grief and curl into bed and fall into a deep sleep and never wake up. But instead she forced herself to open yet another book. Turn to yet another page. And another...

Guinevere hurt her arm today, falling from a tree. She screamed so loudly, I thought at first she had broken her neck! I was so worried...

Guinevere keeps asking to go to town with me. She wants to meet other children her own age. But of course I can't risk it – what if someone recognised her? They'd try to take her away from me forever! Maybe I can conjure up some magical children for her to play with...

Guinevere continues to be afraid of magic. I don't understand it. She would be the most amazing wizard if she just gave it a try. But I won't try to push her too much. She has to want it.

Page after page about Guin. But little she could use to help Arthur. In fact, Mim spoke practically nothing of herself as she rambled on about her daughter. She didn't reveal any weaknesses. She didn't confess any fears. In fact, Mim didn't seem to care about anything at all.

Well, except me, Guin supposed, finding yet another entry. Somehow, despite the sick and twisted origin of their relationship, Mim *did* seem to care about her.

She turned to the last page of the diary.

I can't believe it. I sent Guinevere in to help me get Arthur off the throne and what has she done? She's gone and fallen in love with the boy! In fact, she's sided with him and that blasted Merlin, over her dear sweet mother. After all we've been through together. After all I sacrificed for her. Doesn't that mean anything to her at all? What happened to me and her against the world?

Guin bit her lower lip, her mind suddenly churning. This was it. This was exactly it. Her mother's one weakness. The one thing that might be strong enough to take her down.

But would it work?

She set down the book and rose to her feet. She had to find Merlin. *Now.*

CHAPTER THIRTY-SEVEN
ARTHUR

Arthur awoke in his cell the next morning, his muscles aching from sleeping on the small, flea-ridden pile of hay the dungeon considered a bed. He hadn't slept well, to say the least, though it turned out the cold, hard stone floor of his cell had been the least of his problems. Rather, it was his mind that had kept him awake, refusing to settle, replaying over and over what was meant to happen that day.

Namely, his execution.

He'd tried to stay optimistic. Merlin had sworn he had a plan – and Arthur did believe him. The problem was, that plan appeared to hinge largely on the girl responsible for his being in this situation in the first place. Merlin seemed to think Guinevere had changed, but what if she was still playing her games – still secretly on Mim's side? Wouldn't that be the best trick of all? To convince them that she would help save Arthur, only to undermine them completely and carry out her mother's wishes in the end?

But no, Merlin had insisted she was on their side now. That she had been deceived, but now she knew the truth. That she loved Arthur, and she would do whatever it took to keep him safe.

Arthur wanted to believe it. In fact, there was nothing he wanted to believe more. Because, he realised, he loved her, too. Her smile, her laugh, the way her brown eyes sparkled. Surely all that couldn't have been faked, right? If so, she was the best actor of them all.

And Arthur, the biggest fool.

The jailer approached his cell, rapping on the bars with a metal pole. "Get up, Your Majesty," he jeered. "It's time." Then he approached the Saxon king in the next cell. "You too, barbarian."

Arthur rose to his feet, feeling his heartbeat quicken. He stole a glance at King Baldomar, who shrugged and gave him a hopeful look. The jailer unlocked the cell doors and opened them wide. Four soldiers stepped up behind him, ready to escort their prisoners aboveground.

To their awaiting deaths.

They were chained together, then led upstairs, through

the castle keep, and into the courtyard outside. A stage had been set up since Arthur had last walked through it, and on top were matching pyres of wood.

A crowd had already gathered around the stage, watching the scene with nervous eyes. He could tell they were still unsure about what was going on. And they didn't like it one bit. Arthur even noted Mistress Mabel near the back, cradling Helen of Troy. When she caught sight of him, she gave him a worried look, her face torn with confusion.

The guards roughly led him onto the stage and tied him to the pile of sticks. He glanced over at King Baldomar, who was not faring much better on his pyre. The king wore a look of grim determination, showing not even a hint of fear. Arthur had no idea what his own face looked like at the moment, but he could guess it wasn't so noble or brave. Though who could blame him? He wasn't a warrior, used to hard battles like the king. He was a just a boy.

A boy who would soon be dead if Merlin and Guinevere didn't come through.

The crowd hushed as Mim stepped out from the castle far above, standing high on a balcony, overlooking the scene below. She was wearing robes of purple with ermine trim and a crown that she must have commissioned herself – for it fit her Arthur-shaped head perfectly. She surveyed the courtyard, her gaze roving over Arthur's subjects, a mischievous look in her eyes. She was enjoying the spectacle, that was for sure.

Arthur, meanwhile, searched the crowd, looking for Merlin. Or Archimedes. Or Guinevere, even. Someone – anyone – to give him a hint that this grand rescue was actually about to happen. But he saw no familiar faces at all. Where were they? Were they hiding nearby? Did they have a plan?

"Good morning, my lovelies," Mim called out from her balcony in a perfect replica of Arthur's voice. Though somehow she made it sound stronger and more in control than his typically childish squeaks. "So nice to see you up so early. Are you ready to watch us execute two traitors who conspired against England and planned to turn it over to our enemies?" She clapped her hands in glee. "Won't that be so much fun?"

Arthur could see King Baldomar roll his eyes at this. He couldn't blame him. The bigger question was, how could the crowd actually believe this was him? He'd never talk like that!

And she wasn't finished, either. "This naughty boy," she added, gesturing to Arthur below, "is accused of using sorcery to take on my appearance and try to trick you into believing he was me. But now we know the truth.

The sword in the stone proved it once again in front of everyone, revealing his deception!"

King Baldomar scowled at the crowd. "This boy here in front of you has more strength of character in his little finger than the lot of you do together. And you are all fools if you need a silly sword pulled from a stone to see his worth."

Arthur felt a swell of pride at the king's words. Not that they would do any good, but it was nice to hear them, anyway. And Baldomar was right, too, he realised. Whether the sword in the stone was a true miracle or just a trick, it should not be the only benchmark to one becoming king. A king should have to earn his place by his actions and the love of his people, not through some silly divine intervention that could be easily falsified by magic.

He scanned the crowd again, biting his lower lip. Speaking of magic, where was Merlin? He was certainly taking his time. Whatever rescue he had planned, he'd better hurry up about it, or there would be no one left to rescue.

"Kill them!" cried someone in the crowd. "Light them up!"

Mim smiled like a cat who had just eaten a mouse. "Very well," she said. "If you insist." She clapped her hands. A moment later, a man stepped onto the stage, wearing an executioner's hood to hide his face. He carried a lit torch.

Arthur cringed as he stepped closer to the two pyres. Whom would he light up first? Arthur didn't exactly want to volunteer for the honour – but he also wasn't eager for a front-row ticket to his new friend's murder.

He turned to the crowd. "Please!" he begged. "You're being deceived. Even if you don't care to save my life, please try to save your own. She will tear England apart if you let her. Don't be fooled by her treachery."

Mim yawned. "This is boring," she jeered. "Let's get on with the show!" She motioned to the executioner. He stepped closer to the pyres. The smoke from his torch tickled Arthur's nose, and he fought the urge to sneeze. He didn't have much time left.

Come on, Merlin!

"Wait!" A voice rang out from the crowd. For a second, Arthur thought it must be Merlin. But instead, it was Guinevere who stepped out from the throng. She scrambled up onto the stage, her face filled with defiance and not a hint of fear.

Arthur looked up towards Mim, just in time to see her face turn white. "What are you doing?" she demanded. "I mean – who is this girl?" she corrected quickly. "Get her off the stage!"

"You know very well who I am," Guinevere replied, planting her hands on her hips. "I am the girl who conspired with this boy to take you down. I am here now to turn myself in. I am as guilty as they are and should be made to pay for my crimes in the same manner."

"Guin!" Arthur cried, horrified. "What are you doing?"

But Guin ignored him and marched over to the pyre. She climbed up onto it, behind Arthur, and pressed her back against the wood. The crowd rumbled nervously, not sure what was going on. Mim's face had turned a peculiar shade of purple. She raised her hands and flung them out towards the audience. For a moment, everyone froze in place. But then, just as quickly, they stuttered to life again. As if the spell had fizzled.

Or someone had broken it.

Arthur gasped. Was Merlin here?

Mim scowled. She tried to freeze the crowd again. But they unfroze just as easily. A hum began to rise from the courtyard. The people were starting to catch on that something was happening to them, and they didn't like it.

The executioner stepped up to the pyre, raising his torch.

"No!" Mim cried. "Stop! I order you to stop!"

"Goodbye, Mother," Guinevere said simply, meeting

her mother's eyes with her own. "I hope this has been fun for you. That's what you wanted, right? A little fun?"

"Guinevere! Step away from there! Stop it – you monster – don't burn her!"

The executioner ignored her, lowering his torch. As the flames licked at the wood, his cloak slipped a bit from his face. Arthur gasped.

It was Merlin!

"No!" Mim's voice took on a desperate tone. She waved her hands at the pyre, but whatever magic she was trying to do clearly wasn't working against Merlin's own. "Stop this! Now!"

Smoke began to rise in the air. Guin started to cough. Arthur's eyes stung. Whatever was supposed to happen had better happen soon, or—

"ROAR!"

Arthur looked up, squinting to see through the smoke. When his eyes fell to the balcony, he realised the fake King Arthur had disappeared.

And in his place? A giant purple dragon.

CHAPTER THIRTY-EIGHT
GUINEVERE

The crowd gasped, their eyes on the dragon. Guinevere smiled to herself even as tears slipped down her cheeks from the smoky air. It had worked! Mim had taken the bait, as Guinevere had hoped she would. To save Guinevere – the one thing she cared about in this world – she had given herself away.

A moment later, Guin found herself flying through the air, having been scooped up in Mim's new claws. The dragon deposited her safely on the balcony above, then peered at her with angry eyes.

"Why would you do that?" she asked, her voice filled with confusion and hurt. For a moment, Guin almost felt bad. But then she looked down at the scene below, reminding herself what this woman had done.

"Because, Mother, this isn't right. This isn't fun and games any more. This is someone's life. And maybe you don't care about Arthur. But I do. I care about him. And if you ever cared at all about me, you'll stop this game right now." She swallowed hard. "If you do, I'll ask Arthur to show mercy."

For a moment, Mim said nothing. And Guin dared to hope that maybe, on some level, she'd agree. But then her gaze dropped to the scene below – Merlin had freed Arthur and the Saxon king from their pyres and was now directing the people to pass buckets of water up to the stage to put out the fires.

Mim's dragon face twisted in rage. "No!" she growled. "Because then that cheating wizard will win again. I cannot stand for that! Not after the last time."

"Mother," Guin pleaded. "Who cares about—"

But she was too late. Mim turned on the spot – graceful, actually, for her gigantean size. Then, as Guinevere watched in horror, she dive-bombed towards the ground below, releasing purple flames from her mouth.

"Arthur!" Guinevere called in panic. "Look out!"

Arthur looked up just in time to see the flames barrelling towards him. He dived to the left, but it wasn't enough to avoid the fire. At the last instant, Merlin leapt in front of him, shapeshifting into a giant salamander and shielding his pupil. The flames bounced harmlessly off his slimy back, causing Mim to roar again in fury. Guinevere gripped the railing of the balcony, her knuckles turning white. She wanted to help, but what could she do from up here? Her mother wasn't just going to give up without a fight.

It was then that she noticed the sword, Excalibur – the one Arthur had been wearing the day they'd met. The one he'd pulled from the stone. Mim must have left it behind when she shapeshifted into a dragon, which gave Guinevere an idea.

It might have all been a trick – but it was a real sword. Maybe it would still be of some use.

"Arthur!" she called down to him. As he looked up, she tossed the sword off the balcony. He ran to catch it, grabbing it easily as it fell to the earth. Then he ripped it from its sheath just as Mim dived towards him for another attack. As Guin watched, breathless, he launched Excalibur at the dragon with all his might. The throw was a bit wobbly, but it did the trick, knocking Madam Mim backwards with its force and breaking her spell.

Mim screamed, falling out of her shapeshifted form. She crashed to the ground, her old purple-haired body tumbling over itself three times before settling. Before she could sit up on her own, King Baldomar stalked over to her, grabbed her by the scruff of the neck, and yanked her to her feet.

Merlin turned to the crowd.

"As you can see, this is not your King Arthur," he announced, perhaps unnecessarily, as it was pretty obvious at this point. "May I introduce you to Madam Mim. She's the one who's the true traitor to the realm."

The crowd booed loudly, looking relieved to finally have some evidence in Arthur's favour. A few threw pieces of rotted fruit at Mim's head. Mim glowered at Merlin as apple juice streamed down her rosy cheeks.

"I was just having some fun," she muttered.

"Your days of *fun* are over, sorceress," came a new voice. "I shall personally see to that."

Guinevere's eyes shifted to the crowd, trying to find the source of the voice. A moment later, a strange woman pushed her way through the throng and stepped up onto the stage. She was dressed in silver robes, and her hair fell down her back in tangles of golden curls. She looked strangely familiar, though Guin was also pretty sure she'd never seen her before.

At least not for a very, very long time.

"You, madam, are under arrest for kidnapping a royal princess of the Summer Country," the woman stated.

She clapped her hands, and a squadron of guards appeared in line behind her. But she did not take her eyes off Mim. "You will be tried for treason and be made to answer for your crimes against my country." She turned to King Baldomar. "And for those against yours, as well, sir, if you agree."

The Saxon king bowed his head in her direction. "I thank you for that. Any allies of Arthur's are allies of ours."

"Indeed," Arthur said, patting the king on the back. "We are all in agreement on this matter. Now go and free your men from the dungeons. They have suffered enough."

King Baldomar gave him a grateful look and headed towards the dungeons. Guinevere watched him go for a moment, then turned back to the woman standing before her. She felt her knees wobble. She stared at the woman, tears streaming down her cheeks. "Mother?" she called out in a hesitant voice. "Is that… you?"

The woman's eyes lifted to the balcony. Her jaw dropped. Her hands trembled.

"Guinevere?" She said it as a whisper, but Guin could hear her as well as if she'd been shouting. "Oh, my darling girl!"

Suddenly, Guin felt herself floating; Merlin had created a magical bubble that picked her up and pulled her gently to the ground. Her feet had barely touched down when she found herself running towards her mother, throwing her arms around her, and squeezing her tight. Her mother squeezed her back just as hard. And Guin felt for a moment as if her heart would burst.

"Oh, sweet girl," her mother murmured, stroking her hair. "I'm so sorry for all you've been through. When Archimedes came and told me, I almost couldn't believe it." She shook her head. "All these years… I thought you were dead."

"I thought you were, too," Guin sniffled. "I—"

"Guinevere!" Mim's voice cut through the air like a knife. Guin turned to see the old wizard on her knees, her hands tied behind her back, surrounded by guards. She gave Guin a pleading look.

"Guinevere," she moaned. "Don't let them do this to me!"

Guinevere took a step towards her, looking down at her with steely eyes. She wanted to be angry, furious at what this woman had done. Instead, she just felt horribly sad.

"Please! Don't turn your back on me now!" Mim begged. "It's you and me against the world, remember?"

"There was a time I believed that," Guinevere said softly. "But it was never really true, was it? You were always only out for yourself and I was just your useful pawn. You claim you care about me – yet you stole my entire life away. How can I forgive you for something like that?"

Her voice choked on the words. Mim had been everything to her for so long. But everything had been a lie from the start. Yet another stupid game. With the highest stakes of all.

Mim's face crumbled. Fat tears slid down her cheeks. Guinevere couldn't remember a time she looked so pathetic. So weak. Even when she'd had that dreaded disease, she'd had a spark left in her eyes. Now Guin saw nothing at all.

Then Mim scowled at her, her bravado seeming to return. "You stupid girl!" she growled. "You never were any fun!" She started laughing hysterically. "Not any fun at all!" She kept giggling as the guards began to drag her away.

Guinevere sighed. "Maybe not," she murmured, half to herself. "But at least now I know who I am. And where I'm meant to be."

CHAPTER THIRTY-NINE
ARTHUR

"How do you feel?" Merlin asked as Arthur shoved a big hunk of meat into his mouth at the dining table about an hour later. He couldn't remember the last time he'd had a proper meal. Luckily, the castle cook, Mistress McCready, had been more than happy to throw out all the slug soup Mim had asked her to make and whip up a hearty meal fit for a king.

"Much better now," Arthur said after swallowing down his bite. Merlin wasn't a fan of people speaking with their mouths full. Evidently it was considered 'rude' in the future. "Now that I've had a…" He paused, trying to remember. "What was that waterfall thing you rigged up so I could wash indoors?"

"A shower," Merlin replied with a smile. "A truly remarkable invention of the future."

"Agreed," Arthur said. "I might even be willing to take one of those twice a year."

Merlin sighed. "Or twice a week?" he tried.

"Let's not be ridiculous," Arthur teased. Then he sobered. "So is everything all right? Have they taken Mim away?"

"Guinevere's people left about an hour ago," Merlin said. "With Mim as their… invited guest. Let's just say I don't think we'll have to deal with her for the foreseeable future."

"Thank goodness for that," Arthur declared. "I've had enough purple for a lifetime, thank you very much."

"Agreed," Merlin said. "I'm about ready for things to go back to a nice, boring old—"

He was interrupted by a door opening at the far end of the hall. Arthur looked up to see none other than Guin stepping through, looking at him hesitantly. She was wearing a pale blue silk dress much in the style of her mother's – the proper attire of a princess, he supposed. He just hoped it wasn't too itchy.

"Guinevere," he said, his voice hitching on her name.

"Arthur…"

Merlin raised his eyebrows. Then, without a word, he

snapped his fingers and poofed away in a cloud of smoke. Arthur couldn't help a small smile. The wizard knew when it was time to make an exit.

Guinevere stepped up to the table. Her eyes lowered to the ground. "Hello," she said in a soft voice.

"Hello," he returned, feeling nervous all of a sudden. "I thought maybe you had left with your mother."

She shook her head. "I told her I'd join her soon. But I had some… unfinished business first." Her cheeks turned bright red. "Oh, Arthur," she murmured, looking up at him, her big brown eyes meeting his. He felt his heart pang at the look on her face. "I'm so sorry."

Arthur rose from the table and walked around it until they were face to face. Then he reached out, grabbed her hands, and pulled her closer to him. He threw his arms around her and squeezed her tight. She was stiff at first, but eventually seemed to melt into his embrace. He pulled away and smiled at her.

"Thank you," he said simply.

She shook her head, dropping her gaze. "You shouldn't thank me. This is all my—"

He stopped her words with a kiss, pressing his lips against hers. She reacted with shock at first, then kissed him back. Softly, sweetly. It was perhaps the best moment in the world.

Vanquishing evil was amazing. But kissing Guinevere – well, that was something else entirely.

"You did nothing wrong," he told her when they parted. "You were lied to. Deceived. But when you learnt the truth, you tried to make things better. You *did* make things better! I wouldn't be alive if it wasn't for you. You're a hero, Guin. As much a hero as any knight of the round table."

Her cheeks coloured, and a small smile slipped across her mouth. "I am rather heroic, aren't I?" she joked. Arthur laughed and hugged her again. At that moment, he didn't want to ever let her go.

When they did eventually pull apart, Guinevere gazed upon him with loving eyes. "So how does it feel to be king again?" she asked.

Arthur pressed his lips together. "Funny you should ask."

She cocked her head in question. "What do you mean?"

"I've been doing a lot of thinking," he confessed. "And Mim and even Kay were actually right about one thing. Why should we let some magic sword decide who should be king? The people deserve to choose the ruler they want. Like they do in the twenty-first century." He tapped his head, trying to remember the word. "Merlin called it a democracy. Where people vote for their leaders."

"And you want people to do that?"

"Yes," Arthur said, the idea growing stronger as he thought about it. "We will hold a vote. And every man, woman and child of London will be able to choose the leader they want. Then whoever gets the most votes will be king. Or queen," he added hastily, catching Guin's look.

She smiled at him. "That sounds great, Arthur," she said. "And I know just who will have my vote."

CHAPTER FORTY
ARTHUR

Two Weeks Later

The sun was shining high in the sky by the time Arthur awoke. He'd been up long into the night putting the finishing touches on the voting booths he and Merlin had created. He hadn't realised how exhausted he was until his head hit the pillow and he passed out immediately. And he didn't wake up until he felt Merlin shake him.

"Come on, boy! Are you going to sleep all day?" the wizard grumped, looking displeased. "You have an election to run!"

Arthur stretched his hands over his head, no longer tired. An election! He'd almost forgotten about that!

"Has anyone cast a ballot?" he asked, trying to remember the terms he'd gone over with his teacher.

"Has anyone cast a ballot?" Merlin looked at him incredulously. "You might as well ask me if anyone has not cast a ballot! Half the kingdom has turned out for this election! And they all seem extremely eager to choose their next ruler."

"I wonder who it will end up being," Arthur mused, slipping out of bed and grabbing a tunic and a pair of tights from his wardrobe. "Most likely one of those fancy knights. Sir Morien, Sir Gawain – he's very popular with the people. Maybe even Sir Pellinore – he's old, but smart. Just hopefully not Kay." He made a face. "Surely the people are smarter than that, right?"

Merlin smiled mysteriously. "I guess we'll have to wait and see…" he said.

Arthur nodded. But deep inside he was still nervous about the whole thing. After all, leaving the kingdom's leadership up to the people had never been done before. Who knew what would come of it?

He thought back to when he'd introduced the idea to the people.

"We need to find a proper English king," he'd told them. "Not from some perceived destiny or a jousting tournament. The king needs to be fair and wise and true to his people. He needs to want what's best for them, not just glory for himself. He needs to understand that might does not always equal right. The biggest sword does not give you the right to rule. Instead, we need the biggest heart."

"So who are you appointing?" a woman from the crowd had asked. "Who's to be our next king?"

"We will all decide that together," Arthur declared.

The crowd went wild with this idea. Of course they'd never heard anything like it. *Thank you, twenty-first century,* Arthur thought with a small smile. *Thank you, Merlin.*

They'd spent the next two weeks getting ready for the vote. Merlin was a great help, poofing himself from town to town, creating magical voting booths that would tally up their own results and send them straight to London. Meanwhile Archimedes worked to educate the people on how to use letters to spell out their favourite candidate's name – to help those who could not read or write themselves. Arthur took a few lessons himself – so he could recognise the winner's name when it came time for him to give the results. Guinevere helped with this and promised when the vote was all over she would teach him to read properly.

Once dressed, he headed out of his chambers with Merlin and down the stairs to the great hall. There, Guinevere and Archimedes were waiting for them.

Guinevere had dressed in the same simple yet elegant blue dress she'd worn to the Saxon banquet, and her hair was done up in a new set of complicated braids. She smiled as she saw Arthur, stepping up to give him a hug. He hugged her back, his heart full.

"I voted!" she told him, pulling away from the embrace. "It was very exciting."

"I suppose I need to vote myself," he said thoughtfully. "Who did you vote for?"

She smiled mysteriously. "You're not supposed to tell who you voted for. Merlin said."

"Oh." He blushed. "Well, then I guess I won't tell you who *I'm* voting for, either."

Guinevere stuck her nose in the air playfully. "That's good, because I don't even want to know!"

In truth, there was only one person Arthur could think of voting for, and that was Merlin. He was the smartest man Arthur had ever met, and he believed in peace and education over war and chaos. What better person to lead the realm into a new era of prosperity and goodwill?

He walked out of the castle and into the courtyard, where the voting booths had been set up.

There was still a long line of townsfolk waiting to cast their ballots, but the guards escorted Arthur to the front of the line, and no one seemed to mind. He guessed he might as well take advantage of his kingly privileges while he had them!

After casting his vote for Merlin, carefully spelling out the wizard's name the way Guin had taught him, he headed back out into the courtyard. He could feel a few people in line watching him, and he smiled and waved at them and wished them luck.

"Everything all right?" Guinevere asked, approaching him. "Did you vote?"

"I did and yes," he responded. Then he looked around the courtyard. "Though I have to admit, I'm going to miss this place."

"You're doing the right thing," she assured him. "I'm proud of you for leaving it up to the people."

Archimedes flew down from the turrets. "I hear the first results are starting to come in," he said. He looked a little tired, and Arthur knew it was past his bedtime.

"And...?" he asked, curious. "Who's in the lead?"

"They won't say until everyone's voted," the owl explained. "But it shouldn't be much longer now."

Arthur nodded, feeling a little impatient. Guinevere caught his look. "Let's go take a walk somewhere," she suggested. "Get your mind off things. We'll return when they're ready to announce the results."

And so they did. For Arthur was no longer confined

within the castle walls. He could go where he wanted, when he wanted – a freedom he'd never truly had before.

It was a feeling he'd grown to like quite a bit.

They wandered down the winding river, watching the farmers and fishermen and washerwomen go about their daily tasks. They strode down a forest path until they reached the well where they had first met.

"Remember when you wanted to be a bird?" Guinevere teased. "And fly far, far away?"

"I'm glad I didn't," he admitted. "There's so much right here." Then he glanced shyly at her. "When are you leaving?" he asked. She'd stayed longer than she'd planned to already, wanting to help him set up the election before she returned to her old home.

"Right after they announce the winner," she said. "I'm excited, but nervous. I hope my family likes me."

"How can they not?" Arthur cried indignantly, his heart squeezing at the happiness he saw on her face. Guinevere deserved this – the life she had always been meant to lead. "I'll miss you," he added. "So much."

Guinevere looked up at him with veiled eyes. "I'll miss you, too," she said softly. "But don't worry. I promise to come back soon. Merlin's actually offered to teach me some magic. He thinks I have the makings of a great wizard."

"If Merlin thinks so, then it must be true," Arthur declared. "He's an expert at seeing potential."

Guinevere grinned. "I think I finally understand what you see in him. He's actually pretty great."

"He's the best," Arthur agreed. "Even if he is a little grumpy at times."

Eventually they headed back to the castle, though they took a little more time than perhaps was strictly necessary. When they finally reached the gates, Merlin met them, his eyes alight with excitement.

"It's time!" he cried. "The results are in. Come, come! They're waiting for you to announce them."

Arthur wondered why they needed him for this, but dutifully followed Merlin into the courtyard, where everyone was waiting. The place was packed, and it felt as if the whole town had turned out to hear the election results. Arthur climbed onto the same stage that had once been meant to be his funeral pyre and looked down at the crowd below. Everyone looked anxious and hopeful, and he felt a thrill of excitement race through him.

"Thank you for voting," he told the crowd as Sir Pellinore walked the envelope with the results to him. "You should be proud that you had a part in selecting the new ruler to lead us into the future." He smiled. "And now, I won't keep you in suspense any more."

He tore open the envelope. The crowd collectively seemed to hold their breaths.

He unfolded the paper.

Looked down at it.

Squinted and did a double take.

"Wait, what?" He looked up. "There must be some mistake!"

Guinevere grabbed the paper from his hands, scanning it with her eyes. A slow smile spread across her face. "I don't think so," she said. "I think this is exactly right."

Arthur felt like he was about to fall over. He looked out over the faces of the people in front of him. Their hopeful eyes, their big smiles.

"You— you want *me* to be your king?" he stammered, looking down at the paper one more time as if he expected the name to change without warning. "You voted for me?"

The crowd erupted into cheers. Guinevere bounced up and down. Merlin grinned a wide, toothy grin, and Archimedes slapped Arthur on the back with his wing.

"They want you, lad," Merlin declared. "Not because of some miracle or some feat of strength. But because you have proved to them that you are a kind, fair, capable leader. They believe you are the one who will take them from the darkness and bring them into the light."

Arthur felt too stunned to speak. He glanced at Guinevere. Her smile could have lit up the moon. "Did you know about this?" he asked incredulously.

"Of course I did," she said with a smile. "The Internet said so, right?"

Arthur shook his head, still having a hard time believing it all. But the people had spoken. They wanted him as king.

"So what do you say?" Merlin asked, raising a bushy eyebrow. "Do you want the job or what?"

Arthur forced his head to bob up and down. "I want it," he said. "I would be proud to be their king. As long as you stick around," he added, gesturing to Merlin. "After all, a good king needs a good education."

Merlin nodded approvingly. "I'm glad you recognise that. And I'm happy to do it. After all my travelling, I could use a place to hang my hat for a while. Might as well be here in Camelot."

Arthur smiled, then turned back to the crowd. "Then I accept your offer. And I only hope I prove worthy of your faith in me."

The crowd cheered. People began to dance, and musicians took up a lively tune. Soon everyone was celebrating together. Arthur even spotted a few Saxons in the crowd, dancing and laughing with the rest.

A smile crossed his face. His people. His kingdom. For now and always.

He might not have been some miracle king, but the people didn't care about that. They cared about him. As much as he had grown to care about them.

And for the first time in his life, his true destiny was set in stone.

Mari Mancusi is an Emmy Award–winning former TV news producer and author of more than two dozen sci-fi/fantasy books for kids, teens and adults. Her award-winning series have been translated around the world and have been placed on several US state school reading lists. In addition to writing, Mari is an avid cosplayer, gamer, Disney fan and world traveller. She lives in Austin, Texas, with her husband, daughter and two dogs. She can be found online at www.marimancusi.com or on TikTok under @marimancusi8.

ALSO AVAILABLE IN THE TWISTED TALES SERIES:

WHAT IF TIANA MADE A DEAL THAT CHANGED EVERYTHING?

When the notorious Dr. Facilier backs Tiana into a corner, she has no choice but to accept an offer that will alter the course of her life in an instant.

Soon Tiana finds herself in a new reality where all her deepest desires are realised – she finally gets her restaurant, her friends are safe and sound, and, perhaps most miraculous of all, her beloved father is still alive.

But after a while, her hometown grows increasingly eerie, and Tiana must work alongside Naveen and Charlotte to set things right – or risk losing everything she holds dear.

ALSO AVAILABLE IN THE TWISTED TALES SERIES:

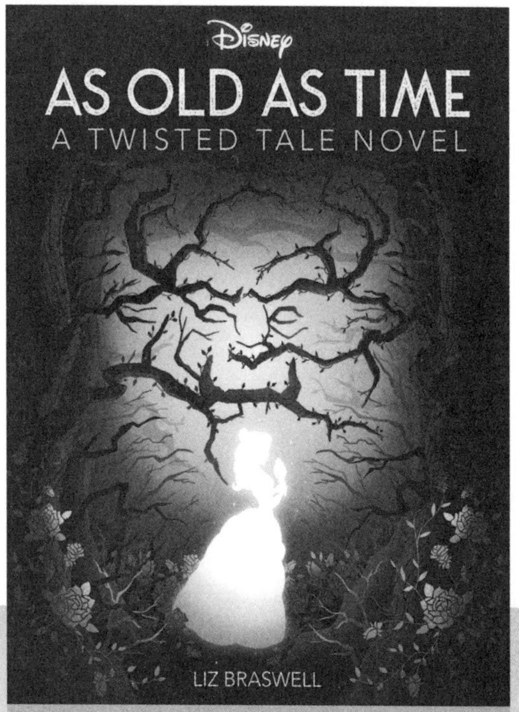

WHAT IF BELLE'S MOTHER CURSED THE BEAST?

Trapped in the castle with the terrifying Beast, Belle learns there is much more to her angry captor when she touches the enchanted rose. Suddenly, her mind is flooded with images of her mother, a woman Belle hardly remembers.

Stranger still, Belle realises that her mother is none other than the beautiful Enchantress who cursed the Beast, his castle and all his staff.

Stunned and confused by the revelation, Belle and the Beast must work together to unravel years of mystery.

ALSO AVAILABLE IN THE TWISTED TALES SERIES:

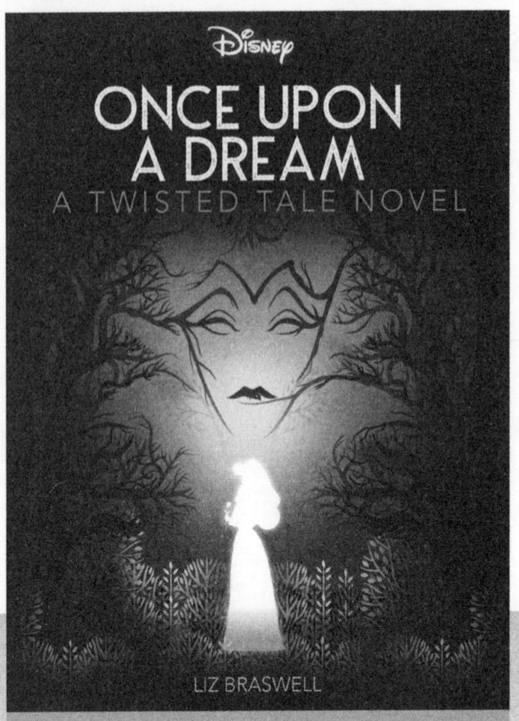

WHAT IF THE SLEEPING BEAUTY NEVER WOKE UP?

The handsome prince is poised to kiss the beautiful sleeping princess and live happily ever after, but as soon as his lips touch hers he too falls fast asleep. It is clear that this tale is far from over.

Now, Princess Aurora must escape from a dangerous and magical land created from her very own dreams.

With Maleficent's agents following her every move, Aurora needs to discover who her true friends are and, most importantly, who she really is.

ALSO AVAILABLE IN THE TWISTED TALES SERIES:

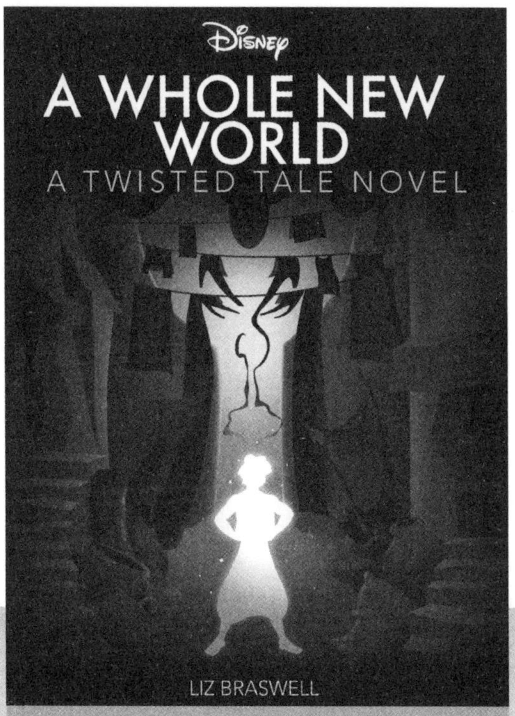

WHAT IF ALADDIN HAD NEVER FOUND THE LAMP?

Aladdin is a Street Rat just trying to survive in a harsh city, while Jasmine is a beautiful princess about to enter an arranged marriage. Their worlds collide when the sultan's trusted adviser suddenly rises to power and, with the help of a mysterious lamp, attempts to gain control over love and death.

Together, Aladdin and Jasmine must unite to stop power-hungry Jafar tearing the kingdom apart in this story of love, power and one moment that changes everything.

ALSO AVAILABLE IN THE TWISTED TALES SERIES:

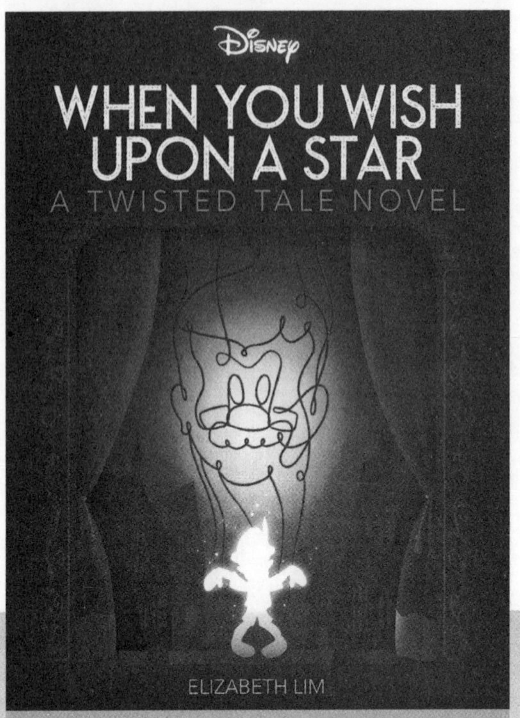

WHAT IF THE BLUE FAIRY WASN'T SUPPOSED TO HELP PINOCCHIO?

Pariva is a village full of magical lore where sisters Chiara and Ilaria grew up together.

Forty years later, Chiara, now the Blue Fairy, defies the rules of magic within Pariva and grants a wish that changes everything for her old friend Geppetto, and for a little puppet named Pinocchio. But, she is discovered by the Scarlet Fairy, formerly Ilaria, who holds this transgression against her.

They decide to settle things through a good old-fashioned bet – with Pinocchio and Geppetto's fate hanging in the balance.

ALSO AVAILABLE IN THE TWISTED TALES SERIES:

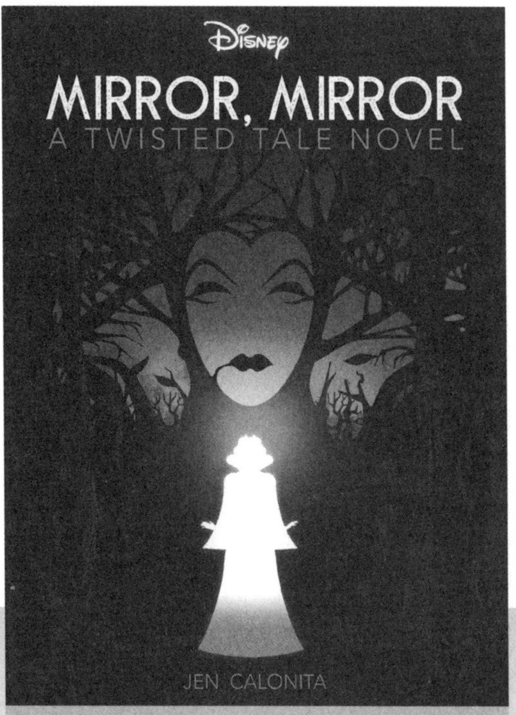

WHAT IF THE EVIL QUEEN POISONED THE PRINCE?

Following her beloved mother's death, the kingdom falls to Snow White's stepmother, known as the Evil Queen.

At first, Snow keeps her head down, hoping to make the best of things. However, when new information about her parents comes to light, and a plot to kill her goes wrong, Snow embarks on a journey to stop the Evil Queen and take back her kingdom.

Can Snow defeat an enemy who will stop at nothing to retain her power… including going after the ones Snow loves?

ALSO AVAILABLE IN THE TWISTED TALES SERIES:

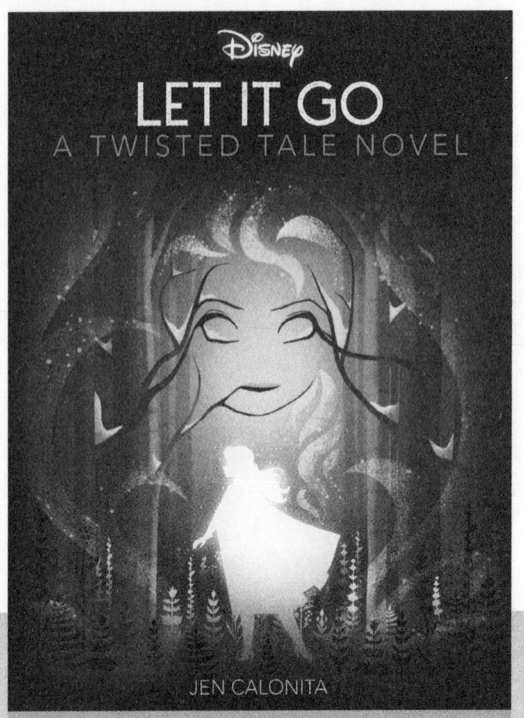

WHAT IF ANNA AND ELSA NEVER KNEW EACH OTHER?

Following the unexpected death of her parents, Elsa finds herself the sole ruler of Arendelle and mysterious powers begin to reveal themselves.

Elsa starts to remember fragments of her childhood that seem to have been erased – fragments that include a familiar-looking girl.

Determined to fill the void she has always felt, Elsa must take a harrowing journey across her icy kingdom to undo a terrible curse... and find the missing Princess of Arendelle.

So you *really* wan

LATIN

BOOK II

Answer Book

© Nicholas Oulton 1999, 2020

Gresham Books Ltd
The Carriage House
Ningwood Manor
Ningwood
Isle of Wight
PO30 4NJ

All rights reserved: no part of this publication may be reproduced, stored in a retrieval system, or transmitted in any form or by any means, electronic, mechanical, photocopying, recording or otherwise, without either the prior written permission of the copyright owner or a licence permitting restricted copying issued by the Copyright Licensing Agency, 90 Tottenham Court Road, London W1P 0LP.

First published in 1999 by Galore Park Publishing.
This edition published by Gresham Books in 2020.

ISBN 978-0-946095-67-4

Also available in the So You Really Want to Learn Latin series:

So you really want to learn Latin Book I	ISBN 978-0-946095-63-6
• Book I Answer Book	ISBN 978-0-946095-66-7
So you really want to learn Latin Book II	ISBN 978-0-946095-64-3
So you really want to learn Latin Book III	ISBN 978-0-946095-65-0
• Book III Answer Book	ISBN 978-0-946095-68-1

CONTENTS

Introduction 3
Chapter 1 4
Chapter 2 8
Chapter 3 12
Chapter 4 17
Chapter 5 21
Chapter 6 24
Chapter 7 27
Chapter 8 29
Chapter 9 32
Chapter 10 36

Introduction

The answers which follow have been compiled with a view to providing users of *So you really want to learn Latin* Book II with an easy to use reference against which to check their work. The answers are in no way meant to be definitive and variations may of course be allowed, in particular with regard to word order and use of vocabulary. Where possible suggested translations are those which it is thought would probably be written by a student who had reached that stage in the course. This has led to some very stilted sentences, my own favourite being "were my words not heard by you?"! However, once the Latin has been understood, the fun of turning it into meaningful and stylish English can begin.

P.S. You can now follow the course on YouTube!

Chapter 1

Exercise 1. 1

1. We saw the huge wood.
2. He killed the soldier with a huge sword.
3. The king was sleeping in a huge bed.
4. We shall throw huge spears at the enemy.*
5. The bold citizens did not fear the huge lion.

*N.B. *in* + acc. = “into”, “on to” or, as in this context, “at”.

Exercise 1. 2

1. *mēnsae ingentis*
2. *mēnsārum ingentium*
3. *puella audāx*
4. *puellās audācēs*
5. *ad silvam ingentem*
6. *cum mīlitibus audācibus*
7. *sine duce audācī*
8. *castra ingentia*
9. *sub mēnsā ingentī*
10. *cum nautā audācī*

Exercise 1. 3

1. The Roman forces were attacking the camp of the Etruscans near the huge river.
2. The Etruscans however prepared a huge camp near the river.
3. Lars Porsenna, the king of the Etruscans, led the bold soldiers towards the Romans.
4. The Romans however did not fear the bold enemy and hurried into battle.
5. The Etruscans saw the bold Romans but did not want to flee.

Exercise 1. 4

1.

brevis	*brevis*	*breve*
brevis	*brevis*	*breve*
brevem	*brevem*	*breve*
brevis	*brevis*	*brevis*
brevī	*brevī*	*brevī*
brevī	*brevī*	*brevī*
brevēs	*brevēs*	*brevia*
brevēs	*brevēs*	*brevia*
brevēs	*brevēs*	*brevia*
brevium	*brevium*	*brevium*
brevibus	*brevibus*	*brevibus*
brevibus	*brevibus*	*brevibus*

2. *fēlīx* *fēlīx* *fēlīx*
   fēlīx *fēlīx* *fēlīx*
   fēlīcem *fēlīcem* *fēlīx*
   fēlīcis *fēlīcis* *fēlīcis*
   fēlīcī *fēlīcī* *fēlīcī*
   fēlīcī *fēlīcī* *fēlīcī*

   fēlīcēs *fēlīcēs* *fēlīcia*
   fēlīcēs *fēlīcēs* *fēlīcia*
   fēlīcēs *fēlīcēs* *fēlīcia*
   fēlīcium *fēlīcium* *fēlīcium*
   fēlīcibus *fēlīcibus* *fēlīcibus*
   fēlīcibus *fēlīcibus* *fēlīcibus*

3. *celer* *celeris* *celere*
   celer *celeris* *celere*
   celerem *celerem* *celere*
   celeris *celeris* *celeris*
   celerī *celerī* *celerī*
   celerī *celerī* *celerī*

   celerēs *celerēs* *celeria*
   celerēs *celerēs* *celeria*
   celerēs *celerēs* *celeria*
   celerium *celerium* *celerium*
   celeribus *celeribus* *celeribus*
   celeribus *celeribus* *celeribus*

Exercise 1. 5

1. *rēgis trīstis*
2. *agricolae trīstī* or *ad agricolam trīstem*
3. *cum mīlite trīstī*
4. *in carmine trīstī*
5. *puellae trīstēs*
6. *sub librō gravī*
7. *in epistolā brevī*
8. *victōriae facilēs*
9. *ducis fortis*
10. *carmen difficile*

Exercise 1. 6

1. The girl sent a short letter to the master.
2. The brave leader was leading many soldiers into the difficult battle.
3. The boys and girls were running down from the hill.
4. Yesterday the inhabitants of Italy were sad.
5. Now he is singing sad songs.

6. The sad leader had led the brave forces into the sea.
7. Our men were fighting in the sea for a long time but were not overcoming the sailors.
8. The sad mother found her happy daughter under the table.
9. Why are you carrying water out of the sea to the city?
10. They heard many shouts in the woods.

Exercise 1. 7

While King Porsenna was attacking Rome he captured many girls. One girl, called Cloelia, wanted to flee. Therefore she swam across the river with her friends and walked into the city. Porsenna was angry and sent soldiers to the Romans. "Where is Cloelia?" they asked. However the Romans had made a treaty with Porsenna and did not want to break the treaty. Therefore they sent the wretched Cloelia back to the camp of Porsenna. Porsenna however was not angry but happy. "The Romans are brave" he said "and worthy of fame. Therefore I shall give Cloelia and many girls to the Romans."

Exercise 1. 8

1. *ducēs audācēs!*
2. *puellae celeris.*
3. *ā mīlite fortī.*
4. *operī gravī.*
5. *in marī altō.*
6. *fēminās trīstēs vīdit.*
7. *agricola laetus cantābat.*
8. *puellam trīstem vidēre cupiēbat.*
9. *dē colle altō.*
10. *fābulam brevem nārrābit.*

Exercise 1. 9

1. *appellō* = I call; appeler = to call
2. *arbor* = tree; arbre = tree
3. *bonus* = good; bon = good
4. *pōns* = bridge; pont = bridge
5. *dormiō* = I sleep; dormir = to sleep
6. *dēscendō* = I go down; descendre = to go down
7. *et* = and ; et = and
8. *habitō* = I live; habiter = to live
9. *malus* = bad ; mal = bad
10. *audāx* = bold; audacieux = bold

Exercise 1. 10

Once upon a time the Romans were waging war against the Volsci. They attacked a town called Corioli but did not capture it. At last Gnaeus Marcius, a Roman soldier, led his forces into the town and killed many (of the) enemy. The bold Romans overcame the wretched Volsci and gave a new name to Marcius: now Gnaeus Marcius was Coriolanus.

Exercise 1. 11

Rōmānī diū Corialānum timēbant. tandem mīlitem superbum ab urbe discēdere coēgērunt. ad castra Volscōrum fūgit et cum Rōmānīs pugnāvit. māter igitur et uxor Coriolānī in castra hostium vēnērunt. māter "cūr" inquit "urbem tuam oppugnās?" Coriolānus verba mātris audīvit et cum mīlitibus discessit. inde Rōmānī fēminās audācēs laudāvērunt.*

* The Latin for "to fight against" is the same as "to fight with", i.e. *pugnō cum* (+ abl.).

Chapter 2

Exercise 2. 1

1. *tibĭ*
2. *mihĭ*
3. *tē/vōs vidēmus*
4. *nōs vidēs/vidētis*
5. *vōs spectat*
6. *tū dormīs/vōs dormītis sed nōs labōrāmus*
7. *librum tibĭ dō*
8. *mē audīvit*
9. *nōs monēbunt*
10. *tē laudābō*

Exercise 2. 2

1. The citizens were listening to me.
2. The swift soldier will watch us.
3. Yesterday I wanted to see you.
4. *We* love the sea but *you* fear it.
5. Today the bold soldiers will capture you.
6. O Romans, look, Romulus is going up/has gone up into the sky!
7. Lars Porsenna captured many prisoners.
8. My mother is walking with you.
9. *We* are reading but *you* are sleeping.
10. *We* gave the gifts to you.

Exercise 2. 3

1. *Coriolānus urbem nostram oppugnāvit.*
2. *fortasse māter cāra Coriolānī castra hostium intrābit.*
3. *Coriolāne, māter tua tē nōn amat.*
4. *ecce, intrā castra nostra vēnit!*
5. *num amor nostrī tē Rōmam oppugnāre cōgit.*
6. *vōs/tē nōn capiam sed discēdam.*
7. *igitur Coriolānus ā castrīs discessit.*
8. *māter tamen nōn laeta erat.*
9. *Rōmānī lacrimās mātris trīstis vīdērunt.*
10. *puerum amāverat sed frūstrā.*

Exercise 2. 4

1. *eum amāmus*
2. *eam amās*
3. *eīs/iīs crēdit*
4. *id amāmus*
5. *eī*
6. *cum eīs*
7. *sine eā*
8. *ea*
9. *id*
10. *is eam amat*

Exercise 2. 5
1. *mihĭ*
2. *ā tē*
3. *eius*
4. *eī mīlitēs*
5. *eīs/iīs*
6. *vōbīs*
7. *nōbīscum*
8. *mē*
9. *eum*
10. *eī*

Exercise 2. 6
1. I gave a gift to you.
2. He gave the gifts to us.
3. His mother.
4. That river.
5. You warn us.
6. I shall prepare his table.
7. I shall send a letter to him.
8. He reads that letter.
9. *You* are walking.
10. You do not trust us, do you?

Exercise 2. 7
1. *mātrem (suam) amat.*
2. *patriam (suam) amant.*
3. *mātrem eius amat.*
4. *patriam eius amant.*
5. *tē/vōs laudāmus nec tamen eum amāmus.*
6. *nōs laudās nec tamen eōs amās.*
7. *eōs laudant nec tamen tē/vōs amant.*
8. *eam puellam amat.*

Exercise 2. 8
1. *frūstrā* = in vain. If one frustrates someone, one prevents them (making their efforts in vain).
2. *cum* + *currō* = I run together. To concur is to agree.
3. *dis* + *crēdō* = not + I trust. To discredit is to refuse to believe or bring disbelief upon someone (note the negative force of *dis*).
4. *captīvus* = prisoner. A captive is a prisoner.
5. *dēscendō* = I come down. A descent is a coming down.
6. *in* + *legō* = not + I read. If something is illegible it cannot be read (note the negative force of *in-*).
7. *iūvenis* = a young person. A juvenile is a young person (or animal).
8. *in* + *fidēlis* = not + faithful. Infidelity is lack of loyalty.
9. *legō* = I read. A lecture is read to the audience.
10. *intrā* + *spectō* = I look within. Introspective means inward looking.

Exercise 2. 9
1. Contravene = go against.
2. Contradict = speak against.
3. Circumspect = cautious, wary (looking around).

4. Inaudible = cannot be heard.
5. Interject = interrupt or butt in.
6. Dispel = drive away.
7. Repel = drive back.
8. Impel = drive in.
9. Expel = drive out.
10. Compel = force.

Exercise 2. 10

1. The king sent the wretched prisoners to his city.
2. The masters led many slaves into the forum; or they led the master's many slaves into the forum.
3. The daughter of the soldier came within the walls.
4. Perhaps she wanted to lead the enemy within the city.
5. The enemy however did not trust the wretched girl.

Exercise 2. 11

1.

capiō	*capiam*	*capiēbam*
capis	*capiēs*	*capiēbās*
capit	*capiet*	*capiēbat*
capimus	*capiēmus*	*capiēbāmus*
capitis	*capiētis*	*capiēbātis*
capiunt	*capient*	*capiēbant*

2.

cīvis	*cīvēs*
cīvis	*cīvēs*
cīvem	*cīvēs*
cīvis	*cīvium*
cīvī	*cīvibus*
cīve	*cīvibus*

3.

ūnus	*sextus*
secundus	*septimus*
tertius	*octāvus*
quārtus	*nōnus*
quīntus	*decimus*

4. *sum* *erō* *eram*
es *eris* *erās*
est *erit* *erat*
sumus *erimus* *erāmus*
estis *eritis* *erātis*
sunt *erunt* *erant*

Exercise 2. 12

1. The patricians were the aristocratic families descended from the original founders of Rome.
2. The plebeians were the common citizens.
3. The plebeians felt aggrieved that the laws were not written down.
4. In 450 B.C. the ten judges were appointed to study the laws of Athens and write down a set of laws for Rome.
5. These laws were called the Twelve Tables.
6. Appius Claudius was one of the ten judges appointed to produce the laws of Rome.
7. Verginia was a girl whom Appius Claudius wished to seduce, despite the fact that she was engaged to someone else.
8. Appius Claudius persuaded a friend to claim that Verginia was a slave belonging to him. At the resulting court case, he (Appius Claudius) would rule in his (the friend's) favour, thus allowing him (Appius Claudius) to go off with Verginia.
9. Verginia's father killed her when he realised that he could do nothing to protect her.
10. The Romans placed virtue above personal safety, indeed above life itself. The shame involved in Verginia's being seduced by Appius Claudius would have been too much for her father to bear. Poor Verginia herself did not get a chance to say what she would have felt about the matter!

Exercise 2. 13

Once a Roman citizen called Appius Claudius loved a beautiful girl called Verginia. But Verginia's father had already promised her in marriage. Appius, therefore, said to his friend "will you help me? I want to marry that girl." His friend entered the forum and captured Verginia. She tried to escape but in vain. However the father saw his daughter and shouted. "You will not capture my daughter. I will save her." Then he took his sword and killed his dear daughter. Thus he saved the wretched girl.

Chapter 3

Exercise 3. 1

1. *manus* *manūs*
   manus *manūs*
   manum *manūs*
   manūs *manuum*
   manuī *manibus*
   manū *manibus*

2. *exercitus* *exercitūs*
   exercitus *exercitūs*
   exercitum *exercitūs*
   exercitūs *exercituum*
   exercituī *exercitibus*
   exercitū *exercitibus*

3. *cornū* *cornua*
   cornū *cornua*
   cornū *cornua*
   cornūs *cornuum*
   cornū *cornibus*
   cornū *cornibus*

4. *oculus* *oculī*
   ocule *oculī*
   oculum *oculōs*
   oculī *oculōrum*
   oculō *oculīs*
   oculō *oculīs*

Exercise 3. 2

1. *exercitum ad portum dūcet.*
2. *dux exercitūs mīles fortis erat.*
3. *hostēs domōs incolārum dēfendēbant.*
4. *omnēs senēs in gradibus sedēbant.*
5. *herī pater meus cornū ingēns servō bonō dedit.*
6. *in gradū domūs sēdit quod mīlitēs genū vulnerāverant.*
7. *dux barbarōrum in cornū sinistrō pugnābat.*
8. *exercitūs ad flūmen dūcēmus.*

Exercise 3. 3

1. The master of the slave gave him a new house.
2. Our men were fighting on the plain with arrows and swords.
3. The leader of the army led his soldiers into the mountains.
4. We were holding the prisoners in the harbour.
5. All the slaves were coming out of the garden and were running towards the harbour.
6. You are walking down from the mountains but we are running.
7. You will not build the houses near the harbour, will you?
8. The leader of the army loves summer, doesn't he?

Exercise 3. 4

Once upon a time the Romans were waging a war against the Gauls. The king of the Gauls, called Brennus, led his army towards the city and prepared to fight with the Romans near a river called the Allia. However the Romans saw the Gauls and immediately fled into the city. Then the Gauls came to the city and entered the houses of the citizens.

Exercise 3. 5

1. *nautae, nāvigāte in portum!*
2. *mīlitēs, este fortēs!*
3. *puer, sedē in gradū!*
4. *puerī, audīte omnēs fābulās!*
5. *Coriolāne, exercitum in bellum dūc!*

Exercise 3. 6

1. *puellae quārtae*
2. *gladiō tertiō*
3. *puerō quīntō*
4. *bellum secundum*
5. *annus decimus*
6. *cum tribus amīcīs*
7. *cum rēge sextō*
8. *ūna castra*
9. *ūnae cōpiae*
10. *agricolae ūnĭ̄us*

Exercise 3. 7

1. Roman fathers were always teaching/always used to teach their sons.
2. They told them many stories.
3. The first king, called Romulus, ruled Rome.
4. Seven kings ruled the city.
5. However the Romans did not love them because they were proud.
6. Brutus drove the king out of the city and for a long time defended Rome.
7. Lars Porsenna with a great army wanted to destroy the bridge.
8. Horatius with two friends defended the bridge for a long time and saved the city.
9. Then two consuls ruled the city.
10. The young Roman men listened to the old men and always feared them.

Book 2 Answers

Exercise 3. 8

1. He was walking home.
2. They had departed from Troy.
3. They were hurrying to Rome.
4. We shall sail to Ithaca.
5. You have sailed from Crete, haven't you?
6. We are walking to the town.
7. He was sailing to the island.
8. I was hurrying to the country from the city.
9. He was hurrying home from the country.
10. They have sailed to Troy.

Exercise 3. 9

The Gauls entered the city because the inhabitants were afraid of them. The women and young men had gone up onto the Capitoline Mountain but the old men were sitting in the forum. The Gauls walked into the forum and for a long time looked at them. The old Roman men were doing nothing. At last a Gaul touched an old Roman man and he was angry. Then the Gaul killed him and his friends killed all the Romans. However they did not find the soldiers because they were remaining on the mountain with the women.

For a long time the Romans remained on the mountain. At last the Gauls climbed the mountain. The Roman soldiers did not hear them. But the sacred geese heard the Gauls and shouted (cackled?). The soldiers got up and drove the enemy down from the mountain.

Exercise 3. 10

1. *lūna* = moon. Lunatics were thought to be influenced by the moon.
2. *senex* = old man. Senile is an adjective used to describe old people.
3. *pāx* = peace. If one pacifies someone, one makes peace with him.
4. *pecūnia* = money. Impecunious means lacking money.
5. *pōnō* = I place. To place is to position and a position is a place!
6. *ignis* = fire. To ignite is to set on fire.
7. *dēfendō* = I defend. Defence is the act of defending.
8. *lūna* = moon. Lunar means relating to the moon.
9. *hostēs* = enemy. Hostile literally means of an enemy, thus unfriendly.
10. *īnsula* = island. Insular means of an island. It comes to mean narrow-minded from the idea that islanders have little or no contact with the wider world around them.

Exercise 3. 11

1. *quīnque annōs*
2. *duōbus annīs*
3. *noctū* (or, less correctly, *nocte*)
4. *annō tertiō*
5. *annō quīntō*
6. *abhinc quīnque annōs* (or *annīs*)
7. *abhinc trēs hōrās* (or *tribus hōrīs*)
8. *septem ante annīs*
9. *octŏ post annīs*
10. *multōs annōs*

Exercise 3. 12

1. For many years the Romans feared kings.
2. In the first year Romulus ruled the city.
3. Many hours before he had killed his brother with a sword .
4. "Many years ago" he said "Aeneas sailed from Asia".
5. Many years afterwards a brave citizen called Brutus drove the king out of the city.
6. The king of the Etruscans, called Lars Porsenna, hurried to Rome.
7. Horatius defended the bridge for many hours but did not overcome the enemy.
8. Many years afterwards the Gauls attacked the citadel of the city during the night.
9. The Roman soldiers were asleep but in the middle of the night the geese shouted (cackled).
10. The Romans fought with the enemy for many hours.

Exercise 3. 13

1. *in Ītaliā quīnque annōs habitāverimus.*
2. *fīlius imperātōris urbem tribus ante annīs oppugnāverat.*
3. *quattuor post annīs Troiā ad/in Ītaliam nāvigāvimus.*
4. *mīlitēs noctū audīvimus.*
5. *decimō annō cīvēs senem ex oppidō pepulērunt.*
6. *nōnne rūs duōbus annīs veniēs?*
7. *multīs post annīs mīlitēs Rōmā discessērunt.*
8. *multīs ante hōrīs fēmina fābulam fīliābus nārrāverat.*
9. *nōnne lūnam noctū vīdistī?*
10. *magister līberōs cōnsulis quattuor annōs docēbat.*

Exercise 3. 14

1. The Romans fought against the Gauls at the Battle of Allia in 390 B.C.
2. The king of the Gauls at this time was Brennus.
3. The Gauls won the Battle of Allia and then marched into the city of Rome.
4. The women and young men had withdrawn up on to the Capitoline Hill.
5. Eighty of the oldest senators remained in the forum, seated on their ivory chairs.
6. The old men were killed once the Gauls had realised they were not statues.
7. The Gauls climbed the mountain because they had spotted the foot-prints of a Roman who had climbed up and down the mountain in an attempt to get help.
8. The Romans were saved by the sacred geese, who cackled and woke them up.
9. Camillus eventually came to the rescue of the Romans.
10. Gaul became part of the Roman empire as a result of Julius Caesar's campaigns in Gaul, 58–51 B.C.

Chapter 4

Exercise 4. 1

1.

(a)	*portō*	*portor*
	portās	*portāris*
	portat	*portātur*
	portāmus	*portāmur*
	portātis	*portāminī*
	portant	*portantur*
(b)	*portāre*	*portārī*

2.

(a)	*teneō*	*teneor*
	tenēs	*tenēris*
	tenet	*tenētur*
	tenēmus	*tenēmur*
	tenētis	*tenēminī*
	tenent	*tenentur*
(b)	*tenēre*	*tenērī*

3.

(a)	*iaciō*	*iacior*
	iacis	*iaceris*
	iacit	*iacitur*
	iacimus	*iacimur*
	iacitis	*iaciminī*
	iaciunt	*iaciuntur*
(b)	*iacere*	*iacī*

4.

(a)	*dūcō*	*dūcor*
	dūcis	*dūceris*
	dūcit	*dūcitur*
	dūcimus	*dūcimur*
	dūcitis	*dūciminī*
	dūcunt	*dūcuntur*
(b)	*dūcere*	*dūcī*

5.

(a)	*aperiō*	*aperior*
	aperīs	*aperīris*
	aperit	*aperītur*
	aperīmus	*aperīmur*
	aperītis	*aperīminī*
	aperiunt	*aperiuntur*
(b)	*aperīre*	*aperīrī*

6.

(a)	*frangō*	*frangor*
	frangis	*frangeris*
	frangit	*frangitur*
	frangimus	*frangimur*
	frangitis	*frangiminī*
	frangunt	*franguntur*
(b)	*frangere*	*frangī*

Exercise 4. 2

1. The farmer is seen.
2. The boys are heard.
3. The gift is given.
4. The army is being led.
5. The slaves are being killed.
6. The soldiers are ordered by the leader.
7. The young men are being praised by the consul.
8. The voice of the girl is heard.
9. The harbour is being defended.
10. The hill is being climbed.

Exercise 4. 3

1. *Rōma regitur.*
2. *monēris.*
3. *laudārī cupiunt.*
4. *servī docentur.*
5. *lacrimae mātris videntur.*
6. *omnēs mīlitēs interficiuntur.*
7. *urbs frūstrā dēfenditur.*
8. *fēminae trīstēs īn forō inveniuntur.*
9. *pōns dēlētur.*
10. *epistola amīcō tuō/vestrō mittitur.*

Exercise 4. 4

As suggested, these verbs are taken as historic presents.

Rome was being attacked by the Gauls. The soldiers climbed onto the mountain but the old men were found by the Gauls. All the old men were killed and the Romans were terrified. However the city was saved by the sacred geese. For the Gauls were driven down from the mountain and were forced to flee.

Exercise 4. 5

1. *superābor*
   superāberis
   superābitur
   superābimur
   superābiminī
   superābuntur

2. *pōnēbar*
   pōnēbāris
   pōnēbātur
   pōnēbāmur
   pōnēbāminī
   pōnēbantur

3. *dūcar*
   dūcēris
   dūcētur
   dūcēmur
   dūcēminī
   dūcentur

4. *iaciēbar*
   iaciēbāris
   iaciēbātur
   iaciēbāmur
   iaciēbāminī
   iaciēbantur

Exercise 4. 6

1. *ab iūdice accūsābuntur.*
2. *iter ā mīlitibus cōnficiētur.*
3. *lēgātī ab imperātōre mittentur.*
4. *servī fēlīcēs gladiō nōn occīdentur.*
5. *legiō Rōmam mittitur.*
6. *ā magistrō monēbātur.*

---

7. *īn flūmen ab agricolā iacientur.*
8. *castra hostium sagittīs oppugnābantur.**
9. *epistola magnā cum cūrā scrībēbātur.*
10. *līberī magistrī tempestāte terrēbuntur.*

* Remember that *castra* is plural.

Exercise 4. 7

Once upon a time a Roman father called Lucius Manlius was being accused by the citizens. For Lucius had sent his son into the fields because he was stupid. But the boy, Titus Manlius, was not angry and loved his proud father. At last the citizens called the old man into the forum. Titus however wanted to help his father. Therefore he entered the home of the tribune and said "I shall kill you because you have accused my father." The tribune therefore freed the old man and Titus Manlius was praised by all.

Exercise 4. 8

1. *in urbe quīnque diēs manēbat.*
2. *Rōmam tribus diēbus oppugnābunt.*
3. *lēgātus rem magnā cum cūrā cōnfēcit.*
4. *rēs urbis ūnum annum gerēmus.*
5. *ad īnsulam parvam abhinc septem diēs nāvigāvērunt.*

Exercise 4. 9

The Gauls wanted to attack Rome. The Roman army was being led by a diligent general*. Among the soldiers was Titus Manlius. The Gauls had not overcome the Romans and were tired. "Won't one Roman fight with one Gaul?" asked a Gallic soldier. The Romans looked at the Gaul for a long time. At last Titus Manlius said "I will fight with that Gaul."

In the fight Titus Manlius killed the huge Gaul and took his necklace. He was praised by the Romans and on account of the necklace was called Torquatus.

Exercise 4. 10

1. *animus* = mind or spirit. Animated means spirited.
2. *fēlīx* = fortunate. Felicitous means lucky or fortunate.
3. *dēspērō* = I despair. If one is desperate one has given up hope.
4. *dīligēns* = careful. Diligent means careful.
5. *fortūna* = fortune. If one is fortunate, one has good fortune.
6. *līberō* = I free. To liberate is to set free.
7. *accūsō* = I accuse. If one accuses someone, one makes an accusation against them.

8. *iūdex* = judge. Judicious means sensible or of sound judgement.
9. *lēx* = law. Legal means of the law.
10. *cīvis* = citizen. Civil means of citizens. For example a civil war is one fought between fellow citizens.

Exercise 4. 11

1. He has fallen
2. They call
3. They have climbed
4. After the poem
5. With you
6. He will be
7. They are
8. To be
9. Do! / make!
10. Why?

Exercise 4. 12

1. The plebeians wanted more land, less tax, less oppression and to hold political power.
2. The conflict was resolved in 376 B.C. with the passing of the Licinian Laws.
3. Rome's defeat at Allia had seriously damaged her reputation with her neighbours.
4. In 340 B.C. the Latins and the Campanians revolted against Rome.
5. The rebels wanted half of the Roman senate to be made up of Latins and one of the consuls to be a Latin.
6. The consuls at this time were Manlius Torquatus and Publius Decius. They led their armies to meet the rebels near Capua.
7. The consuls dreamt that a giant had come to them and said that the army whose general sacrificed himself to the gods of the underworld would be victorious.
8. Manlius Torquatus's son rode out to kill one of the Latins who had insulted the Romans. When he got back to his own lines, his father killed him for disobeying orders.
9. Manlius Torquatus killed his son to show the importance of obeying orders, whatever the circumstances. His men never disobeyed orders again.
10. Seeing that his troops were being pushed back by the enemy, Publius Decius rushed out into the enemy to face certain death. Thanks, then, to the oracle, the Romans, whose general had sacrificed himself to the gods of the underworld, were victorious.

Chapter 5

Exercise 5. 1

1. *monitus sum*
   monitus es
   monitus est
   monitī sumus
   monitī estis
   monitī sunt

2. *rēctus sum*
   rēctus es
   rēctus est
   rēctī sumus
   rēctī estis
   rēctī sunt

3. *audītus sum*
   audītus es
   audītus est
   audītī sumus
   audītī estis
   audīti sunt

4. *captus sum*
   captus es
   captus est
   captī sumus
   captī estis
   captī sunt

Exercise 5. 2

1. Few ships have been sent to the island with many legions.
2. The soldier has been accused by the new ambassador.
3. For a few nights the city was being attacked by the enemy.
4. The girl has been led through the gates of the city.
5. The victory has been announced to the Roman people.
6. "Our men will never be overcome by the Gauls" he said.
7. Now bread is being carried into the town by the children of the consul.
8. We knew the name of the new ambassador.
9. "Help has been given by the new forces" they said.
10. Many stories have been told.

Exercise 5. 3

1. *puer vocātus est.*
2. *puella vocāta est.*
3. *bellum parātum est.*
4. *puerī doctī sunt.*
5. *puellae spectātae sunt.*
6. *bella gesta sunt.*
7. *peditēs ab hostibus vīsī sunt.*
8. *urbs ā paucīs servīs dēlēta est.*
9. *Rōmānī ā rēge novō territī sunt.*
10. *pars fābulae ā magistrō tuō nārrāta est.*

Exercise 5. 4

1. *monita erit.*
2. *territus eris.*
3. *dōnum puerō parvō datum erit.*
4. *hostēs ā Rōmānīs superātī erunt.*
5. *cōnsulēs iam lēctī erunt.*
6. *septem ante diēbus fugere coāctus eram.*
7. *quīnque ante annīs interfecta erat.*
8. *cūr nōn monitus erās?*
9. *rēx ex urbe noctū pulsus erat.*
10. *pōns multīs post hōrīs dēlētus erat.*

Exercise 5. 5

1. The boys and girls had been terrified by the master.
2. All the slaves had been driven into the forum.
3. The wretched girl had been forced to remain in the citadel for five days.
4. The barbarians will soon have been driven out of the fatherland, won't they?
5. The son of the consul had been seen under the table.

Exercise 5. 6

cīvis Rōmānus, quod pater eum nōn amābat, in agrōs missus erat. populus Rōmānus īrātus erat et cīvem accūsāvit. puer autem senem servāre cupiēbat. pater enim ā fīliō amābātur. puer igitur domum tribūnī vēnit et "in agrōs" inquit "missus eram sed patrem amō et eum servāre cupiō."*

*A nice trap for the unwary; *populus* is singular in Latin and thus must be followed by a singular verb.

Exercise 5. 7

Manlius Torquatus was consul with Publius Decius. The Romans were waging a war with the Latins. Once upon a time Manlius called his soldiers and said "I do not want to fight with the enemy." But a Latin horseman shouted in a loud voice "the Romans do not want to fight; the Romans are afraid of the Latins." The son of Manlius Torquatus heard his words. Therefore he took his sword and ran into the enemy. The Latin horseman was wounded and killed by the brave Roman.

The father, however, was angry. "Were my words not heard by you?" he asked. "Why did you fight with the enemy?" Then the wretched son was taken by his father and killed with a sword.

Exercise 5. 8

eō annō duŏ cōnsulēs, Mānlius Torquātus et Pūblius Decius, somnium habuērunt. deus eīs "imperātor" inquit "interficiētur sed exercitus suus hostēs superābit." in pugnā, igitur, quod Rōmānī ā Latīnīs fugere cōgēbantur, in hostēs Pūblius Decius cucurrit. "patriam meam" inquit "servābō." cōnsul interfectus est sed Rōmānī mortem eius vīdērunt et in cōpiās hostium cucurrērunt. Latīnī superātī (sunt) et fugere coāctī sunt.

Exercise 5. 9

While the Roman forces were overcoming Italy, they waged three wars with the Samnites. In the second war the leader of the Samnites, Gaius Pontius, pitched his camp near Caudium. Then he adopted a plan as follows: he ordered ten foot-soldiers to walk in the woods. The foot-soldiers were captured by the Romans. "The army of the Samnites" said the foot-soldiers "has already departed to the city of Luceria." The Romans hurried towards Luceria because they wanted to save the city.

Two roads led to the city. There was a long route near the sea, and a short route (which led) through the mountains. The Romans took the route through the mountains and in a narrow pass, called the Caudine Forks, they were overcome by the Latins. The Romans were forced by the Latins to seek peace and all the soldiers were sent under the yoke.

Exercise 5. 10

1. Firstly the boys had to learn to farm; second they had to study the Twelve Tables and the *mōs maiōrum*.
2. The Twelve Tables contained the laws of Rome, first written down in c. 450 B.C.
3. The *pater familiās* was the father in each household.
4. The Roman quality of *pietās* involved respect for the gods, for one's parents and for one's fatherland. We get the word piety from this.
5. *gravitās* was, literally, seriousness, and we get the word gravity.
6. Young Romans were encouraged to achieve *pietās* and *gravitās* by emulating the actions of their forefathers.
7. Children went to school at the age of about seven.
8. The children were taught to read and write by the *litterātor* or *lūdī magister*.
9. The children were taught grammar and literature by the *grammaticus*.
10. The art of rhetoric was taught by the *rhētōr*. Rhetoric is public speaking.

Chapter 6

Exercise 6. 1

1. *dūrior* *dūrissimus*
2. *laetior* *laetissimus*
3. *cārior* *cārissimus*
4. *īrātior* *īrātissimus*
5. *altior* *altissimus*
6. *ingentior* *ingentissimus*
7. *dīligentior* *dīligentissimus*
8. *fortior* *fortissimus*
9. *felīcior* *fēlīcissimus*
10. *audācior* *audācissimus*

Exercise 6. 2

1. *puellae trīstiōris*
2. *rēgēs fortiōrēs*
3. *bella longiōra*
4. *magister īrātissimus*
5. *fēminae laetissimae*
6. *imperātōrī fēlīcissimō*
7. *cum mīlitibus audācissimīs*
8. *in monte altiōre*
9. *prope flūmen altius*
10. *agricolae laetissimī!*

Exercise 6. 3

1. *rēx quam cōnsul fortior est;* or *rēx cōnsule fortior est.*
2. *Rōmānī bellum longissimum gessērunt.*
3. *mīlitēs Rōmānī audāciōrēs quam barbarī sunt;* or *mīlitēs Rōmānī barbarīs audāciōrēs sunt.*
4. *māter nostra trīstior quam pater tuus est;* or *māter nostra trīstior patre tuō est.*
5. *mihĭ mitte epistolam longiōrem!*
6. *Rōmānī ā peditibus audāciōribus superātī sunt.*
7. *ducem habēmus fortiōrem quam tū.*
8. *montēs altiōrēs quam urbs sunt;* or *montēs altiōrēs urbe sunt.*

Exercise 6. 4

Once upon a time a Roman boy was being taught by his very angry father. The boy learnt many things about brave Romans but always feared the dangers of war. Therefore the father sent the wretched boy into war. For a long time he fought among the bravest soldiers and often made very long journeys. At last the boy returned home and saw his father. "Once I did not love you" he said "but now I am bolder than all the soldiers. I am a very fortunate Roman citizen. I am very grateful to you (literally: I send you many thanks)."

Exercise 6. 5

1. *līberior, līberrimus*
2. *miserior, miserrimus*
3. *minor, minimus*
4. *pulchrior, pulcherrimus*
5. *peior, pessimus*
6. *maior, maximus*

Exercise 6. 6

1. *urbis maximae*
2. *in flūmine altissimō*
3. *carmina pulcherrima*
4. *perīcula pessima*
5. *mīlitibus audāciōribus*
6. *opus difficillimum*
7. *in itinere facillimō*
8. *in itineribus faciliōribus*
9. *post bellum longissimum*
10. *ante pugnam maximam*

Exercise 6. 7

1. Best; optimist
2. Worst; pessimist
3. Smallest; minimum
4. Biggest; maximum
5. He shows/has shown; ostensibly, ostentatious
6. Sign; signal
7. Of the allies; social
8. They had replied; respond
9. Letter; epistle
10. He has left; relic

Exercise 6. 8

Now Rome was the greatest city of Italy and many (people) were seeking help from the Romans. However the citizens of Tarentum did not like the Romans and sought help from the Greeks. There was in Greece a king called Pyrrhus. Pyrrhus* wanted to rule many lands. After the citizens of Tarentum had sought help, Pyrrhus came into Italy with very many soldiers. He overcame the Romans near Heraclea but very many Greek soldiers were killed.

After the battle the king said "If I have such a victory again, I shall journey home without an army."

*Note how in English we often repeat proper names. In Latin this is rarely done, a pronoun being preferred.

Exercise 6. 9

1. *ante diem tertium Īdūs Mārtiās*
2. *prīdiē Nōnās Ianuāriās*
3. *ante diem ūndecimum Kalendās Iūliās*
4. *Kalendīs Aprīlibus*
5. *ante diem octāvum Kalendās Ianuāriās*
6. *Īdibus Octōbribus*
7. *Nōnīs Novembribus*
8. *ante diem tertium Kalendās Augustās*
9. *prīdiē Nōnās Februāriās*
10. ….

N.B. If your birthday happens to fall on February 29th, you have problems! The Romans dealt with leap years by counting February 24th twice.

Exercise 6. 10

1. 29th March
2. 6th July
3. 22nd November
4. 5th August
5. 13th June
6. 3rd November
7. 10th February
8. 1st October
9. 15th March
10. 18th April

Exercise 6. 11

1. The dates of the 1st Samnite War were 343–341 B.C.; the dates of the 2nd Samnite War were 327–304 B.C.; and the dates of the 3rd Samnite War were 298–290 B.C.
2. The result of the Samnite Wars was that Rome was left effectively master of all Italy.
3. The people of Tarentum appealed to King Pyrrhus because they did not like having Rome as their master.
4. King Pyrrhus was the king of Epirus in Greece.
5. King Pyrrhus won the Battle of Heraclea but lost very many men in the process.
6. Fabricius was sent to Pyrrhus by the Romans to negotiate for the return of prisoners.
7. Pyrrhus thought that Fabricius would be easy to bribe because he was poor.
8. Having failed to bribe Fabricius, Pyrrhus tried to scare him with an elephant.
9. Fabricius was unmoved and told Pyrrhus that he could be persuaded neither by money nor by fear of elephants.
10. When the doctor offered to poison Pyrrhus, Fabricius immediately informed Pyrrhus of the doctor's treachery.
11. At the Battle of Asculum the Romans were defeated by Pyrrhus.
12. A Pyrrhic victory is one which is gained only at a great cost to the victor.

Chapter 7

Exercise 7. 1

1. *puer, quī cantat ...*
2. *puella, quae ambulat ...*
3. *bellī, quod gerimus ...*
4. *cum puerō, quem vidēmus ...*
5. *fēminae, quibus damus ...*
6. *agricolae, quī labōrant ...*
7. *cum mīlite, cuius ...*
8. *cōnsulum, ā quibus ...*

Exercise 7. 2

1. The master, who is in the garden, is angry.
2. The girl, who is in the field, is singing.
3. The war, which was long, terrified the women; or
   the war, because it was long, terrified the women.
4. The master, whom we love, is wretched.
5. The girl, whom we see in the field, is singing.
6. The war, which the Romans were waging, terrified the inhabitants.
7. The master, whose slave is tired, is always angry.
8. The girl, whose mother is sleeping, is always singing.
9. The army, whose leader everyone fears, was journeying to the town.
10. Now the master, to whom you gave a gift, is happy.

Exercise 7. 3

1. *magister, quī librum scrībēbat, laetus erat.*
2. *puella, quae mēnsam parābat, īrātissima erat.*
3. *mīles, quem vīdimus, pugnābat.*
4. *fēmina, quam monuerāmus, discessit.*
5. *imperātor, cuius exercitus pugnābat, audācissimus erat.*
6. *dea, cuī cantābāmus, Minerva erat.*
7. *incolae, ā quibus spectābāmur, in montibus habitābant.*
8. *equī, quī in agrō erant, aquam bibēbant.*
9. *flūmina, quae vīdimus, altissima erant.*
10. *peditēs, quōs dux īn silvam dūxerat, fessī erant.*

Exercise 7. 4

1. Pyrrhus, whom the inhabitants of Italy were calling, was king of Epirus.
2. The Romans had fought with the inhabitants whom the king was helping.
3. Tomorrow I shall read the books which you gave to me.
4. The leader, whose army we were watching, is king Pyrrhus.
5. We waged a war against the Gauls, who had attacked the city.
6. You were leading the band of men through the streets of the city which it (or he) had attacked.

7. We are fleeing from our fatherland on account of the danger, which everyone greatly fears.
8. He found gold in the wood which is near the city.
9. The sister of the leader returned home and warned her mother.
10. The customs of our fathers will always rule the best citizens, who love the city.

Exercise 7. 5

1. *fēminam, quae herī nōbīs dōna dedit, amāmus.*
2. *exercitum, quem Pyrrhus in patriam dūcit, spectant.*
3. *imperātor manum in perīculum maximum prō patriā suā dūxit.*
4. *librum quem mihĭ dedistī legēbat.*
5. *prope portam, quam cīvēs aedificāvērunt, stābimus.*
6. *prīnceps, quem Rōmam dūxerāmus, ā custōdibus noctū interfectus est.*
7. *prīmum magistrō novō, quī opus cōnfēcit, pārēbimus.*
8. *Gallī, postquam cīvēs discessērunt, urbem intrāvērunt.*
9. *senēs, quī ab hostibus nōn territī sunt, īn forō manēbant.*
10. *peditēs imperātōrī quīnque diēbus respondēbunt.*

Exercise 7. 6

While the Romans were waging war with Pyrrhus, a Greek citizen was captured. The citizen came to the Roman general, called Fabricius, and said "If you give me much money, I shall kill the Greek king."

However the words of that citizen did not move Fabricius. "The Romans will overcome the enemy with weapons, not treachery" he said. Then, to a guard who was standing near him he said "Go away and tell everything to the king!" The king, who was greatly moved, gave many prisoners to the Romans.

Exercise 7. 7

1. Pyrrhus left Italy in order to assist the Sicilians in their struggle with the Carthaginians.
2. Pyrrhus went to Sicily because he wanted to gain control of the island.
3. At the Battle of Beneventum Pyrrhus attacked the Romans (with a herd of elephants) but was driven back when the elephants were stampeded by burning arrows and lighted barrels of tar.
4. After the battle, Pyrrhus returned to Greece.
5. Pyrrhus died in Argos when he was hit on the head by a roof-tile.

Exercise 7. 8

1. *vulnerātus est.*
2. *monita est.*
3. *portātum est.*
4. *necātī / interfectī / occīsī sunt.*
5. *iussa erit.*

Exercise 7. 9

1. With bolder soldiers.
2. Under the biggest table.
3. Into the smallest wood.
4. By the most fortunate friend.
5. The difficult work.

Chapter 8

Exercise 8. 1

1. *hic mīles*
2. *eās puellās*
3. *huius bellī*
4. *illīs puerīs*
5. *hōrum magistrōrum*

Exercise 8. 2

1. Of those farmers
2. These wars
3. Of this woman
4. By that master
5. Of those forces

Exercise 8. 3

Note *is* or *ille* would be equally correct in most of these sentences.

1. *illī mīlitēs illam urbem oppugnābant.*
2. *hās lēgēs iam intellegimus.*
3. *Mārcus Brūtusque sunt mīlitēs. ille fortis est, hic superbissimus.*
4. *illī rēgēs hanc urbem multōs annōs rēxērunt.*
5. *omnēs cīvēs propter illud perīculum pācem petēbant.*
6. *illa dōna in hāc mēnsā relinquet.*
7. *illīs/hīs/eīs pārēbimus.*
8. *ille poēta eum nōn amābat.*
9. *cūr nōn ab illā terrā discessistī?*
10. *arma per viās illĭus urbis portābat.*

Exercise 8. 4

At last the Romans compelled those enemies to flee from Italy. The king of the enemy, who had wanted to help the inhabitants, led his army into the ships and made the journey home. Now the Romans had overcome all the land and were feared by the inhabitants. But they always wanted greater glory and were soon wanting to overcome other lands. The Roman soldiers were very brave and were often sent in their ships on behalf of the fatherland.

Exercise 8. 5

1. *fidēlis, fidēlior, fidēlissimus*
2. *fidēliter, fidēlius, fidēlissimē*
3. *fēlīx, fēlīcior, fēlīcissimus*
4. *fēlīciter, fēlīcius, fēlīcissimē*
5. *pulcher, pulchrior, pulcherrimus*
6. *pulchrē, pulchrius, pulcherrimē*

Exercise 8. 6

1. *Rōmānī fortius quam Gallī pugnāvērunt.*
2. *illae nāvēs tempestāte maximā dēlētae sunt.*
3. *illō tempōre rēgēs in urbe sapienter regēbant.*
4. *tēla audācius iēcimus.*
5. *plūrimōs captīvōs imperātōrī Rōmānō trādidit.*
6. *virtūtem illōrum (virōrum) fortium laudāvimus.*
7. *hostēs ducī nostrō multōs (virōs) trādere cupīvērunt.*
8. *nostrī ā Gallīs, quī fortissimē pugnāvērunt, victī sunt.*
9. *iuvenis manum in ignem audācter posuit.*
10. *cīvēs hostibus aurum argentumque celerrimē trādere cupīvērunt.*

Exercise 8. 7

The Romans fought bravely with the Greeks but did not defeat them. For the Greek king, named Pyrrhus, was a very brave leader and led his army very bravely into battle. Once a Greek foot-soldier was captured and sent to the Roman leader. This foot-soldier said to the Romans "if you give me silver and gold, I shall kill the Greek king." However the Romans were not moved. "We Romans" said the Roman leader "shall conquer the enemy by means of the courage of our soldiers and the skill of our leader. I shall soon hand you over to your king. Perhaps you will be killed by your own soldiers." When Pyrrhus heard the words of the Romans he was greatly moved. "In this way" he said "the Romans will conquer and I shall be overcome."

Exercise 8. 8

1. If one is victorious one has conquered one's rival; *vincō* = I conquer.
2. To reverse is to go backwards; *vertō* = I turn; *re* = back.
3. Tempestuous = stormy; *tempestās* = storm.
4. To promise is to give one's word; *prōmittō* = I promise.
5. If one has vitality one is full of life; *vīta* = life.
6. Trade is the process of exchanging commodities for money or other commodities; *trādō* = I hand over.
7. Traction is the dragging of a body along a surface; *trahō* = I drag.
8. Incendiary = inflammatory; *incendium* = fire.
9. Mode = way or manner; *modus* = way or manner.
10. Oculist = eye specialist; *oculus* = eye.

Exercise 8. 9

1. The consul carried on the affairs of the city very badly.
2. The Roman soldiers fought very well in the battle.
3. The Greek king was greatly moved by the words of the leader.
4. The mother warned her daughters very often.
5. Finally the leader pitched his camp near the river.

Exercise 8. 10

1. He will hear
2. He rules
3. We were warned
4. I have been heard
5. You are being captured
6. You will be captured
7. Listen!
8. I have led
9. To be led*
10. To rule
11. To be
12. He has been
13. They were
14. We are
15. You are fighting
16. In the battle
17. Into the sea
18. In the sea
19. Under the bed
20. After these things

*Not to be confused with *ducī* = to the leader!

Exercise 8. 11

1. The Trojan War was in c. 1250 B.C.
2. Rome was founded in 753 B.C.
3. Romulus attracted women into his city by inviting the Sabines to a festival and then capturing the Sabine women.
4. Tarpeia was the traitress who tried to let the Sabines into the city.
5. Romulus became the god Quirinus.
6. There were seven kings of Rome between 753 and 510 B.C.
7. After the expulsion of Tarquin the Proud, Rome was ruled as a republic.
8. Horatius Cocles, Spurius Lartius and Titus Herminius defended the bridge against the Etruscan army.
9. Lars Porsenna was the king leading the Etruscan army.
10. Scaevola means left-handed. Mucius was named Scaevola after burning his right hand in the flames to prove to Lars Porsenna that Romans fear no pain.
11. When Cloelia swam safely back to Rome she was returned by the Romans to the Etruscans.
12. Coriolanus's mother was angry with him because he attacked Rome at the head of an army of the Volsci.
13. The patricians were descended from the original founders of Rome; the plebeians were the common people.
14. The Battle of Allia was in 390 B.C. In the battle, the Gauls defeated the Romans.
15. The Gauls entered Rome and killed the senators after the Battle of Allia.
16. Camillus saved Rome from the Gauls.
17. Julius Caesar was responsible for the conquest of Gaul (58–51 B.C.).
18. Manlius Torquatus killed his son because he disobeyed an order.
19. Pyrrhus was King of Epirus. A pyrrhic victory is one which is won at great cost to the victor.
20. Fabricius was a jolly good Roman because he refused a bribe, conquered his fear (of elephants) and showed great integrity by reporting the treachery of Pyrrhus's doctor.

Chapter 9

Exercise 9. 1

1. *amor*
   amāris
   amātur
   amāmur
   amāminī
   amantur

2. *mīror*
   mīrāris
   mīrātur
   mīrāmur
   mīrāminī
   mīrantur

3. *amābor*
   amāberis
   amābitur
   amābimur
   amābiminī
   amābuntur

4. *hortābor*
   hortāberis
   hortābitur
   hortābimur
   hortābiminī
   hortābuntur

5. *amābar*
   amābāris
   amābātur
   amābāmur
   amābāminī
   amābantur

6. *morābar*
   morābāris
   morābātur
   morābāmur
   morābāminī
   morābantur

Exercise 9. 2

1. *amātus sum*
   amātus es
   amātus est
   amātī sumus
   amātī estis
   amātī sunt

2. *hortātus sum*
   hortātus es
   hortātus est
   hortātī sumus
   hortātī estis
   hortātī sunt

3. *amātus erō*
   amātus eris
   amātus erit
   amātī erimus
   amātī eritis
   amātī erunt

4. *mīrātus erō*
   mīrātus eris
   mīrātus erit
   mīrātī erimus
   mīrātī eritis
   mīrātī erunt

5. *amātus eram*
   amātus erās
   amātus erat
   amātī erāmus
   amātī erātis
   amātī erant

6. *morātus eram*
   morātus eras
   morātus erat
   morātī erāmus
   morātī erātis
   morātī erant

Exercise 9. 3

1. *agricolās hortātur.*
2. *puerum mīrābāmur.*
3. *castra invenīre cōnābantur.*
4. *mīlitēs meōs hortābor.*
5. *multa dōna mīrābātur.*
6. *multās hōrās mē hortārī cōnābāris.*
7. *diē quīntō fīliam hortābitur.*
8. *fēminae īrātae puerum hortātae sunt.*

9. *mīlitēs fortius quam hostēs pugnāre cōnābantur.*
10. *imperātor propter tempestātem morātus est.*

Exercise 9. 4

1. *laetus esse vidētur.*
2. *in hortō vīsa est.*
3. *fābulam amāre videntur.*
4. *ab uxōre agricolae vidēbuntur.*
5. *vidērī nōn amat.*

Exercise 9. 5

1. The Romans will not dare to attack the city.
2. The Gauls were accustomed to fight in the woods.
3. Roman girls had been accustomed to help their mothers.
4. All were rejoicing on account of the victory.
5. The poet was praised on account of his poems.
6. After the messengers had departed, all the inhabitants rejoiced.

Exercise 9. 6

1. They warn
2. They are warned
3. They will rule
4. They will be ruled
5. We shall listen
6. We shall be heard
7. He has captured
8. He captures
9. He will capture
10. They see
11. You are seen / you seem
12. It has been seen / it has seemed
13. She has been seen / she has seemed
14. To be loved
15. I have begun
16. To be begun
17. To be captured
18. I have been
19. To be
20. You are being killed

Exercise 9. 7

1. The Romans were advancing towards the camp of the enemy.
2. All wonder at the words of the soldier.
3. The master was angry with the wretched slaves.
4. The enemy will use many arrows, won't they?
5. The ambassadors wanted to speak in the forum.

Exercise 9. 8

1. *in bellō mīlitēs cōtīdiē morientur.*
2. *hostēs fortius quam Rōmānī pugnāre videntur.*
3. *tempestās magna tertiō diē orta est.*
4. *gladiīs nostrīs ūtēbāmur sed tandem ā custōdibus captī sumus.*
5. *ducem exercitūs in collēs sequēminī.*

Book 2 Answers

Exercise 9. 9

The Romans were fighting the Carthaginians. The leader of the Romans, called Regulus, won many victories but he had not captured Carthage. Regulus therefore addressed his soldiers as follows: "Will the Romans be overcome by the enemy? All of Italy has now been conquered by the Romans. The island of Sicily was once ruled by the enemy but now it is ruled by us. We are called to arms, (we are called) to the greatest glory. When the sun rises again we shall be dining in the city of the enemy."

The battle raged (*pugnābātur*) on the plain for many hours but at last the Romans were overcome by the enemy. Many died for their fatherland, but Regulus was captured and led into the city. After this ambassadors were sent to Rome, among whom was Regulus. The latter, before he set out, was ordered to speak for (i.e. in favour of) peace. However Regulus was not persuaded. He went into the Roman forum and spoke in favour of war. "I do not fear Carthaginian arms" he said "nor do I want peace with the enemy. Now I shall go back to the enemy and die for my country." Thus the brave Roman left his friends and returned to the barbarians.

Exercise 9. 10

1. *post proelium imperātor hostium aliud cōnsilium cēpit.*
2. *antequam cēterī victōriam aliam peperērunt prōfectī sumus.*
3. *postquam Rōmānī hoc cōnsilium cēpērunt, cēterī cīvēs gāvīsī sunt.*
4. *mīlitēs fortissimī multās hōrās pugnābant sed cēterī fūgerant.*
5. *apud alterum cōnsulem cōtīdiē cēnābāmus.*

Exercise 9. 11

1. An alternative is (strictly) one or the other of *two* options (although in English now it can refer to more than two options). *alter* = the other (of two).
2. Sequence means the order in which things follow one another. *sequor* = I follow.
3. Progress involves moving forward. *prōgredior* = I go forward.
4. Irascible means irritable or easily angered. *īrāscor* = I am angry.
5. Loquacious means talkative. *loquor* = I speak.
6. A mortuary is where dead bodies are stored. *morior* = I die.
7. The Orient is the east, where the sun rises. *orior* = I rise.
8. Admirable means excellent, i.e. worthy to be wondered at. *mīror* = I wonder at.
9. An ingress is a going in. The verb *ingredior* = I go in.
10. An egress is a going out. The verb *ēgredior* = I go out.

Exercise 9. 12

1. *amāmur*
2. *amātī sunt*
3. *amāberis*
4. *amābātur*
5. *monēbiminī*
6. *monitus erat*
7. *regēmus*
8. *regar*
9. *rēxerit*
10. *audītī sunt*
11. *audīrī*
12. *est*
13. *erit*
14. *erant*
15. *esse*
16. *fuimus*
17. *capit*
18. *capiuntur*
19. *capī*
20. *monērī*

Exercise 9. 13

1. The 1st Punic War (264–241 B.C.) was fought between the Romans and the Carthaginians.
2. The people of Messana appealed to the Romans in 264 for help in evicting the Carthaginians.
3. After driving the Carthaginians out of Messana the Romans decided to push them out of Sicily altogether.
4. At the Battle of Mylae in 260 the Romans destroyed the Carthaginian fleet.
5. In 255 Regulus's army was defeated near the city of Carthage and he himself was captured.
6. Regulus showed great courage in speaking in favour of war with Carthage before returning to his captors to face certain death.
7. The story of Regulus's courage was an ideal example for later Romans to follow, combining as it did great bravery and integrity (there was after all no reason for him not to remain safely in Rome rather than return to Carthage).
8. Hamilcar was a Carthaginian general sent to Sicily. He won battles at Mount Hercte and Mount Eryx but was then defeated in a sea battle off Drepana.
9. Following the defeat at Drepana the Carthaginians sued for peace, renouncing all claims to Sicily and agreeing to pay an indemnity of 3,200 talents.
10. Map from p. 79.

Chapter 10

Exercise 10. 1

1. *potest*
2. *ferēbant*
3. *poterunt*
4. *ferimur*
5. *fers*
6. *ferētur*
7. *ībāmus*
8. *nōn poterāmus*
9. *ībit*
10. *poterō*

Exercise 10. 2

1. They approach
2. They were going in
3. You are able
4. To carry
5. We were able
6. He goes out
7. To be able
8. You are being carried
9. You will be carried
10. To approach

Exercise 10. 3

1. Tomorrow they will carry water outside the walls.
2. Yesterday you were carrying food to the house of the general.
3. The Roman soldiers were not able to capture Carthage.
4. Regulus was able to bear the pain at the hands of the Carthaginians.
5. You will return into the wood and carry water to the city, won't you?

Exercise 10. 4

1. *iuvenis diū dolōrem ferre poterat.*
2. *prīmō domum lēgātī adībimus.*
3. *nōnne arma ad mīlitēs Rōmānōs ferēbātis?*
4. *pecūnia ad līberōs rēgis ferēbātur.*
5. *mīlitēs, nōnne hostēs superāre potestis?*

Exercise 10. 5

1. *tulērunt*
2. *īstī* or *īvistī*
3. *potuit*
4. *tulimus*
5. *exieritis*
6. *tulerant*
7. *lātus erō*
8. *tulerit*
9. *inīstī*
10. *domum rediērunt*

Exercise 10. 6

1. He will guard the guards themselves.
2. The same soldiers will fight again.
3. The king himself hurried into the war.
4. The money was carried by the same slaves.

5. The city was ruled by the same king.
6. *este fortēs, mīlitēs!*
7. *Mārce, dūc servōs domum!*
8. *puer, fer aquam in oppidum ipsum!*
9. *Flāvia, dūc eāsdem puellās ex urbe!*
10. *Brūte, dīc illa verba rēgī ipsī!*

Exercise 10. 7

After Regulus had returned to Carthage, the Carthaginians waged war again with the Romans. They sent a general called Hamilcar into Sicily. Hamilcar led the army from there into Italy. Hamilcar soon won victories near Mounts Hercte and Eryx. Therefore the Romans led their forces across the island and attacked the enemy. The Carthaginians had very few soldiers but were able to withstand the attacks of the Romans for a long time. At last however the Romans prepared a fleet and overcame the Carthaginians, who had already sent many ships home, near Drepana. The Carthaginians were conquered and they sought peace. They left Sicily and after this battle did not return.

Exercise 10. 8

1. *rēx ipse prīmā lūce profectus est.*
2. *īdem rēx equitēs suōs quīnque diēs cūrābat.*
3. *hinc proficīscēmur et illūc ībimus.*
4. *Rēgulus ipse Poenōs nōn timēbat.*
5. *īram deōrum ferre nōn possumus.*
6. *nēmō̆ fīliō cōnsulis crēdere potest.*
7. *labōrēs servīs eīsdem dare potest.*
8. *gaudium mātris maius erat quam dolor fīlī;* or
   gaudium mātris dolōre fīlī maius erat.
9. *quam celerrimē ad castra proficīscēmur.*
10. *equitēs illinc in campum prōgredī possunt.*

Exercise 10. 9

1. Something that is possible can be done. *possum* = I am able.
2. To transfer is to carry across. *trāns* = across; *ferō* = I carry.
3. Mortality relates to mortal nature, i.e. the fact that one is subject to death. *mors* = death.
4. If something is laborious it is hard work. *labor* = work.
5. A cure is achieved by looking after someone. *cūrō* = I care for.
6. An exit is the way out. *exit* = he/she/it goes out.
7. Extra means coming outside a thing. Thus extra-curricular activities fall outside the main curriculum. *extrā* = outside.
8. Ire is anger. *īra* = anger.
9. A curator has the care of something put into his charge. *cūrō* = I care for.
10. If one refers to something, one goes back to it. *re* = back, *ferō* = I carry.

Exercise 10. 10

cōpiae Rōmānae cum incolīs Ītaliae multōs annōs bellum gerēbant. ōlim rēx Graecus, nōmine Pyrrhus, cum exercitū magnō in Ītaliam vēnit. auxilium hostibus Rōmae tulit sed frūstrā. post hoc Rōmānī cōpiās Pūnicās (or *Carthāginis*) *timēbant et eās dēlēre cupīvērunt. Rēgulus autem mīlitēs in Africam dūxit sed captus est. inde in Ītaliā iterum pugnātum est* (or *bellum gerēbātur*). *sed tandem imperātor Poenōrum, nōmine Hamilcar, cum Rōmānīs marī pugnāre coāctus est et victus est.*

Exercise 10. 11

1. The dates of the 2nd Punic War were 218–201 B.C.
2. Carthage wished to expand into Spain in order to seek new sources of revenue.
3. Rome was distracted by a war with the Gauls.
4. Hamilcar was the father-in-law of Hasdrubal and the father of Hannibal.
5. In 219 B.C. the town of Saguntum appealed to Rome for help against the Carthaginians.
6. Hamilcar had made his young son swear an oath never to make friends with the Romans.
7. Hannibal's army was unusual in that it contained elephants.
8. Hannibal marched through Spain, up over the Alps and down into Italy.

Exercise 10. 12

1. An essential guide or handbook.
2. Sane.
3. I think, therefore I am.
4. I came, I saw, I conquered.
5. Good faith.
6. Seize the day.
7. Nurturing mother.
8. From stronger (cause).
9. Proportionately.
10. For this (purpose).